BROKEN CHINA

BROKEN CHINA

LORI

AURELIA

WILLIAMS

SIMON & SCHUSTER
New York   London   Toronto   Sydney

—— ALSO BY LORI AURELIA WILLIAMS ——

When Kambia Elaine Flew in from Neptune

Shayla's Double Brown Baby Blues

SIMON & SCHUSTER
1230 Avenue of the Americas, New York, New York 10020
Book design by Greg Stadnyk
The text for this book is set in Janson Text.
Manufactured in the United States of America
10 9 8 7 6 5 4 3 2 1
Library of Congress Cataloging-in-Publication Data
Broken China / Lori Aurelia Williams.— 1st ed.
p. cm.
Summary: China Cup Cameron, a fourteen-year-old single mother with only her paralyzed Uncle Simon for support, takes on tremendous personal debt in hopes of a beautiful funeral after her daughter dies.
ISBN 0-689-86878-2 (hardcover)
[1. Teenage mothers—Fiction. 2. Mothers and daughters—Fiction. 3. Single-parent families—Fiction.
4. Poor—Fiction. 5. Uncles—Fiction. 6. African Americans—Fiction. 7. Death—Fiction. 8. Funeral rites and ceremonies—Fiction.] I. Title.
PZ7.W66685Br 2005
[Fic]—dc22   2004000151

FIRST
EDITION

For those young people who will experience childhood and parenthood at the same time.

CHAPTER 1

I had to take Amina to the clinic today. She caught a bad cold on Saturday from my best friend Yolanda's little girl Eboni, the youngest of six snotty-nosed kids whose only talent seems to be getting on their mother's last nerve—and mine. That's why I don't like to fool with them too much, but it was Yolanda's twenty-seventh birthday, so I gave in. I agreed to hang out in the backyard with her, barbecuing hot links, and talking about her favorite subject, Eboni's sorry-ass father, Jamal. Jamal is about to go down again for jacking some white chick's brand new Jetta. While giant puffs of mesquite smoke poured out of the barrel pit, and I screamed my voice harsh, yelling at her kids to keep their germy hands away from my two-year-old daughter, Yolanda went on and on about how Jamal just hasn't gotten a fair chance in life. "He got some serious moves, China," Yolanda told me, sitting up in the lounge chair and pulling her spandex tank top over "the Road Map," her name for her seriously stretch-marked belly. "He could play B-ball for the Houston Rockets or maybe even the San Antonio Spurs. He just needs a chance, that's all. The brother needs somebody to open up a few doors."

"I know what you mean, girl," I started to lie. Whenever Yolanda started going on about how talented Jamal was, I just said whatever I thought she wanted to hear. But before I could even get the fib out, Eboni ran over to Amina and gave her a big sloppy kiss on the cheek. I cringed, already seeing Amina laid up with her fourth cold this year.

"Stop that, Eboni," I yelled, hopping out of my plastic lawn chair. She just giggled and rushed off with braids flying and mucus running. I ran over to Amina and started wiping her soft skin with the tail of my broomstick skirt. She batted me away with her chubby little hand, then she broke into giggles too, and toddled after Eboni with the little silver bells on her white tennis shoes jingling like crazy.

"Come back here, girl!" I cried.

"Aw, leave her alone. I swear you act like an old mother hen, and you ain't but fourteen," Yolanda said, picking up her empty beer can and tossing it toward a tall stack of half-crushed aluminum cans and beer bottles resting against the broken-down back fence. The can landed on the ground next to the stack, spilling the last few drops of champagne-colored liquid onto the crunchy sunburned grass. Eboni ran over and picked it up.

"Put that down, girl. It's nasty," I said.

"I ain't," she said, laughing.

I frowned and tried grabbing it from her, but of course she just sprinted out of a huge hole in the back fence, running as fast as her tiny four-year-old legs could carry her.

"Girl, don't you go off from here running like a fool and end up getting hit by a car or something in the street!" Yolanda yelled. Eboni didn't even turn around.

"Ain't you gonna go get her?" I asked, walking over and grabbing Amina by the arm to keep her from going through the hole too.

"Hell naw, I ain't stressing myself about that child. She always running off like she ain't got no sense. Anyway, if she don't come back soon Vonda, Fatima, or Keisha will get her," Yolanda said, motioning to a trio of skinny, knobby-kneed little girls hanging out underneath a large fig tree at the other end of the small backyard. The overripe figs had started to fall from the tree a few days ago and the girls were busy smashing the large purple fruit into the black dirt with their ashy bare feet.

"Hey, cut that out, ya'll gone end up tracking that mess all over the place," I yelled at them.

"Hey, cut that out, ya'll gone end up tracking that mess all over the place," echoed Peter and Percy, Yolanda's six-year-old droopy-eyed twin boys. They were standing next to the fence throwing LEGOS at Mrs. Mayfield's tiger-striped cat, Happiness, who didn't seem none too happy at all to be a target. His fur was arched on his back in a mohawk, and he was hissing madly at the boys, as if they were a couple of stray tomcats trying to grab a bite from his feeding bowl.

"Lord help these silly kids," I muttered under my breath.

"What did you say?" Yolanda asked.

I shook my head. "Y'all better quit screwing with that cat before he jumps the fence and scratches the fool out of y'all!" I shouted at the boys.

"Damn, girl, quit hollering. You 'bout to break my eardrums," Yolanda said, rolling her eyes. "Kids is just gonna be kids. Ain't nothing you can do about it."

"True that. I suppose I was just wasting my time and vocal cords," I said, sitting Amina down in my chair and wiping her face again with the tail of my skirt.

"Aw, shoot, girl, she'll be all right. Eboni ain't got nothing that's gone kill her. It's just a cold. I swear, girl, you don't know nothing about being no mother. Lord knows she ain't gone die from a little slobber on her face."

"I know she won't. I just don't want her to be sick. I can't afford to take no more time off from school to stay with her, plus I don't like it when she's ill. It freaks me out."

"Look, you worry too damn much. Sickness and babies go together," Yolanda said, popping the top on another beer with a loud hiss. "You better just get used to it, if you gone *try* to be some-body's mama."

"I'm not *trying*. I already am somebody's mama, but I don't know about you," I snapped angrily, and glared at her like she had just capped on the new fly tank top I purchased from the One Price Store. She knew that I wasn't just trying. She knew that I put my heart and soul into raising Amina. Hearing her say that I wasn't doing a good job made me want to pour the can of beer over her head. I was a good mother to my child. I changed her diapers long before the little teddy bears on them started to fade, and gave her a bath every morning and night, no matter if she looked dirty or not. I washed her bibs in the bathroom sink by hand with some of that fancy overpriced baby soap, and rubbed her sore gums with Orajel when she had teething pain. She had on the latest pair of baby Reeboks, when I hadn't had a new pair of sneaks in a year, and a 10k gold earbob stuck out of each of her tiny ears, while fake silver hoops dangled from mine. I always did right by Amina even though it was sometimes major difficult to take care of a daughter that I loved with all my heart, but never wanted in the first place.

Before I had Amina I had seen pregnant girls on TV that were only a little older than I was when I got a big belly. They were always crying and saying that they wanted a child because they just wanted somebody to love. I thought that was crazy. I wasn't like those girls. Amina was my reason to get up in the morning, but she was still a mistake, the kind that even though you get through it you pray every night that it don't happen again. It was dumb what I did. It was just one afternoon when me and my best friend, Trip, was messing around while his moms was down at the bingo parlor try-ing to win the thousand dollar prize. It was raining out, so hard that even Noah's neighbors would have built an ark, and there was noth-ing on TV but boring infomercials and cartoon reruns. There was jack to do, so we just started fooling around some, kissing, touching and stuff. That was as far as I wanted to go, but Trip said it would be okay if we went further. He said that a lot of the kids at our school did it all the time. "It's no big deal, China," he said, unhooking my cotton training bra. "Everybody messes around like this sometimes."

That was true, and I knew it. Only a month before, a few of the girls in my English class were chillin' in the bathroom when my girl Lila came in talking about what she and her new boyfriend had done behind some wooden crates in her grandfather's tool shed. "Child, we did it all. And let me tell you something, it was the best time we ever had," she said, standing in front of the cracked mirror, pushing her shiny corkscrew curls back into place.

"I'll bet it was, girlfriend. What all did y'all do?" the other girls asked, as they pressed in closer to hear the Triple X details. I walked away. I didn't need to stay for the 411. I had a pretty good idea of what they had done. I also had a good idea a week later in the lunchroom, when Trip's cousin Rick started telling us why his moms had put him on lockdown. "My moms found my girlfriend's underwear underneath my mattress when she was cleaning my room. She shut my behind down for three weeks. I can't go nowhere but school and church, but it's cool, 'cause you know I still got them drawers. I'm still the man. Let me fill you in on it, dog," he said, laughing and scooping up a spoonful of runny mashed potatoes.

"I hear ya, man. It's all good," I heard Trip say, as I suddenly found a reason to go and discard my half-eaten stale turkey sandwich. Later on I wished that I had stayed and listened, because Trip was wrong. It wasn't all good. It was awkward and uncomfortable both times we did it that afternoon in his twin bed, on his Michael Jordan sheets. Maybe it was because we were only twelve or maybe it was because we weren't used to being with each other like that. I don't know. What I do know is that it wasn't fun for either one of us, so after it was over the second time we swore we would never do it again. We went back to being plain ole friends, spending our rainy days playing games on his Nintendo and shooting hoops in his backyard. We didn't go to school and brag about what we had done that afternoon. We hid it from our class-mates, and even from ourselves. When I started getting nauseous each morning we blamed it on the burnt toast and watery eggs they served for breakfast in the cafeteria, and when my period did-n't come we frantically searched the nurse's office for pamphlets that said skipping a period was not unusual for girls my age. "They say it happens all the time," I said, handing the brochure to Trip so that he could take a look.

We convinced ourselves that nothing was wrong, mostly because we didn't know what else to do. At school we had gotten the talk about menstruation, wet dreams, and stuff like that. "Body Changes and Growing Up," the speech was called. It was simply an hour-long chat about what happens when your hormones start to kick in, but there was nothing to tell you how to take care of yourself after they did. What we knew about sex came from the other kids. So when my stomach started to swell we found an excuse for that, too. I started wearing Trip's big T-shirts to hide it, and we joked with each other about my drinking too many Kool-Aid drinks. "All that sugar gives you a fat belly," Trip said, patting my expanding abdomen.

"Yeah, I got to quit drinking that berry punch," I said, pulling his D.A.R.E. shirt down farther to cover it.

It wasn't until the warm afternoon that we sat on the wooden bleachers at my school, watching the junior varsity football tryouts, that we had to admit what was really going on. We were setting on the third row when Trip's cousin sprinted down the field for a touchdown. We both hopped up out of our seats and started clap-ping; that's when I felt Amina kick. It wasn't anything major. It was just a soft thump against the inside of my belly, but it felt more like a hard kick, a kick to let us know that we couldn't fool ourselves anymore. I sat down and cried, and not ladylike tears, but gut-wrenching sobs that made Trip apologize every few minutes and ask if I was going to be okay. Through the sobs I somehow told him that I was, but it was a lie. I knew that I wasn't going to be all right for a long time. Two days later we went to the free clinic and lied about our ages. It was there that I got the horrible news, and a lecture from a baby-faced doctor who looked like he could still get into movies on the kid's price just like me. "I don't know how in the world you got yourself into this situation, but you really need to bring your parents in and let me speak with them, little girl. You're way too little to deal with something like this. Your body is still going through all kinds of changes. You're simply too young to be someone's mother," he said, writing the name of a prenatal vitamin down for me on his prescription pad.

"I guess not, because it looks like I already am," I said, leaning over to take the small, white piece of paper from him as he tore it out. I shoved it in my pocket and left his office before he could give me the "If you were my daughter" speech. On the way back out to the waiting room I felt Amina kick again. It was a kick that was going to brand me with the title of mother for life. That's what I am now, a mother, and both me *and* Yolanda know it.

"What the hell is that supposed to mean!" Yolanda shouted, her light brown face turning nearly as red as the nylon braids she had woven into her short black hair. "What do you mean, you don't know about me?"

"What the hell do you think I mean? I mean if I were you I would get up off my lazy behind and go find out where my child took off to down the street!" I shouted back.

"I'll get up when I'm damn good and ready! Don't nobody tell me what to do."

"I know, that's your problem," I said, and with that I picked

Amina up and headed for the same hole that Eboni had run through.

"Go on, leave. As far as I'm concerned you can take your behind off and not come back, little witch. I don't need you. I can celebrate all by myself. Do you hear me, cow? Don't come back!" I heard Yolanda yell behind me. I didn't even think about responding. The words were like chalk dust to me, something that would cling for a moment but was easily brushed off. I knew good and well that Yolanda was just trippin'. There was no way that she would really tell me to get lost. Since the day I met Yolanda down at the planned birth clinic I've been her only girlfriend, the one sister in our neighborhood, Fifth Ward, who would put up with her.

With the exception of Eboni, all of Yolanda's children are by married dudes. And no, it's not because she's ugly or dumb. Even with the stretch marks, Yolanda can hang with any of those sexy, tight-dress-wearing girls at Perry's 24 and 7 Beer Joint. She's long-legged and curvy, with a butt like Jennifer Lopez's, and cheekbones like that Grace Jones chick in the 007 movie. In short, she has it going on, but she's also smart. When it comes to math, Yolanda can work some digits. She can sum up totals quicker than the solar calculators that we use in my fifth-period math class, and when we go shopping at the Cash & Carry she always tells the cashiers our totals before they can ring them up. No, Yolanda doesn't need to date other sisters' men. She just does it because she says they don't put "the grip" on her, meaning that all they want is to have a good time. The little four-room shack that she lives in, her five-year-old hatchback, and the three raggedy bunk beds where her kids sleep were all given to her by guys who just wanted to kick it with her. Yolanda says that she likes it that way. When she gets tired of spending time with the men, she can simply wash 'em out of her life as easily as she washes the braid sheen oil from her hair. "Girlfriend, I don't need no man holding me down, telling me how to live my life. Let 'em go home and tell they wives what to do. Freedom is power," she told me one morning after she had kicked one of her lovers to the curb. "Let a man stick his razor in your bathroom cabinet for good, and before you know it he'll be telling you what type of toothpaste and soap you can buy. I don't need that kind of drama in my life. That's why I just date brothers who will only be around until they wives figure out what they sorry behind is doing."

"I understand you, girlfriend," I said, but I didn't really. I don't see anything good about Yolanda's lifestyle. It seems like a raggedy way to treat herself and her kids, but I would be lying if I didn't admit that I admire her in some small way. She may not make the best decisions in the world, but she's free to make them anyway, good or bad, and nobody gets on her back about it. It's not like that for me. I'm a kid with a kid. The only freedom I have is choosing the kind of baby wipes I clean my daughter's face with.

"Wanna play Eboni," Amina said as we headed away from Yolanda's yard.

"I don't know where Eboni went to," I told her. But out of the corner of my eye I spotted Eboni's pale blue T-shirt and red shorts a block over. She was in the middle of the littered street playing kick-the-can with an aluminum beer can. A yellow SUV came rolling down the street and quickly swerved around her.

"Wanna play Eboni," Amina repeated. I picked her up and continued walking. On the way back to the house the sneezing started. The next day it was sneezing, coughing, wheezing, and a low fever. Today when I skipped my first period English class and took her to the clinic she was all stuffed up and her forehead was hotter than the burning charcoal in Yolanda's old, rusty barbecue pit.

"You worry too damn much," I heard Yolanda's voice say as Amina wriggled and screamed from the shot that the heavyset nurse gave her in her bare bottom.

I think Yolanda is wrong. I think I don't worry enough.

Amina and I hung out at the clinic until her fever broke and the nurse was certain that the shot Amina received wouldn't make her any sicker. It took much longer than I expected. It seemed like forever before the nurse finally gave me a free sample of some Hawaiian Punch–looking liquid antibiotic and sent us off. By then it was around 9:30 A.M., and though I didn't want to, I dropped Amina and the antibiotic off at Mrs. Mayfield's, who keeps her most of the day. Before I left I laid her down on Mrs. Mayfield's sofa and made sure that Mrs. Mayfield understood the instructions on the medicine bottle.

"Of course I do, baby. I understand everything. You just go on and get out of here, girl. I done kept many a sick baby before. She'll be all right with me. Everything will be just fine," Mrs. Mayfield said, patting Amina on the back with her flabby hands.

"Okay, ma'am," I said, giving Mrs. Mayfield's soft, pudgy body a bear hug. She grabbed me and squished me to her like my Grandma Attie used to do before she died.

"You're a good mama," she said. "Don't you worry even a little bit. Me and little Miss Amina will be okay."

"I won't worry at all," I lied. I bent down and kissed Amina on the side of her face.

"Mama will be back as soon as school lets out," I said. She smiled weakly at me, and I left the house.

When I got to school a few minutes later I headed straight for my English class so that I could explain to my teacher, Mrs. Jerome, why I had missed another important exam. It wasn't actually my fault, and I was certain that homegirl would be understanding and come over with some mother-to-mother sympathy. Her husband had just died in a car accident a few months ago, leaving her alone with their three small boys. I figured she had to know what the struggle was like. I guess she did, but so what, big deal. Before I could hardly get my story out, she told me that there was a price to be paid for being a teenage mom, and that price was gonna be to receive a zero on my test. "I'm sorry about this, China, but I've given you tons of chances that I haven't given the other students. You simply have to figure out how to juggle your schoolwork and motherhood. I know that your situation is unique, but life just isn't always fair, and I believe that you and I are both living proof of that," she said.

"I guess so, ma'am."

"Trust me, we are, China." She tugged a blue ballpoint out of one of her thick cornrows and began scribbling something on an orange notepad.

"What's that, ma'am?" I asked.

"I'm out of hall passes," she said, tearing the page out and handing it to me. "Here, take this note and go down to Principal Nesby's office. She sent word earlier that she needed to see you."

"About what?" I asked.

"I'm certain that you can figure it out. If you can't figure out how to get to school on time, or anything else, you ought to be able to figure this out," she said sternly.

I sighed. She was right. I could definitely figure out why the principal wanted to see me. I slung my purple backpack over my shoulder and headed off to what I knew was going to be my second scolding of the day.

As I left the room I ran straight into Trip. He was dressed pretty much like me in sneakers, faded jean shorts, and a black T-shirt, but on *his* T-shirt in creepy dripping red letters were the words THE OUTER REALM, the name of his favorite TV program. Trip has every episode of the show, the old black-and-white tapes and the new color versions that come on each Saturday night. According to Trip, the greatest shows ever made are all sci-fi and fantasy shows, and to him *The Outer Realm* is the best of the bunch. He says that nobody can beat the alien, robot, time travel, and horror stories that they feature each week. He's major into the program, so into it that he even sends them ideas, but so far all he's got in return is the T-shirt.

"What's up, my dark sister?" he asked, sliding my heavy backpack off my shoulder. He was good like that, always helping me carry stuff, and opening doors, like we were married or something.

"Not much, I just got seriously sweated by Mrs. Jerome for missing another English exam. Girlfriend gave me a big red zero."

"A zero? That's cold, but you did miss your third exam this year."

"Tell me about it. I kinda like English, especially the poetry. It's easy to read, and sometimes we get to study a poem that deals with all the junk I have to put up with," I said, taking off down the hall with Trip. The second period bell had already rung and there were only a handful of kids still hanging out. They were standing near their shiny orange lockers rapping about what couple recently broke up and who got kicked out of school last week for fighting in our smelly bathrooms. I noticed my ex-girlfriend, Kembra, a sensitive, light-skinned sister with a short blond fro, was nearly surrounded by a group of cheerleaders all decked out in their burnt-orange-and-blue uniforms. As usual Kembra was sporting the newest designer threads—turquoise Fubu T-shirt, khaki shorts with the name Tommy Hilfiger embroidered on one leg, and what I knew had to be the latest pair of Air Jordan sneaks. It was those fancy rags that made Kembra more popular than Half-Price CD Week down at Street Tunes Music Store. Trip and I waved at her as we headed to my locker, but she didn't wave back. I thought it was kind of funky of her, but I was okay with it. I didn't expect Kembra to be too much on the friendly side. It wasn't like that between us anymore.

Back in the day, me and Kembra were tight, but things changed between us. Some kids think it was because Kembra suddenly got that afternoon office job that paid for all of her nice clothes or because her new stepfather bought her a brand new sports car to drive, but it was really because of Trip.

Kembra is two years older than me and Trip, but the age difference had never stopped her from having a big-time crush on him, and I couldn't blame her. Trip was a smooth piece of special dark chocolate with a buff bod, an almost-mustache that would really look like something in a year or two, dimples, and deep brown saucer eyes that always seemed to be smiling at you. The girls in school all thought he was Da Bomb, especially Miss Kembra. Back when we used to go swimming down at MLK Pool, Kembra would do everything she could to get Trip to notice her. She was Miss Teen USA pretty, but with a Miss America figure. She would always come strutting out to the cool blue water in one of her older sister Lela's barely-there bikinis. Whenever Trip saw her like that his eyes would pop out of his head like my science teacher's black mollies. He would leave me and go over to her side of the pool to mack, but Kembra was way too shy. No matter what Trip said she would hardly even speak to him, and when she did it was in a voice as soft as the sound of bare feet on rose petals. She was nothing like me, outgoing and chatty, so Trip just didn't know what to say to her. He would sit there staring at her chest until she got embarrassed and hopped into the water. Later, as we shimmied out of our suits in the steamy girls' shower room, she would tell me how much she really liked him, and how she wished she could figure out how to let him know.

"Just tell him, girl. He doesn't bite," I would say, drying off with my rainbow beach towel. But she never did, and I don't know why, but I never mentioned it to him either. We all just remained friends, until the day that I showed up at her house with a maternity blouse on. I tried to explain to Kembra that it wasn't what she thought, and that me and Trip were really only good buddies, but she called me a liar, and said that I had played her for a fool. It was the first and last time I heard her raise her voice above a whisper. Today I still feel bad about our friendship, but not bad enough to accept her calling me a liar. I wasn't like that. I would have let her know straight up, face-to-face if I was even thinking about going that way with Trip. Besides, it was a long time ago. She had no reason to still be so ugly to me, or to Trip.

"Kembra didn't say hi to us again," Trip said as we stopped in front of my locker.

"I know," I said, turning my red combination lock. "I guess she's still too mad. I thought she would be over it by now. Why girlfriend got to be like that? She knows I wasn't trying to mess over her. I wish she could stop trippin' and see that I didn't mean her no harm. Shoot, I guess she's never going to speak to us again. Oh well, I can't do jack about it. I'm already waist-deep in quicksand. Just one more thing happen to me today, and damn if I won't be all covered up."

"It be's like that sometimes," Trip said, reaching over and pulling my lock apart. He yanked it off and held it while I tugged the door open.

"Gross, I really have to clean this thing out," I said, peering at the crumpled notebook papers, gym clothes, half-full baby bottles, and beat-up textbooks stuffed into the small rectangular space.

"No kidding, a bunch of rats would be living large in there. And why you got all them baby bottles? Amina ain't wanted a bottle in months," Trip said.

"I know. Every time I dropped her off last year I forgot I had an extra one stuck in my purse and it ended up here. I was gonna clean it out last month, but I started talking to Marty about her prom dress and I forgot about it."

"Marty is going to prom? Who with?"

"Some senior over at Cashmere. She got a new dress and everything. It's purple satin, and backless. She got it at Dillards when she went to Austin to see her aunt. Man, I know she's gonna have a good time. Shoot, I wish I was her." I frowned at my locker. "Great, great, I'll take those stupid bottles home and wash 'em as soon as I get a chance, or as soon as the smell runs me away from my locker," I said. I grabbed my European History book and slammed the locker shut with a loud bang.

"Man, girl, take it easy," Trip said, reaching over and replacing the lock. "These old, tired lockers can't take too much."

"I can't either," I said, walking over to the water fountain. When I turned the metal knob on the side the cool water rushed out, splashing my face.

"Aw, shoot!" I cried, dabbing my face with the bottom of my T-shirt.

"Is it all that?" Trip called to me. "Calm down, girl. You look like you 'bout to freak out and go Terminator on somebody."

I laughed. "Naw, I'm just tired. Besides, you know that I'm not big on making my problem somebody else's."

"True that. Anyway, why were you late this time?"

I opened my mouth to answer him, but he cut me off.

"Oh wait, hold up, hold up. I want to tell you about my new *Outer Realm* story idea," he said waving his hands.

"What about it?"

"Okay, okay, this is really cool. Picture this, this dude goes to lunch one day with some friends from his office. When he gets to the restaurant everybody starts acting all strange, including his friends."

"What kinda strange?"

"Sugar," he said. "They're putting sugar all over everything, on their steaks and catfish, green salads, baked potatoes, even on their coconut cream pie, and you know that don't need no sugar."

"I guess," I said. "I don't like coconut cream pie."

"Okay, it don't matter," he said, waving his arms again. "What matters is that it's all odd. The dude leaves lunch not knowing what the heck is going on. He finishes his workday out and goes home, but the same craziness is going on there, too. His wife and kids is putting sugar on everything at dinner. The dude still doesn't know what to think of it. He gets all weirded out, but he doesn't know what to do, so he just decides to play Leroy Normal and not say anything to his family. He eats real quick and goes to take the trash out, but when he opens the lid and starts to pull out the aluminum cans for recycling—*bam*, guess what he finds?"

"A bunch of smelly banana peels," I said, shrugging my shoulders.

"Naw, girl, damn, use some imagination," he said. A big grin spread across his face. "A pod, he finds this giant, wrinkled brown pod that looks like a big peach pit."

"A pod? That's what he finds? It sounds like *Invasion of the Body Snatchers.*"

"Naw, naw, it's gonna be way better than that, way more cool."

"If you say so," I said with a sigh. "You're the sci-fi guy."

"True that, but okay, okay, what's the deal?" he asked, not at all annoyed that I wasn't into his story plot. "Go on and tell me why you couldn't bring your behind to school on time."

"I couldn't bring my behind to school on time because Amina's sick again. I had to run her up to the clinic," I said, glancing at my digital watch and starting down the hall toward the principal's office.

"What's up with my little Bunny Face?" Trip asked, falling into step beside me.

I laughed to myself. Bunny Face is the only thing that Trip calls Amina, not "baby" or "daughter." When Amina was born I decided to let him choose how he wanted to refer to her. We had both made a bad mistake, but I didn't think that Trip had to pay for it too. I put his name down on the birth certificate, but I told him that I didn't expect anything from him. He didn't have to give up his sci-fi movie poster money to buy her rattles and booties or miss his drama club practices to take her to checkups, and when she was colicky, he didn't have to come over at night and walk her up and down the hardwood floors until his feet hurt, as if he had just finished a ten-mile run. Trip wasn't ready to be called "daddy" anymore than I was ready to be called "mama," so I didn't push Amina on him. He chose the nickname Bunny Face to refer to her, and I let him know that he could change it whenever he felt like it. "You can start calling her your baby any time you like," I said, while we peered through the nursery-room glass at her. "Lord knows she ain't taking off for nowhere. She'll be here when you're ready, when you want to start taking her for those father-daughter trips to the zoo and stuff."

"It's cool," Trip said. "I'll let ya know when I'm ready to be Bill Cosby or somebody."

So far he's not ready, but I'm still fine with it. Trip is my soulmate. Whenever I'm down about something I always go to him. He either finds a way to make me double over with laughter or cries a river of tears with me. When he's ready he'll be a good father to Amina, much better than my father, who I've never even met.

"So what's wrong with my little Bunny Face?" he asked.

"Your little Bunny Face has another cold. She caught it from Yolanda's little girl Eboni last Saturday. It's no biggie," I said, trying to convince both of us. "She's only stopped up kinda bad with nasty congestion."

"How bad?"

"Regular ole bad, you know how babies and colds are," I said. "I took her to the clinic. The doctor put her on some medicine and told me that she should start feeling better by this afternoon. When I dropped her off at Mrs. Mayfield's she still didn't look too hot, but Mrs. Mayfield said she would be fine, and I believe her. She's taken care of all kinds of kids, plus I know she'll give me a ring if I need to come and get your little Bunny Face."

"Come get her for what? I thought you said that it was just a cold and she got some medicine?" Trip said, with more concern in his voice than I expected. I checked out his face. A worry frown was doing a number all over his *GQ* looks. It was the kind of frown that a daddy might make. I guess he was getting closer to turning into a Bill Cosby after all.

I threw up a huge smile to try and make us both feel better. "For nothing, Trip. Trust me. Everything is okay. Amina is fine. Right now, I'm the one all screwed, and screwed up."

"I see that, but are you sure my Bunny Face is all right?"

I nodded. "Trust me. She's much better than I am. Shoot, what the heck is the principal gonna say to me this time?" I asked.

"You won't know until you go," he said, handing me back my backpack.

"Yeah, I know. Anyway, I better get my behind over there before I get into more trouble. I'll see ya at lunch."

"Naw, not today. My mom told me to come home for lunch. She got something to show me. I'll bet it's that new DVD player I been trying to get her to buy me for my birthday. I can't wait. A brother will be seriously living large with that."

"I guess you will. Later," I said.

"Much later," he called back. After that, he pushed open the metal double doors and stepped out into the courtyard. I waved good-bye as he passed the light-green tinted windows and I took off down the hall.

A couple of minutes later I stepped into Principal Nesby's secretary's office. Both she and Principal Nesby were out. I drank a paper cup of water from a cooler next to a couple of metal folding chairs and walked into Principal Nesby's space. I flopped down in another folding chair in front of her huge oak desk. On top of the glass desk cover, right in the middle of a stack of leather grade books and pink message slips, was a manila folder with my name written neatly on the side of it in fine-print, navy-blue magic marker. I cringed big time when I saw it. I was about to grab it and stick it under the grade books when Principal Nesby came strolling into the office. As usual she was dressed more like a talk-show host than a principal. She was wearing a fancy cream suit with gold braid around the sleeves, and a matching pair of cream leather pumps with gold trim around the heels. Her shoulder-length, salt-and-pepper hair hung in heavy curls around her oblong face, and she was wearing enough makeup for five models. She looked like she was about to interview some major actor.

"Good morning, ma'am," I said, as she passed my chair. She nodded and took her seat on the other side of her desk. I braced myself, wondering what she was going to do to me. I figured that it had to be a lot worse than a big red zero.

She cleared her throat. "China, do you remember when we talked earlier this year?" she asked.

"Yes, ma'am," I answered.

"At that time we had a nice little talk and we discussed a lot of things about your life past and present," she said, placing one of her manicured hands on my folder.

"Yes ma'am, I remember," I said, hiding my short, chewed-up nails in my lap. She pulled her chair closer to the desk. I noticed that her eyebrows were even more together than her hands. They were perfectly waxed in half moons over her heavily outlined eyes. Just looking at them reminded me that I hadn't had time to do anything to my face in months, no makeup or even a warm wash with cold cream. In the mornings I was always in a rush to get me and Amina out of the door, and at night I was always in a hurry to get me and Amina in bed.

"I'm sure you do recall it," she said. "At that time you told me about your birth and how you got your first name. You told me that when you were born your mother wasn't very happy about it. She was only seventeen and in an alternative school for disciplinary problems. You told me that having you was a punishment from your grandfather. It was his way of making your mother pay for all the anguish she had caused him and your grandmother with her school problems."

"Yes ma'am. It was really mean, but he told her that she had caused them a whole world of misery, and she had to make it right. He told her that struggling with her own child would let her get a taste of how miserable they were when she got on drugs and ended up being suspended twice for pulling a knife on another girl, and for messing around with the school's janitor in an empty classroom. He said they would be right there to watch her trying to raise me, and it would make them feel better seeing her in pain for a change. My mama was okay with it. She loved her mom and dad, and deep down she was sorry for all the trouble that she put them through. She said that she was just going through some ugly phase, and she didn't know how to get out of it. She agreed to quit school and have the baby, but it didn't matter. The day I was born my grandfather decided that he didn't even want to look at her anymore. He told her that we couldn't live with them. Then he gave her three hundred dollars and he and my grandma left."

"I remember," Principal Nesby said. "You said that your mother got really depressed for a day—then she got angry. In fact, she was so angry at her parents that when the physician's assistant asked her what name she wanted on your birth certificate, she said that she could care less. She threw an ugly fit and screamed that she could name you whatever she wanted. She pointed around the room and yelled that she could call you *chair, window, bedpan, mattress,* or anything else she saw lying around, because it didn't matter one darn bit to her—so the assistant did."

"Yes ma'am, I guess the PA wasn't in a great mood either. She named me China, after the cup that Mama had been drinking tea out of. China Cup, to be exact. That's the name that went down on my birth certificate."

"China Cup Cameron," she said.

"Yes, ma'am," I said, wondering why she had called me into her office to go over something that we both knew, something that didn't appear to have anything to do with my not making it to school on time.

"I love that story," she said. "I've heard a lot of stories in my fifteen years as a principal, but that's my favorite one, because it has a very happy ending. Your mom ended up out on the street with you, but she figured out how to take care of herself. She got a job at a furniture factory, and provided you with a pretty decent place to live. She even managed to get her GED and eventually go on to beauty school. She was a beautician for several years in a nice beauty shop. . . ."

"Until she died of brain cancer," I reminded her.

"I know," she said with a heavy sigh. "And I wasn't trying to be insensitive. I just wanted you to know that despite your mother dying so young she was a woman that a lot of young people could look up to. Excuse my language, but she knocked the hell out of some pretty bad odds. I know that being a young mother with no help at all had to be extremely difficult and scary for her."

"I guess it was. But ma'am, it's scary and difficult when you do have help, at least it is to me," I said.

"I know, and that's why I called you in here. I wanted to tell you that no matter how scary and hard it is, you're just going to have to suck it up and do better." She opened my file and took out a stack of yellow legal-pad pages. "You see these," she said, shaking them at me. "Complaints. These are all complaints from your teachers about your tardiness, sleeping in class, and missed assignments. Your teachers say that you're holding onto a rope that's about to be cut."

"I am?" I asked, as if I had no idea.

"Yes," she said, putting the pages back. "Look, China, you're a bright kid with lots of promise, which is why your teachers even bother to send me updates on you, but they all say that you have simply got to get your act together or you're not going to make it through the school year."

"I'm doing the best I can," I said defensively. "It's hard trying to take care of Amina and get schoolwork done. I hardly ever get time to do things for me because I have to make choices. Amina always has to come first. That's what my uncle Simon taught me. He says a true mother gives her child a slice of bread before she takes one herself."

"I like that," she said. "My mama used to say that a mother sleeps on stones while the child sleeps in a featherbed, or something similar to that. Your uncle is a smart man. But tell me this, what does he honestly think about you and Amina?"

I sighed and shifted uncomfortably in my seat. What did Uncle Simon think about me and Amina? I wasn't sure what she meant. Did she mean what did he think about me and Amina and my bad school grades? Or what did he think about me and Amina period? The second question I could answer easily. Uncle Simon thought me and Amina had hair of spun gold, and when we walked, beautiful maidens in silk dresses went before us sweeping the dust from the ground. We were empresses of Rome, goddesses of Egypt, African princesses wading in the River Niger under the bright hot sun—that's what Uncle Simon thought of us. To him we were more than special, we were his entire world. Now, what he thought of me and Amina making a mess out of my grades, I didn't know. I hadn't told him. It would hurt him too much, and he didn't deserve that.

When Mama died three years ago Uncle Simon packed his stuff up and moved into our tiny house with me, though it was an incredibly difficult thing for him to do. Since high school Uncle Simon's been in a wheelchair. When he was in the tenth grade he got into an argument with another boy at a football game. During halftime the boy walked right up to Uncle in the bleachers and got in his face over some fly Jamaican chick that the boy had been dating before Uncle hooked up with her. Uncle didn't really like fighting, and tried to step-off, but when he was walking away the boy threw a glass bottle of Dr. Pepper at him and struck him in the head. Uncle lost his balance and fell twenty feet below onto the hard concrete. His spine got damaged, and after that he couldn't walk anymore. For years Uncle Simon was really down about it. He finished high school through homeschooling and tutors, and when it was over he never really did anything else. He spent his days listening to classical music and building a miniature replica of our hood out of red clay. In his replica every house and store was populated with faceless people, people who had no eyes to stare at him when he rolled by them in his wheelchair. They were people who couldn't see him, and the people that he himself didn't want to see—including me and Mama. When Grandpa and Grandma were alive I would sometimes go and visit them. He never ever came out of his room to greet me. I would knock on his door and say hello, but all I ever got was a grunt in return. He acted like he wanted nothing to do with me, but when Mama died he out of the blue decided to step up to the plate. He let the social worker assigned to my case know that I didn't belong anywhere but with him. "My legs don't work too good, but my heart is just fine. I don't know anything about raising a little girl, but I can figure it out. I'll adjust, and so will she. It ain't gonna be easy for either one of us, but I'll make sure that she stays in school and becomes the lady that her mama knew she could be. That's the way I believe it should be, family always looking out for each other. Just give me a chance. I'll make sure that she don't go without the care and attention she needs," he said the afternoon we all sat down to a conference.

And Uncle Simon was true to his word. After he got the state to come in and lower just about everything in the house to his height, Uncle turned into June Cleaver on wheels. He cooked meals, washed clothes, helped me with my math and sociology homework, and even rolled over to the school with me each morning. He did or tried to do most of the things that Mama used to do for me. When I told him that I was pregnant, that was the worst I've ever felt. "I'm sorry, Uncle. Me and Trip were fooling around one day, and now the doctor says that I'm gonna have a baby in little while," I cried one afternoon, while we were folding a load of laundry to put away. I thought that he would erupt like Mount St. Helens when I told him, but I should have known better. Instead of fussing me out he reached up and took my hand. He held it for a second, then gently pressed something smooth and hard into it. I unfolded my fingers for a look. Resting in my palm was a little miniature me. Her eyes, her hair, even her double-pierced ears were exactly like mine, but the thing that stole the breath right out of my mouth was her stomach. It was round and swollen, as if she had swallowed a miniature pumpkin. I rubbed her belly and cried heavy tears that washed six months of fear and guilt from me.

"I made that two months ago," he said, picking up a terry washcloth and dabbing at my eyes. "All this time I just been waiting for you to tell me the truth. I can't walk, China, but I can see a robin resting on a fence five blocks down the street. Do you get what I'm saying?"

I nodded.

"Good," he said. "Then get and understand this, if you get into a mess, we both get into a mess, and the two of us will figure out how to get out of it together. You got that?" he asked.

"I got it," I said.

"Good, because we can find a way to mold a mistake into something decent, but there's no way to reshape a lie so that it comes out right. Just be honest with me, girl," he said. "All I want you to do is tell me the truth."

"I will. I promise that I won't ever lie again," I said, and I've kept that promise, up until now. Principal Nesby could never understand. There was no way that I could tell Uncle Simon the truth about my school grades. I couldn't let him down. The day he gave me the figurine a new bond formed between us, one that centered around great respect and trust. That's what Amina's name means: it's an African word for *trust.* And it was Uncle who gave it to her, right after he cut her umbilical cord. He said that it would be a symbol of the confidence that he would place in me to not make another mistake and get pregnant again, and a reminder that I could always count on him to be there for me when I needed help. *What the willows don't know won't make them weep.* It described how I felt about cluing Uncle Simon in on my present problem, and was also a pretty cool line from a poem in my English class.

"My uncle says that I'm going to have to start concentrating more in school, and only miss when I have to," I answered, which wasn't really a lie, because it was exactly what Uncle would have said if he knew the truth.

"Does he?" Principal Nesby asked.

I nodded and uncrossed and crossed my legs nervously. "He does. He told me just last night that I had to start getting my stuff together. He said that my mama wouldn't like it if I flunked my school year and got left back."

"He's right, she wouldn't, but China, what I want to stress to you today is that you need to be concerned about flunking out on your future. Amina won't be a baby forever. She's going to be a little girl, with really big needs, and you're going to have to figure out how to meet them. I have to admit in many ways you're a lot more mature than some of the other teen mothers that we have here in the school, but China, you're still just a girl, a little girl with a big responsibility. Tell me, what do you want to be when you're all grown up?"

"I guess . . ." I started, but the words got stuck to the roof of my mouth like the peanut-butter-and-molasses sandwiches Amina and Uncle Simon eat during their cartoon afternoons. What did I want to be? She was trippin', right? I wanted to be a doctor, strutting around in a long white coat ordering X-rays of broken elbows and scribbling prescriptions for drugs that my patients couldn't pronounce. I wanted to be a poet, sitting in front of a window on a foggy fall morning, writing a sonnet about a lost love that I met one cold night under the soft glow of a new moon. Or I could be a flamenco dancer, tapping my feet and twirling around in a flaming red dress and slingback red heels while a mesmerized audience clapped and cheered. All of those were things I wanted to be when I grew up, but right now all I could see written on the wall for me was the word *mother* in huge flashing neon letters, the same red color as my dancing dress.

"I'm not sure, ma'am," I answered. "I guess I want to be what everybody wants to be when they grow up. Happy—and not broke."

"I see, and how do you plan on doing that?" she asked.

"I guess—" I started. The beige multibutton phone on her desk buzzed, cutting me off. Principal Nesby picked up the receiver.

"Yes—of course, okay, okay—I sure will, thank you, Mrs. Espinoza, right away," she said, and pushed the clear hold button. She glanced over at me.

"What's up, ma'am?" I asked.

"China, the lady who keeps your daughter says that it doesn't look like the medicine the doctor gave your daughter is working right. She thinks that perhaps you had better come home and check on her. Her breathing seems a little labored."

"I know. She was having a little trouble and breathing funny last night, that's one of the reasons why I had to take her to the doctor this morning. She was wheezing a lot, but I guess I forgot to fill Mrs. Mayfield in on that. Okay, tell her that I'll be there in a little bit," I said, but I quickly changed my mind. I knew my daughter. It wasn't unusual for medicine to not work on her the first time. Sometimes she was really resistant to stuff. I would probably have to take her to the clinic again to get her prescription changed. We would be there most of the day, and once again I would miss my classes. Man, I loved Amina, but I had to have time to catch up, or I was gonna fail and let Uncle and my mama down for sure. I had a study period after my next two classes, surely she could wait until it came around. Then I could take her back to the doctor and get her something that would actually open her head up.

"Just tell Mrs. Espinoza to tell the baby-sitter to drop Amina off at my house," I said. "My uncle can look after her for a while until I get there. I'm sure she's just fine. This happens all the time. Last month I had to take her to the doctor three times to get her medicine changed. It's just an Amina thing."

"Are you certain?" Principal Nesby asked.

I nodded again. "I'm certain, ma'am. She'll be fine."

Principal Nesby punched the hold button and relayed the info to her secretary. When she was finished she replaced the receiver and glanced over at a round wall clock sitting over a long, forest-green bulletin board. "Darn, I have a meeting in a bit, so I guess this isn't going to be a good time for either one of us to continue our talk. But, China, I really want to speak to you about your classes and your future, so I'm going to set up another meeting for us before the week is out. For now just go on to class. I'll have Mrs. Espinoza get back to you by tomorrow."

"Yes, ma'am," I said, gladly getting up from my chair. I walked into the waiting room and said good-bye to Mrs. Espinoza, a friendly, fifty-something Hispanic lady, whose personality was even warmer than the fresh basket of homemade sweet-potato empanadas and Mexican pastries that she kept on her desk for the problem kids who ended up in the office. As I passed her she handed me a hamburger-shaped bun with pink icing crisscrossed on top. I thanked her and stuck it in my bag to snack on later.

I strolled through the open office door and stepped out into the vacant hall, already beginning to feel just a tiny bit guilty about Amina, but knowing that she *would* be okay with Uncle Simon until I got home. He was really cool with her. Wherever she was, he was. There were so many times I had seen him catch her busy hands before she touched a hot skillet full of fried okra or picked up one of our sharp carving knives. I had even seen him wheel after her in the yard and catch her before she toddled into a giant mound of red ants underneath our pomegranate tree. He was like a second mother to her. She would be okay with him until I could knock out a couple of classes.

With my mouth watering from the lemony smell of the pastry in my backpack, I walked through the open courtyard doors at the end of the hallway and allowed my thoughts to roll over to my history class. We were having a quiz on the French revolution, and so far I hadn't had five minutes to go over the material I was supposed to read. I was major hoping that my teacher, Coach Cruz, was going to lay one of his true-false quizzes on us. With any luck I could make at least a fifty, and maybe add twenty points or so to my grade next week with a short essay. Coach Cruz was usually cool that way. He was always willing to let a girl get extra credit—at least, I was praying that he still was. After this morning I couldn't be sure about any of my teachers. They had all ratted me out to Principal Nesby. I couldn't trust any of them.

I passed the concrete statue of Harriet Tubman and headed for a shortcut through our ancient gym so I could holler at Trip during his workout. Last year the senior class had gotten together and raised money to buy some used exercise equipment from a fitness club that was going out of business. All they could afford was some rusty weights, a couple of worn treadmills, and a punched-out punching bag, but unlike the equally crappy equipment that the football boys trained on, it was open to all the kids. With their exercise teacher's permission, Trip and a few of the other buff guys in his class usually spent their entire gym hour just working on their muscles. I wasn't at all surprised when I yanked open the weight room door and found him there running on one of the treadmills, his thick muscular legs making long strides over the black rubber. "Trip, I got out pretty quick, so I stopped by, hey what's up?" I hollered.

"Hey what's up back, my dark sister?" he yelled at me.

"Yeah, hey what's up back, my dark sister?" yelled Tommy, a handsome Korean guy working out on the treadmill next to Trip. Trip and I both laughed.

"Man, you a fool," Trip said.

Tommy winked at him and laughed.

"Hey, Tyra Banks," he yelled at me. "You don't need to work out. You already look good to me. Hey, you wanna come have a spring roll with me later?"

"You can't get a spring roll around here," I yelled back.

"Yes you can, at my house," he said. "I'm a great cook. Come on over for lunch, and I'll show you."

"You wish," I said. "I don't even like spring rolls."

"That's not what your girlfriend Alejandra told me. Now come on girl. You know you all into me. Don't be hating on me 'cause my folks came from across the water."

"Most everybody's folks came from across the water," I said, and laughed.

"I know. That's what I'm talking about. So be for real, girl. Come on over and hang out with me."

"Wait on it," I said.

He laughed and turned up the switch on his treadmill. The motor made a loud whirring sound. "I can wait," he said over the noise. "I'm extra special. You'll come around; all the girls do."

"Yeah right!" I said.

"Man, you a fool," Trip said, shaking his head at him. "Quit bugging girls that don't want you and finish working out." Trip turned off the treadmill and hopped off, dripping big beads of sweat. "Hey, fill me in on the office visit," he said, walking over to me. "What kind of trouble you in now?"

"I'm not sure yet," I said. "I have to go back."

"Well, give me the lowdown so far."

I stood in the doorway and filled Trip in on what went down in Principal Nesby's office. I told him about her asking me how I was gonna take care of Amina when she got older, and about how many of my favorite teachers had ratted me out. Trip said that he thought the teachers telling on me was pretty cold, and we started talking about how sometimes even good teachers do dumb things. We talked about the teachers who had turned in some pretty decent students just because they caught them smoking in the bathroom or kicking back a few beers in the parking lot after school. We went on and on about the teachers who gave you detention if you were late a couple of times, and the ones that told your parents if they caught you making out with your boyfriend or girlfriend between classes. It was a long conversation, too long. Before we knew it the end-of-period bell had rung, and it was time for us to tear ass to our next classes.

"Oops, we better book. I gotta get to my quiz on time today," I said, glancing down at my watch.

"Shoot, you right. I better be getting out of the door too. I got to get to science class and set up my microscope. I'll see you later," Trip said, and rushed through the double doors back into the main gym. I waved at Tommy, who was just finishing his workout, and left.

I meant to hurry to my history class, but I made a stop to grab a peanut cluster candy bar from the snack machine in front of the teacher's lounge. Then I went to bum a blue ballpoint from my girl Alejandra, who was in study hall trying to sleep off the effects of a party she had sneaked out to the night before. She said her stomach was upset and her head was pounding, so I gave her some Pepto pills that I had in my backpack, and four or five baby aspirins. She swallowed it all down without any water and started telling me how much fun she had at the party. I hadn't gone to a party in forever. I couldn't wait to hear the details.

"Girl, the party was off the hook! Do you know what I'm saying?" Alejandra said.

"Of course, girl. I know exactly what you saying. Who all was there?" I asked. "Did that poser Kira show up? She gets on my nerves sometimes, always acting like she better than everybody else, 'cause her mama work at some computer company. Did she show up?"

"You know she did. She came with some basketball player that goes to another school. All she did the whole night was talk about what everybody else had on."

"Yeah, that sounds like her. And what about that really hot guy, Akeem, who Shardae used to date? Was he there? I used to think he was cool before he stopped going around with Shardae and dogged her out."

"Yeah, he did her dirty. Anyway girl, everybody was there but you. Like I said, the party was seriously off the hook, and you know I got Jaime to drive me home later. That was the best, girl!" Alejandra said.

"Really? Jaime took you home?"

"Oh hell yeah, girl. And he asked me to go to another party with him next week. You know I'm going. I don't care what my parents say. If I gotta go to confession every week, I might as well have something to confess to. You know what I'm talkin' about?"

"Yeah, but girl, you sure are crazy."

"Crazy like a girl 'bout to get a new boyfriend. You know how long I been liking Jamie."

"Yeah, I know. You been all into him since sixth grade."

"Oh, for real."

"Anyway, I hear you, girl. Man, I sure wish I woulda been at that party."

"Me too, but let me finish telling you what all happened."

"Ooh yeah, girl. Tell me, and don't leave nothing out. I want to know exactly what I missed!" I said.

What I missed was everything. According to Alejandra, I had skipped the event of the year. All kinds of things went on. I loved hearing everything she had to say, and when she was finished she even managed to top the party info by taking me to the bathroom and showing me her new secret tattoo that she got only a few days before the party.

"My cousin Michael did it for me. Ain't it major cool?" she asked, yanking down her shorts and showing her hip to me. I surprised myself and looked at it a little green-eyed. I normally didn't like tattoos, but I had to give it up to girlfriend. The red butterfly was an asset to her tan skin. I figured it would look just as good on someone a little bit darker shade of brown.

"Man, it is cool," I said.

She laughed. "See, I knew you would want one too. Don't be looking all jealous. You know I'll hook you. You my girl. I'm always gonna take care of you," she said with a big grin. "I'll let you know where my cousin Michael's place is. He'll do it for cheap, and I'll also tell you what other kinds of tattoos he makes. He can do anything, so don't even sweat about it."

"Thanks, girl. I just might let him do a butterfly or something on me. I really like the way yours looks," I said, writing down her cousin's address. As I scribbled she added in more information. She told me how long it took to get the butterfly done and what the process felt like. When I finally looked at my watch again the very last class bell had rung, and I had to run like mad to get to my history period at the other end of the school.

By the time I reached the large portable located by the back gate, the rest of the students had already gone into class. I hurried down the concrete walkway as quickly as I could, hoping Coach Cruz would still be cool and let me in, but a few feet from the porch something jammed me up—Principal Nesby. She was standing at the wooden railing of the portable in her Oprah suit talking to Coach Cruz. I couldn't believe it. They were face to face, deep in conversation about something serious. I could tell because Coach had his massive hairy arms plastered to the side of his burnt-orange sweat suit like he always did when he was talking to somebody big. Like Trip's mom, Shronda Faye, he was ex-military. He was used to standing at attention when he was being talked to by someone higher up. Anyway, I swallowed hard, and drug myself down the rest of the walkway. I knew they were talking about me. Principal Nesby had obviously gotten through with her meeting a little early, and instead of going back to her office she had rushed over to my classroom to get in my business again. I could just hear her asking Coach how many times I had been late, and telling him that she needed me back in the office. Damn, what was up with that? Principal Nesby was getting on my last nerves. She acted like she wanted to help, but what I really needed was for her to quit riding me. I already had enough to deal with. She was kind of a nice sister, but she was still beginning to piss me off. I felt myself getting madder with each step, and by the time I reached the portable stairs I had what teachers call "an attitude." I was about to go off, really go ahead and make my problems hers, since she was all into them anyway. I stomped up the stairs actually ready to ask her why she was making things more difficult for me—but it didn't happen. The second I stepped up on the porch she turned and stared at me, and I froze, completely turned to ice. Something wasn't right. I could see it in her too-calm eyes, but mostly I could feel it. It felt like I was standing still, and yet falling at the same time, falling fast and hard away from something. It wigged me out, but I still couldn't move, couldn't try to steady myself or even take a step. Principal Nesby walked over to me. Her face had the same kind of calm as her eyes, but I could tell that it was an act. She was covering something. I played cards with Trip all the time, and I always won. I knew when somebody was covering, trying to force all the emotion out.

I really started to freak. Something bad was going down. "What happened? What's going on?" I asked, and girlfriend instantly fell apart.

"Oh China, I'm so, so sorry," she said in a pained voice, placing her hand on my shoulder gently. "My secretary and I have been looking for you for a while. I'm so sorry, but your daughter, she . . ." I barely got the rest. The minute she said *daughter* I was somewhere else, gone. I heard her talking, but it was like she was talking from the bottom of a well, or from the other end of a long hallway. It came to me distant, distorted, like the sound from a warped record. I could hardly make out the words *your baby, stopped breathing, ambulance,* and *your uncle needs you to come right away.* I hardly heard any of it, but I didn't need to. I felt it, even stronger as she tried to get the words out, and I knew what it was. I remembered. It had been a long time since I felt it, but I remembered. The evening I pressed my face close to Mama's as she passed away, I felt it. It was that mother-child connection, the feeling that you get when something has just been severed forever, cut apart. *Souls separated and floating freely*—another line from a poem in my English class. That's what I felt, my daughter's soul separating from mine.

"You have to go home," I heard Coach Cruz say. "Principal

Nesby needs to be here on campus, so I'm going to run you over while she watches my class." He came over and took my arm to walk me down the steps. He was a gigantic guy with a strong grip, but even he couldn't get me to move. I couldn't take a step. I couldn't do anything at all.

CHAPTER 2

We buried Mama on the worst day that I can ever remember there being in Houston. It was frigid and freezing rain poured from the sky, making our final good-bye to her even worse than I thought it would be. Three months earlier, when I learned that Mama wasn't going to survive her cancer, I had prayed for a warm day filled with the beautiful purple sage bushes and tall yellow sunflowers that grew untouched between the grave sites in our neighborhood cemetery. Mama loved flowers. In the spring she would always take time out to plant a flower bed. Her favorite flowers were roses and pansies, and I was certain she would like the sage and sunflowers too, even though she couldn't actually see them. But Mama died before winter turned to spring, so all I could do was sit silently in a folding chair beside Uncle Simon, blowing into my cold red hands and hoping that the service Mama had written herself would come to a close quickly. "Put your hands in your pocket, child. It's a day that would make even the dead shiver," a wrinkled old neighbor lady on the opposite side of me had whispered in my ear. For a moment the comment struck me as funny. I imagined the corpses lying quietly beneath the frozen brown grass suddenly popping up from their wooden coffins, hugging themselves, and going *brr*. I thought it would be a really cool sight to see, but then I realized that Mama would soon be one of those corpses beneath the grass too. I started to tear up. "Don't you do it," the old lady whispered to me, pointing her gloved hand up toward the gray overcast sky. "Don't you utter a sob. When I was little my mama used to tell me that when a child cries, an angel dies. One of God's own creatures topples from the nice white clouds and tumbles into the burning pit of Hell with every tear a little girl like you sheds."

"Excuse me, ma'am?" I whispered back.

"No excuses," she said, shaking her finger at me. "What we do below always affects what happens up above. Remember that, child. Remember and endure."

"Yes, ma'am," I said, and immediately wiped my face with the tail of my corduroy coat. Deep down I knew that the old sister was just trippin'. I didn't believe that angels could die, and I sure didn't see how just a few waterworks from a little girl could cause anything to be cast into Hell forever. But I was just a little kid back then, and misery was piled up on me higher than the mound of black dirt that the undertakers were waiting to shovel onto Mama's grave. I know it sounds silly, but there was no way that I could deal with Mama's passing and angel-death guilt, too.

Mama and me didn't go to church much. Sunday was the only time that she could rest her sore feet after standing twelve hours a day, six days a week in the beauty shop. We usually only went to our church, Bethel Hill Chapel, on special occasions like Christmas. During that time angels would be everywhere. Every bulletin board in the church had some kind of celestial winged creature tacked up to it. In the children's schoolroom, where I actually loved listening to the Bible stories and coloring the handouts, the angels were all cherubs. They were plump, baby-faced toddlers with cheeks the color of Santa Claus's red suit. I always enjoyed seeing them. They were usually floating around in some starlit sky, or hovering over some happy little children's heads while they joined hands and sang around a huge Christmas tree. It was all joy with the cherubs, and when I thought about what the old lady was saying to me, I knew that there was no way I could do them any harm. I dried my tears up, and I used the horrible image of those rosy-cheeked cherubs falling into a fiery pit to get me through the funeral, the mourner's dinner, and Uncle Simon moving his stuff into Mama's room when everything was over. "When a child cries, an angel dies," the old lady told me. Sure, she was just messing with my head, but what she said kept me from wigging out. It was like rubber cement to hold me together. I used it then and kept using it. It helped me out when Uncle Simon went to the hospital to have minor surgery on his back and somehow slipped into a coma for a month, when I broke two ribs in a car crash with Trip and his mom, and when we had to sell almost everything that Mama left me to pay the bills for those ribs.

I didn't shed a single tear during any of those incidents, or anything else that I've faced since Mama passed away. I repeated what the old lady said to me, and told myself that falling apart would hurt the cherubs, and it worked. I felt strong, like I could beat down anything that came my way, but not yesterday. Yesterday when my daughter went away for good too, I tried repeating the warning to myself, but not even the threat of blistered angel skin and scorched wings could help hold me together. I didn't care about cherubs or seraphim or anything else in the sky up above. I just cared that my baby was lying still and without breath on a old, raggedy sofa that I had left her on not even two hours before. I threw myself on her and I screamed and cried enough tears to topple the entire Heavenly Host. I sobbed and yelled until Trip and Mrs. Mayfield pulled me off her, then I watched in horror while a burly man from the coroner's office gently placed her in a black body bag and took her away from me forever.

"Oh my Lord," Mrs. Mayfield cried, as the man went out of the door with my child. "Baby, I just don't know what could have happened. I ain't never had nothing happen like this before. I just don't understand. She had a cold, that's all. I done kept plenty of babies with bad colds. I just don't believe it!"

Neither did I. I didn't believe it, not even this morning when the tired, moody coroner sat down outside of her office and tried to explain to me and Uncle what had happened. I just watched her blankly as she pushed her stringy blond hair out of her sleep-encrusted eyes and tried to put my child's death into words that we could understand.

"Your little girl had a preexisting heart condition that apparently was never detected," she said, reading from a beige folder. "She was born with a heart malfunction that sometimes caused her heart to get an irregular heartbeat. It would be very hard for me to put it in terms that you and your uncle could comprehend easily, but somehow her heart condition reacted to the medicine the doctor gave her. Her heart started beating very slowly until it simply stopped. I don't think that she was in any real pain. She probably had a short period where she wasn't breathing very well, and that's about all. I think for her it was probably very much like going to sleep."

"Like going to sleep," I mumbled.

"Yes, I think so. I think her heart just stopped pumping, and couldn't start itself back up. I'm so sorry," she said, patting my knee with a clammy hand. "I've already told the police that I don't believe anyone was at fault here. Neither you nor your baby-sitter could have seen this coming. It was just something that was a long time in the making, and finally caught up to her yesterday. Does heart disease run in your family?"

"My father and grandmother both died of heart complications," Uncle Simon said, placing his head in his hands. "But I just thought that it was something that happened because of their lifestyles. They were both pretty heavy, and loved just about every part of the pig. They had problems with cholesterol and clogged arteries, but I was never told about any irregular heartbeats. I don't know. Maybe the doctors just didn't see it with everything else that was going on inside them."

"Maybe, and what about your mother? You just mentioned your father and grandmother. Were there any heart problems in your mother's history?" the coroner asked.

Uncle shook his head. "Not that I know of. My mother never seemed to get very sick like most people her age. She would get a cold maybe every other year, or her arthritis would give her a fit occasionally, but for the most part she was pretty healthy until the day she died."

"And how was that?" she asked.

"She was staying with a sick friend when one of the lady's grand-babies set the house on fire with a cigarette lighter. The smoke got to her and she never got out."

"Oh, I'm sorry."

"Me too, but she was a good woman, and I know when God took her home she was ready to go. But to answer your first question, I don't know if she had any problems with her heart. If she did she never said anything to me. My God, if I would have known that there was even the slightest chance that something could have been wrong, I would have had that baby checked out. I would have made sure that the doctor knew that something funny could be going on," Uncle said, shaking his head.

"Don't blame yourself, sir. There's no way you could have known, and it's possible that what happened to her wasn't genetic at all," the coroner said.

"Well what was it? I'm a good mama. Amina was only two. I take her to the doctor all the time. How could the doctor not know? Couldn't he hear her heart if it was doing something strange? I'm sorry, ma'am, but that just doesn't make any sense to me. I don't understand none of what you just said. It doesn't make sense does it, Uncle?" I asked Uncle Simon.

"I don't know, baby," he said, shaking his head.

"These things are often difficult to catch. It's really hard to say how it happened or how it was missed. It's possible that Amina's problem was uniquely her own, and for some reason her doctors never caught it, but it's also possible that someone in your family did have the same irregularity as Amina and it was just never diagnosed. The truth is we may never know. Doctors aren't perfect. They can only diagnose an internal problem if they see or hear some evidence of it. I suspect your daughter's dangerous heart condition never showed up during an exam."

"But how couldn't it? She has examinations all the time. I never miss any of her appointments. I make sure that she gets all her shots and everything. This is just whack!" I snapped. "I don't believe you. I woulda known if something was wrong with my child. I don't think you even bothered to look her over right. I think you just made something up."

"No ma'am, no ma'am. I did not make anything up, Ms. Cameron," she snapped back in a surprisingly funky tone. I guess I had woken *something* in her up.

"Look, I'm sorry, but there's no more that I can tell you," she said. "I know that this is a horrible loss for you, but these things happen, they just do. But you don't have to take my word for it. You have a right to seek answers from anyone that you choose. You can pick up a copy of the official report at the front desk, and you and your uncle can pay for another independent coroner to look over my results. I'm certain that he'll just confirm what I told you, but it is your right to try to get all the answers." She stood up and brushed the wrinkles out of her light blue hospital scrubs as easily as I knew she was about to brush me off. I stood up too and waited.

"If you're going to have someone else look at your daughter they can get in touch with me through the main office. If not, you can make arrangements at the front desk to have her picked up by the funeral parlor of your choice. I have no reason to hold her here any longer," she said.

"Yeah, right, whatever," I said, as she headed for the glass door at the end of the hall.

"Thank you, ma'am," Uncle Simon called after her. But the minute the sliding doors slid back into place he shouted, "Damn insensitive bitch!" It was a shout that made the tough-looking security guard at the end of the hall look our way, and one that I was totally unprepared for. Uncle is always polite and courteous to women. He's what the sisters in my hood call "the last decent brother," the kind of guy who always treats women like he understands what a woman suffered to bring him into this world. He never goes through a door in front of a lady even though he's in a wheelchair, and he always lets them go ahead of us in the grocery store checkout line. He holds your purse while you run to the dressing room to try on a blouse and pair of shorts, and tells you how lovely you look no matter how lame your outfit is. Hearing Uncle call a woman a "damn bitch" is like seeing the Pope hanging out at a rap concert with gold chains and a pair of baggy jeans, it's just not right—but Uncle's not right.

He spent most of the night in his room molding and shaping figurines of Amina out of blocks of clay. Amina sitting in his lap tugging on his soft black beard, Amina picking red ripe tomatoes off the tomato bushes in our backyard, Amina and him flying bread-bag kites in the vacant lot down the street from our house, Amina playing with her favorite stuffed tiger on the front porch, and Amina pretending to paint his lips with one of my empty lipstick tubes. "That's it, make me beautiful, girlfriend," he always teased when she did it in real life.

"You'll be the supreme diva of the ball," I would laugh as I watched them from the kitchen doorway. To me Uncle's figurines of Amina were special. Just standing in his room holding them made me feel a little less shock and grief. But when I told Uncle Simon how much I liked them he just yelled for me to take them away. "Get them out of here, China. Throw them in the trash can outside or carry them down to the bayou and toss them in the water. I don't care what you do with them, just get them as far away from me as you can," he said in a voice thick with pain. Then he rolled past me into the bathroom. I rapped on the door to see if he was okay, but all I got was silence. I didn't know what else to do, so I closed my eyes and held the figurines to my breast, wishing the whole time that they were my precious daughter.

I remembered one of Trip's ideas for an *Outer Realm* set in Africa. In his story a mother traveling on a long journey to her homeland loses her only son to a hungry hyena. The wild animal just comes out of nowhere while the woman is sleeping and carries off her baby for a midnight snack. In the morning the mother searches high and low for the boy until it's clear that he has met with foul play. Then, broken and teary-eyed, she makes the trip back to her village alone. When she gets there she goes to see a powerful witch doctor, who immediately carves a clay figurine of her son and does a magical fire dance around it. After that, he tells the mother to go home and sleep in a fetal position, all curled up like a baby. Of course the mother does exactly what he tells her to do. In the morning when she wakes up she finds herself nine months pregnant. She throws up her hands and rejoices. A few hours later she feels the pains of labor, and a new son is born to her. When she has finished giving birth she walks to the doorway of her hut with him in her arms, and tells the whole village that the fire god has blessed her with a reason to be happy again.

I liked Trip's idea when I heard it, and I still like it now, but I know that it could never really happen. In real life no lump of clay can bring your child back to life. Uncle was right to want to toss the figurines away. No matter how much they looked like Amina, they weren't her. They didn't contain the soft feel of her hand in mine when I walked her to Mrs. Mayfield's each morning or the look of joy on her face when I picked her up again in the afternoon. They just couldn't contain who she was.

I walked over to the open window behind Uncle's bed and threw them as hard as I could through the burglar bars. They instantly became hidden from me in the tall weeds and dandelions. I slammed the window closed and beat on the glass with my fists until it shattered, sending huge shards of broken glass all over Uncle's pillow and piercing my right hand with sharp splinters. I didn't mind the pain though. It was real, concrete, something that I could understand. It wasn't like what I was feeling on the inside. That pain I would never be able to comprehend. It was a mother's pain, anguish that only someone who had been in labor for thirteen hours could understand.

"China, what's going on out there?" I heard Uncle yell through the bathroom door. "Are you all right?"

"Yes, sir. I'm just fine," I mumbled. Then I sat down at the foot of his bed and pressed my hands together until the sharp pain of the glass splinters made it almost impossible for me to feel anything else. That was the way I got through last night. Now here it was the next day, at the coroner's office, and nothing was working anymore. I could feel everything. It was making me ill inside and out.

"Damn unfeeling bitch!" I heard Uncle mutter, as he pushed the forward button on his wheelchair. "Let's go get our baby and take her to somebody who cares."

"I'm nauseous. I think I'm going to be sick, Uncle," I said, and ran for the bathroom at the end of the hall.

"Wait, China, let me see if I can get you some help," I heard him say as the heavy bathroom door slammed shut behind me. I couldn't even respond.

I spent the next ten minutes with my head over a toilet. I threw up everything that I had in my stomach: the gum that I had chewed nervously and swallowed before we walked into the building, the breakfast of scrambled eggs and cheese grits that Uncle Simon made me eat even though I told him that I didn't want anything. I threw it all up, but deep down I knew that what I was really trying to get out of me was guilt. It wasn't Uncle's responsibility to have Amina checked out. It was mine. I also knew that Amina had two relatives who had died from heart problems. I should have remembered that each time I took her to the clinic. I should have asked them to give her some kinda test. All this time I thought I was a good mother, but a good mother knows when her child is ailing. A good mother also doesn't leave her baby with somebody else when she's not feeling good. I should have gone and gotten her from Mrs. Mayfield the minute she called me. Maybe I could have seen something going on with her that a sixty-five-year-old lady couldn't. I thought of all I had gone through or given up for her. I had messed up my relationship with Uncle, nearly flunked out of school, lost my best girlfriend, and basically missed doing all the dope things kids my age got to do, and for what? So that I could take care of a baby, a baby that I didn't even have anymore because I didn't really take care of her. Like my English teacher Mrs. Jerome would say, it was ironic; ironic and all screwed up. All this time I had been calling my homegirl Yolanda a bad mom, but Yolanda never killed her kid. As sorry as she was she never made a horrible mistake like that.

I got up off my knees and pushed down the hot water faucet handle with my hand. The sharp splinters still in my fingers from the night before dug in deeper, but I didn't cry out. I caught a cupped hand full of warm water and swished it around in my mouth for a while. When I was through cleaning up I joined Uncle Simon in the hall again. Together we went to the desk and I asked for the form that would ship my child to a funeral home in our hood. When the paper was all signed we called on Uncle's emergency cell phone for a yellow cab van with a wheelchair lift and went outside to wait on it.

As we waited a young white lady with auburn hair and dark sunshades stepped out of the backseat of a blue Dodge followed by a laughing toddler, who immediately took off running down the walkway as if he had just spotted a litter of frisky puppies. I wanted to yell at the woman and tell her to go grab his hand before he ran into something, or somebody took off with him, but how could I? I couldn't even look out for my own child. I watched the boy running down the walkway until his mother finally got a clue and chased him down. "Cody, I told you about running away from me," I heard her say in a stern voice. It was just what I would have said to Amina, if I still had an Amina to say it to. I leaned against Uncle's chair and prayed for the van to come soon.

A couple of miles from the funeral parlor I decided to give Trip a ring. When Uncle and I left the house, Trip was sleeping in the wooden rocker next to my bed. It was where he had spent the night bear-snoring, while I cried over Amina and wished that I could sleep through anything too. Sleep was like a gift to Trip. No matter what kind of trauma the day ushered in, Trip could always get away from it the minute he crawled under the covers, and it had always been that way.

A couple of springs ago he and his mama, Shronda Faye, went down to South Texas to go fishing. They arrived somewhere near Corpus late in evening and rented two cheap hotel rooms not too far from the water. They went right to sleep, and while they slept a common Texas downpour suddenly turned into an angry storm. Excessive rainfall and high waves caused flash flooding. Parts of the hotel starting filling up with water, so the manager set off an alarm system. As soon as the loud sirens sounded everybody came tearing out of their rooms but Trip. He didn't hear a thing. His mama banged on his door for nearly five minutes until one of the housekeepers came running with a key and let her in. She woke him up and all was fine, but ever since then his mama makes him leave his door cracked each night before he goes to bed.

Trip doesn't really like doing it. He gets on Shronda Faye all the time about treating him like a baby, and taking away his privacy, but

Shronda Faye doesn't care. She says leaving the door open keeps Trip safe from anything that he can't see coming, and that it's her job to protect him from the things that might cause him harm. I guess that also includes me.

Even though Shronda Faye was pretty good friends with Mama when she was alive, she was never okay with me having a baby for Trip. Since Amina's birth she's only come to see her once, the day that we got out of the hospital. When Uncle and I pulled up in the cab, she and Trip were sitting on the front porch playing dominoes at a folding card table. The minute they saw us Shronda Faye threw her dominoes back in the cardboard box and ran down the stairs like she had purchased a lotto ticket from me, and I was bringing her the winnings. It really shocked me.

Shronda Faye is a beautiful woman. She wears her hair in really cool dreds, and she has Trip's dimples, special dark skin, and cocoa-brown saucer eyes, but after she left the military she got really depressed and let herself go. She smoked a lot and put on a great deal more weight than she should have. She wasn't yet roly-poly fat, but she was a long way from the fine sister she was at boot camp. I've seen her walk down to Clinton's store for a pack of Salems, and stroll easily over to Glen's corner store for a bag of chocolate chip cookies, but I had never seen her run. Yet she dashed down the steps and pulled back Amina's blanket for what I thought was just a short peek, but was I ever wrong. She checked Amina out for a good five minutes. She peered at every part of her, going over her like an assembly line supervisor going over a freshly put-together object. Finally, she mumbled something about Amina's eyes and also her straight hair looking just like Trip's, which hung to his shoulders when he didn't feel like tying it up. Then, before I could even agree or disagree with her, she walked right past me to her wide-load pickup truck and climbed in. The next thing I knew girlfriend was off, screeching her wheels like a Saturday night drag racer.

"Man, what's up with her?" I asked, handing the baby to Trip so I could push Uncle up the wooden ramp on the side of the porch.

"Nothing," Trip mumbled, rocking Amina back and forth, keeping his eyes fixed on her face.

"I'm sure she just had somewhere she had to be," Uncle said as I pushed him forward.

"She probably just remembered that she left the Crock-Pot going. She does that sometimes," Trip added.

"I'm sure that's exactly what happened," Uncle said.

"I guess you guys are right," I said.

Later I found out that both Trip and Uncle were lying. Shronda never said one word to me, but when I was in the hospital she told Trip that Amina was probably some other boy's, and she told Uncle that she would never believe that Amina was her son's until Amina had a blood test. But when she saw Amina lying in the baby blanket, looking way too much like Trip, Shronda had to give in and admit that Amina was indeed Trip's little girl. "I guess she could be Trip's, if you done checked all them other boys off the list," she told me one morning at Johnson's drugstore, while I was purchasing a package of BC powder for Uncle. The statement made me so mad I cursed her out for old and new, which made Trip not speak to me for an entire week. It was the first time that I could ever remember us being on the outs. I was glad when he finally came over and apologized. He said that he was sorry, and his mama was too. So I accepted his apology, but not hers. I was certain Shronda wasn't sorry, and it wasn't long before that proved to be true. Shronda never told me Amina wasn't Trip's again, but she also never bought Amina so much as a baby doll from the dollar store. I couldn't count on her for Christmas or birthday presents, or even a bag of candy corn on Halloween. It just didn't make sense to me. I knew how much she loved Trip. I couldn't see why she couldn't love his daughter as well.

"You know my mama. It's not easy for her to make adjustments in her life," Trip said, while he and I were trying to put together a zoo-animal mobile for Amina's crib. "She likes order and control. She's not real good at dealing with situations that just pop up."

"Amina's not a situation, she's a baby, and your mama had nine months to deal with it," I said, handing him a laminated cardboard ostrich. "I'm not asking her to play Grandma. I'm just asking her to admit that the baby even exists."

"I don't know what to tell you, China. Mama is just Mama. I gotta go," Trip said, and left the room with the ostrich still in his hand. It was the last time we ever had a conversation about his mama and our baby. I understood then that Shronda would never come around. I finished putting the mobile together without the ostrich. When it was completed I hung the lopsided toy over Amina's crib, and dangled it for her until she fell asleep. While she slept I wondered how one day I would explain to her that she had a grandma, but didn't have a grandma. I wondered how I would explain Shronda not wanting anything to do with her.

"Don't worry about it too much, China. The wind sometimes changes directions. She might one day decide to be the best grandma in the world," Uncle advised me, as I was giving Amina her afternoon feeding.

"She might one day, before it's too late," I agreed, placing Amina in his lap. But it looks like I was wrong about that, too. It was already too late. I dialed my home number. When Trip finally picked up the phone I told him what the coroner had said about Amina, and asked him to meet us at the funeral home. I didn't even bother asking if he had told his mother about our baby. I didn't really care.

By the time I clicked the phone off and handed it back to Uncle Simon we were in front of Ivy, the only funeral parlor in our community which was actually named after a dog. Its owner, Phoebe Aldrich, named it for her favorite black Lab, who was struck and killed by a group of speeding teens on their way home from a college step show. The funeral parlor was located in a large, goldenrod yellow, newly renovated house, and was originally meant to be a place where grieving pet owners could send their faithful friends to a final rest, but Phoebe Aldrich soon found out that no matter how much folks in the hood loved their cats and dogs they weren't going to spend their grocery money burying them. With a few modifications the home was now a place where two-legged folks met their final good-byes. When the van driver opened the door I hopped out and waited for Uncle to come down the lift. As soon as he was safely on the ground, Uncle paid the driver, and we went up the concrete ramp on the side of the funeral home to wait. "I wish this day was already over," Uncle said, looking at me with watery eyes.

"Me too," I said. "I hate this. Why did this have to happen, Uncle?"

"It didn't have to, baby. It just did."

"I wish the whole day would just go away," I said. "I wish it would all just be over."

After we waited for thirty minutes, Shronda's pickup rolled to a stop in front of the building. Trip hopped out of the driver's side, and I expected to see Shronda take off, but to my surprise she climbed out of the truck too. I left Uncle's side to greet Trip. As I approached him I could see that Trip didn't look much better than he had the night before. He was wearing the same crumpled *Outer Realm* T-shirt and shorts. His straight hair was a tangled mess, and his eyes were puffy and red. Shronda, on the other hand, was all decked out. She had on a black pleated suit with long black gloves, and a black pillbox hat like the kind Grandma used to wear to church. She looked like she was already on her way to a funeral, on her way to bury a child that she had never spent any time with. I honestly wasn't big on violence, but the sight of her made me swollen with anger. The closer she got to the porch steps the more I wanted to sock her dead in the face. She had no business showing up in a mourning outfit for my child. I gritted my teeth and balled up my fist, but Trip must have sensed what I was ready to do. He skirted around Shronda Faye and ran up the steps. "She's my mama, China," he whispered, pulling me back away from the edge of the porch. "You know how wrong she can get about stuff. This is bad enough on everybody. Don't get to swinging and make it worse. I don't want to be caught between ya'll today. Just chill. We can all get through this together."

"What *we* Trip?" I asked. "She shouldn't even be here. Why did you bring her? When did she give a damn about my child?"

"Hold it, China Cup," Uncle said, rolling over to us. "You don't want to do this here, not on this day. Let Shronda Faye do whatever she gone do. You just handle your business, be a lady, be a mother."

"I'm trying, Uncle," I said.

"Try harder," he said in a voice thick with sadness. "Let's just get through this. I don't want Amina looking down from Heaven and seeing all of us acting a fool. We didn't do that when she was alive, and we ain't gonna do it now. Does everybody understand me?"

"Yes, sir," me and Trip both said. I turned to see Shronda Faye step up on the porch. She took her hat off and fanned her sweaty face as she walked up to me.

"I'm so sorry, baby. I'm so very sorry about my little grand-daughter. I'm sorry I never got a chance to spend time with her," she said, placing one of her ridiculous gloved hands on my shoulder. In my mind I saw myself slapping that hand off, and telling her frontin' ass what she could do with her sorry. It was what I wanted to do more than anything, but what Uncle said was true. It wasn't the time or place for me to throw a fit. I nodded my head. Then I walked to the parlor entrance, and opened the door for Uncle to go in without giving her stupid behind a second thought. "Come on, Mama,"

I heard Trip say to her, in an exasperated voice, as I walked in behind Uncle. I instantly felt sorry for Trip. In fact, I felt sorry for us all.

The minute Uncle Simon and I went into the foyer of the funeral home I felt like death was standing right beside me. It was the way I felt on the afternoon that Uncle and I went to make arrangements for Mama's funeral, like the Grim Reaper greeted us at the front door and followed us from room to room as we planned our services. It wasn't a scary feeling. It was just a feeling that you really wanted to be someplace else. I felt that way again as soon as I looked around the sitting room and saw the ugly purple crushed-velvet sofa and the matching purple velour curtains that looked like they could easily have gone into the Munsters' living room. It was so dark in the room you could only see the whites of Phoebe's eyes in the numerous portraits of her that hung on the cedar-paneled walls.

"Man, this place is a little creepy," Trip said. "A brother wouldn't want to stay in here too long."

"An Uncle wouldn't either," Uncle Simon said. "China, yell back there and let somebody know that we need some help."

I walked over to an open doorway and hollered out, "Is anybody there?" down a hallway that was too dimly lit to see the end of. A moment later an elegant crystal chandelier hanging from the arched ceiling flickered on, bathing the room in soft white light.

"Whew! That's a little better," Trip said. Any other time I woulda teased him about loving sci-fi and horror flicks, and still being afraid of things that go bump in the night, but my heart wasn't in it.

"May I help you?" a voice said from the other end of the hall. A tall, handsome brother dressed in a colorful African dashiki stepped through the doorway. From the waist up he looked like he had just stepped off the plane from the motherland, but he was wearing a fly pair of Seventies windowpane jeans that I had seen in the vintage clothing shop next to our school only a week earlier.

"Are you the mother of that beautiful sweet child that just arrived a few moments ago? What can I do for you, my sister?" he asked Shronda Faye, in a voice that sounded way too smooth and cool for somebody that spent all his time working with folks that couldn't even hear him talk. I thought that I would have liked the brother, if he hadn't messed up and assumed that heifer, Shronda Faye, was the mother of my child.

"No, Amina's my baby. She's just somebody that showed up," I said icily. Uncle and Trip both gave me a "that-wasn't-called-for" look. I didn't even pretend to care.

"Oh, she's your child?" the brother asked just as smoothly, obviously not a bit shocked at how young I was. I guess it wasn't a big thing for him. I'm sure he had other teen moms come in from time to time.

"Yes sir, she's mine," I said.

"Of course, little sister. Please excuse me. I'm really sorry that you're going through something like this at such a tender age. I'm Brother Agee. Your little girl just arrived in the back. Why don't you come with me to the office and I'll get you all fixed up," Brother Agee said, starting up the hallway. Me and Uncle followed him, with Trip and Shronda bringing up the rear.

The back office was *really* a trip to the motherland. It was like something out of an African museum exhibit. The sand-colored walls were covered with all sorts of strange animal masks. Bronze fertility gods with protruding bellies sat atop a metal file cabinet, wooden giraffes and elephants stood proudly atop a round marble table, two giant animal-hide drums sat next to a brown leather wing chair, and a huge portrait of four onyx-skinned Sudanese women walking with heavy cloth bundles on their heads hung over the leather sofa that me, Trip, and Shronda flopped down on. When we were comfortably seated, Brother Agee pulled a rolling chair from his mahogany desk over to me, and started working on what he referred to as my "terribly sad situation." The first thing he did was ask what kind of life insurance I had on Amina. The question drew a blank stare from me. I couldn't afford any life insurance, and even if I could, why would I have life insurance for a child that was supposed to live longer than me? It was dumb, like a Fifth Ward brother pretending to be Shaka Zulu. "I don't have any." I said.

"Yes you do, or at least I do," Uncle corrected. "I have one on the baby. People die pretty young in my family. I wanted to make sure that we were all covered just in case. I got a little policy on all three of us. Here's the information on Amina, so you can verify it," he said, pulling out a goldplated money clip with a blue plastic card on top. He handed the card to Brother Agee, who immediately started looking it over.

"It's current," Uncle said. "I make a payment each month when I get my disability check."

"I'm certain it is up to date, but let me just check it out," Brother Agee said. He clipped the card to the clipboard that he was holding and dug a small flip-top cell phone from his jeans pocket. While we waited quietly he called the insurance company and confirmed that Uncle had a policy for three thousand dollars on Amina. After that, he replaced the phone and filled me in on the type of services the parlor offered.

There were memorials, burials, and even cremations. They could hook you up with a coffin or an urn, and if you had enough cash, a family mausoleum. If you didn't belong to a church, there was a minister and a choir on the payroll who would come and give your loved ones a real Christian send-off, and if Bible-thumping really wasn't your style they had a lady poet who would write and recite a poem that best described your feelings about the deceased. "You only need to tell her your best memories of your daughter, and she'll compose something spectacular," Brother Agee said.

I smiled at him. I liked the idea of someone writing a poem about

Amina, a poem just about her that couldn't apply to any other child in the world. "That sounds really nice," I said.

"It does sound nice," Trip echoed beside me.

"I want some prayers said over that child," Uncle interrupted. "Poetry is beautiful, but it ain't never took no soul to Heaven. I'm not that big on preaching and praying, but it just seems like sometimes the Good Word is needed."

"Of course," Brother Agee agreed.

"Can we do both?" I asked.

"You can do whatever your funds will allow. I'll let you know if we can put together a combination service as soon as we take care of the big stuff. I'm assuming that you're going to want a traditional burial, so I suggest that we go look in our display room. We do have a few lovely boxes that you can choose from."

Brother Agee rolled his chair back so that we could all get out easily. Trip and his Mama stood up, but I didn't. I couldn't move again. Just the thought of putting my child in a box broke me into pieces, but what could I do? I turned to Uncle. "I don't want to see it, Uncle," I said. "I don't want to go in any display room." Uncle Simon wheeled his chair closer to the sofa. He placed his hand on my knee. He eyes were filled with enough concern and compassion for twenty Chinas.

"I understand, sweet-face. You don't have to do anything that you don't want to do. I know this hard. It's eating me up too. Do you want me to go in and pick out something nice?"

I shook my head. "No, I wanna do it. I just . . . is there a picture or something that I can look at instead?" I asked Brother Agee.

"Yes, of course," he answered. "I understand how you feel. Preferring not to go into the display room isn't unusual. I always have a few clients who don't want to pick something out in person. I do have a catalog you can look at instead."

"That would be great," Uncle said. Brother Agee got up from his chair and walked over to the filing cabinet.

Trip came over and sat beside me. Brother Agee returned with a thin white catalog with a glossy cover. He handed it to me. I opened it and glanced inside. There were coffins, twelve pages of them—small ones, just big enough to lay a tiny, precious person inside. Some were simple, plain boxes painted carnation pink, lemon-drop yellow, ivory, or ocean blue. Others were fancier—polished oak and cherrywood, knotted pine and walnut, shiny copper—but the one that caught my eye was a beautiful bronze coffin that had charming tulips and roses all over it. I didn't want to see Amina placed in any box, but if she had to be in one I wanted it to be covered in flowers, the same flowers that couldn't bloom the day that we sent Mama off. No matter what weather came our way, Amina would still be surrounded by the loveliness of nature.

"I want this one, Uncle," I said, handing the book to him. He looked at it, and a smile came to his thin lips for the first time since sorrow came into our lives.

"It's beautiful, China Cup," he said, running his hand over the glossy photograph. "Sweet-face, this is the perfect casket for our little princess."

"Can I see it?" Trip asked. I took the book from Uncle and handed it to him. Shronda walked to the other side of the sofa and peered over his shoulder.

"I wish she would go on and see the thing up close, but it is really nice," she said to Trip. Trip nodded.

"You chose a good one, China," he said, handing the catalog back to me. I glanced at the photo again and handed it to Brother Agee with my finger pointing at it.

"How much is that one?" I asked. He shook his head.

"That's a new one," he said. "We just started carrying it about a month ago. It's elegant and stylish, but I'm afraid you won't be able to get it for your little girl."

"Why not?" I asked. He gave me a pitiful look.

"This box runs about twenty-seven hundred. It's a little out of your price range."

"Oh, too bad," Uncle and Trip said at the same time.

"Maybe we ought to pick something else, sweet-face," Uncle added.

"No, Uncle. I don't want anything else," I said defensively. "Amina has to have that one. I know she would like it the best. It's the prettiest!"

"It is lovely, it's lovely, but look, we have some almost as pretty," Brother Agee said, thumbing through the catalog. He stopped at a page in the front of the booklet. I knew without looking that it had to be the page with pastel painted coffins because they were the cheapest.

"Why don't you try one of these, young lady?" he said, handing the catalog back to me. "They are reasonably priced, and I think if you choose one of these we'll be able to plan a nice little service for your daughter."

"Maybe," I mumbled. I took the catalog and glanced again at the pink one for girls, and frowned all the way down to my soul. It was bubble-gum colored, and the acrylic paint that they finished it with made it look plastic and fake. It looked like it belonged in a Barbie Playland. I could see Barbie in her micromini black dress and black high heels, standing in her snap-together Barbie cemetery, crying over her plastic child, but Amina wasn't plastic. She was real, as real as the sticky oatmeal that I washed from her face each morning, and as real as the cotton bunny-rabbit pajamas that I helped her wriggle into each night. She didn't deserve a box that was just pretty, she deserved a box that was pretty special. In life all I could give her was a mother who never wanted to be a mama in the first place, and a father who didn't even refer to her as his daughter. I loved her more than I loved Uncle, Trip, even myself, but I made a huge mistake with her and now she was dead. The least I could do was send her away in the best. I owed her that. I owed her everything.

"I don't like those," I said, handing the catalog back to Brother Agee. He took it from me and began thumbing through some of the other pages.

"Okay," he said. "There's a couple more in here that I think will fit into your price range."

"I don't want a couple more," I snapped. "I want the one I picked out."

"I know, I know," Brother Agee said, closing the catalog with a sigh. "I know that you want the one that you picked out, but I'm afraid that it's impossible."

"Why is it impossible?" I asked. "You said that it was twenty-seven hundred. We got three thousand."

"Yes, but you have to understand that there will be more costs associated with the service, costs that will run you much more than the three hundred that you will have left over."

"What kind of costs?" I asked, uglier than I intended to. "How much could it cost to dig a small hole?"

"We do more than just dig a hole. We are a full-service mortuary. We take care of all your needs," Brother Agee said in a flustered voice. I guess my question hit homeboy the wrong way. His face was all screwed up as if I had just broken one of his fancy African masks.

"All of my needs. You take care of all my needs." I repeated the phrase to myself. It struck me as funny, and almost sick. What I needed was my child back. I needed to have her sitting in my lap, playing with the dangling gold hoops that I stuck in my ears this morning because I knew that she liked to play with them. There was no way that he could meet my needs. I had to settle for just my want being met. "I just would like the coffin that I picked out," I said. "That's all I want."

"I know, young lady, and I'm trying to explain . . ." Brother Agee started again. Uncle stopped him.

"We need a family moment, Mr. Agee," he said calmly. "Would you mind excusing us for a moment, sir."

Brother Agee nodded. He gave me another pitiful look and left the room. Uncle turned his chair around and faced me. My heart dropped when I saw that he had the look, the sad, watery-eyed look, like he had just watched *Old Yeller* or *Bambi*. He always gave me that look when he had to tell me something that he didn't really want to. Last year I got it when he had to tell me that he couldn't afford to get me the coat I wanted for Christmas. The year before I got it when he told me that my social security check had to be used to pay off his portion of a new wheelchair. I didn't mind seeing that look on those occasions. I understood it, but not this time. How could he say no to something for Amina, regardless of what the price tag said.

"Wait, Uncle, I know what you're going to say, but we can do this," I said, before he could even open his mouth. "I know that it's kind of high, but it's for Amina. Please, Uncle. I want her to have the best. I don't want her to be buried in some casket that looks like it belongs in a toy box. I want her to have the best."

"What do you mean by that?" Shronda asked dipping her nose into my Kool-Aid. "I glanced at that catalog. I didn't see nothing too crappy. There's all kinds of nice cheap caskets in there you can put your little girl in."

"That's right, my little girl. She's mine, and I don't recall asking your opinion about a damn thang!" I yelled at her.

"Well, she's also my grandbaby!" she yelled back.

"Since when?" I asked. "Since you found out you were off the hook, and would never ever have to do anything for her!" I screamed. I jumped up from the sofa ready to go after her ass for sure. Trip grabbed me by the arm.

"Okay, okay, I know we all stressed out, but just wait a minute,

China," he said, trying to tug me back down onto the sofa next to him. "Just wait one minute. I know you don't like it, but I think Mama might be right. That coffin is way too high, China. We need to choose something a little less fancy."

"How less fancy, Trip? How cheaply do you think we should bury your child?" I snapped.

"China, that's cold. It's not what I meant, and you know it. I loved Amina just as much as you. You're the one who decided that I should play friend, and not daddy. To be honest with you I never even liked that arrangement. I just didn't want to fight with you about it," Trip said with way too much sadness and anger playing in his voice. I felt as if he had slapped me in the face.

"What does that mean? Trip, I just didn't want you to be tied down like me. I did what I did for you. It's not fair for you to be angry at me about it. How can you sit there and act like I did something wrong?"

"I didn't say that you did anything wrong. I just . . . Look, China, we don't have any money right now to contribute," he said, looking up at Shronda shamefacedly. "My mama just lost her job. She told me this morning on the way over. She got laid off from the packing plant. We don't have any extra cash to spend right now. We won't be able to help out much with the funeral expenses."

"Well what the hell are you here for then?" I wanted to yell, but it was Trip, and I had seen him a lot of things before, but never ashamed. Two years ago some of the brothers at our school learned that even though he had his mother's rich, deep skin tone, Trip's father was actually a white, German schoolteacher that Shronda Faye met while she was in the military. His father was there to teach the troops basic German. He and Shronda Faye kicked it for a little while until Trip's dad got a job teaching in Italy. When some of the guys found out about it they started giving Trip a really hard time because they didn't like the way their girls were always hanging on him. For several weeks after school they followed Trip home calling him a black Nazi, and asking him did his mom serve him sauerkraut for dinner. It was a painful time for Trip, so painful that he wouldn't even bother swinging at the guys, and he never tried defending his heritage to them either.

He didn't tell them that the words *African American* were down on his birth certificate just like they were down on theirs. He just pumped pride into his shoulders and kept walking down the street as if they weren't worth the time he would spend turning around to talk to them. When we got to my house he would do sit-ups on my living room floor until the sweat and soreness had worked all the anger and unhappiness he was feeling out, but he never allowed the boys to bring shame to his face. He went through the situation back then without dropping his head once, but today he was all down in the face because he didn't have any cash to help bury his daughter. It was hitting him hard. What kind of friend would I be if I made him feel bad about it? I knew how difficult it was for him to tell me that his mama was laid off again. It was the third time Shronda had been let go in three years. She worked my nerves big time, but she and Trip seriously suffered each time she stopped bringing a paycheck into the house, and I didn't want to see either one of them go through that again. "It's okay. Don't worry about it. I'll just have to come up with something myself," I said.

"Come up with what, China?" Uncle spoke up again. "Look, China Cup, that baby meant the world to me, but Brother Agee is right. We can't afford that coffin."

"Why not? Why can't we have it?" I asked in the little-girl voice that I always used when I wanted to get my way. It didn't work. He took my hands and placed them in his lap.

"China, sweetie, I know you want the best for Amina, but there's just no way that we can get that coffin and pay for the rest of the funeral too. There's going to be fees for everything. I know it isn't fair, honey, but we have to have the money to pay for them, too. As much as we all would like to see Amina in the best, I'm afraid we're just going to have to get her what we can afford."

"Your uncle's correct," Brother Agee said, stepping back into the room without even being asked. He walked over to his desk and retrieved a small stack of notebook papers. "I'm sorry, I didn't mean to intrude," he said. "I just forgot some estimates that I wanted to look at for another client, but what your uncle said is true. With the coffin you picked out your total costs will run you about eight thousand, and that's figuring cheaply."

"Eight thousand?" Trip said.

"Eight thousand," Uncle repeated.

"I haven't worked it all out, but that's about right. With the cost of that coffin, the hall rental for the wake and perhaps funeral, the programs, the limousine service, the poet, and a modest headstone, yes you would be looking at a figure in that ballpark," Brother Agee said, heading back to the door.

Uncle took a deep breath and let it out. "I'm sorry, China," he said. "Honey, we can't do this. It's just impossible. The prices have gone up since we put your mother away."

"So, we can still do it. We can pay for it in installments or something. I can use my social security check that I get each month. Can't we pay for it a little at a time?" I asked Brother Agee.

"We're a smaller mortuary, so we don't like to make too many long-term agreements, but we do have a six-month plan for people who find that they just can't cover all their costs at once."

"See, Uncle!" I said. "We can do it that way. We can pay it off in installments with my checks."

"Oh no, no we can't!" Uncle Simon said, shaking his head. "That money is just enough for you to live on, and maybe put a little something away for college. You can't use that for this. I promised your mother that I would make sure that you always had a roof over your head and food in your mouth. I wish I could do it alone, but we both know that I can't. We need your checks to help keep things running."

"But, Uncle—"

"No, no buts, China Cup. We're not going to do it. What we're going to do is pick something cheaper, and let Brother Agee come up with a figure that we can deal with, and that's that!" he said in the firmest voice he's ever used with me.

"I don't want anything cheaper!" I said just as firmly. "I want what I picked out, and if I can't use my check, I'll just get a job and pay for it myself."

"Don't be silly, China," Uncle said. "Girl, there's no way that an after-school job will pay off a eight-thousand-dollar bill in six months."

"It's only five. We have three," I said. "I only need the rest."

"Even still."

"Even nothing!" I yelled. "I don't want to argue about this, Uncle. I'm not going to give in. It's what I want, and you know that you can't stop me. You know you can't." My statement left silence in the room. For a moment it was like everything and everyone had just up and left. Uncle just stared at me or I should say stared right through me, as if all he could see was the back of the sofa. I didn't want to do it, but I had played a card that he had forgotten was still in the deck. Earlier this year Uncle learned that he was going to have to have another operation to remove some bone fragments that had been giving him problems since his fall. It was another risky operation, the fourth one he had had since he moved in with me. The last two just came up out of the blue, but this one he was totally prepared for, and he wanted me to be prepared too. When he found out about it, he decided that it was a good idea to take me down to the courthouse and have me declared independent. It was just a precaution. He wanted to make sure that if anything happened to him during the operation I could pull the plug if I had to, but he also wanted to make sure that if I had to pull the plug, me and Amina wouldn't be left homeless. It was just his way of taking care of us all, but it *was* legal. It meant that in all things I had the right to make my own decisions, no matter how dumb Uncle thought they were.

"You're gonna use my sickness against me, China Cup?" he asked in a shocked voice. "You're gonna try to get your way by using something that I did to protect both of us? I know you know better than this. I didn't raise you to be cruel."

"I'm not. I'm not trying to be cruel, Uncle, you don't understand," I said calmly. "I'm not trying to hurt you, but you just don't get it."

"No, I don't, you're right about that," he said, his face turning to sadness. "I don't get it at all. I loved that baby just as much as you, and you know that." He looked up at Brother Agee.

"Yes, sir?" Brother Agee said.

"Write up whatever she wants,'" Uncle told him. "She's right. Amina was her baby. This is her business. She should be the one to handle it. Give her whatever she wants."

"Whatever she wants!" Shronda snapped. "And who gone pay for it?"

"The insurance company will pay for it up to three thousand. After that, it's left up to her and God. Now I'm going outside to stick my face in the sun. It's a little too cold in here for me," Uncle said, rolling around Brother Agee to the door. I got up to walk beside him, but he waved me away, made it to the door and went out. I stood there watching him roll off, feeling just as hurt and alone as I know he felt. I just couldn't understand why he wouldn't agree to do everything he could to get the best for Amina. On TV when people passed, their loved ones always went to the funeral home teary-eyed and said *"spare no expense."* It was what you did when there was nothing else left to give the one you loved. It was the right thing to do. Everything in me told me that it was.

"I better go check on him," Trip said, and hopped up from the sofa.

"This gal got a will of concrete. Ain't no need for me to be here. I'll go with you, so that I can get a smoke," Shronda said, and moved toward the door too. I stepped outside so that they could get out.

"I'll be back in little bit," Trip told me as he closed the door behind them. I nodded my head, but I knew he wasn't coming back. I returned to my place again on the sofa.

"Well, should we finish your arrangements?" Brother Agee asked.

I nodded, and for the next thirty minutes he helped me pick out the best service for my little girl. We chose the casket that I wanted and the poet, two limos, some floral arrangements, the programs, a white lace shroud, and several other things that I had no idea were needed to send someone off. When we finished my bill was well over seven thousand dollars, and Brother Agee dropped the bomb on me that we still needed to figure in a monument. I had already spent way more than I needed to, but I couldn't stand the thought of Amina not having a stone. I thumbed through another catalog he retrieved from his desk and chose a square red granite stone with a cherub carved into the top. Underneath the cherub would be the words AMINA, PERFECT DAUGHTER, PERFECT NIECE, PERFECT CHILD, ALL OUR LOVE—GOOD-BYE. When that was over there was nothing left to do but sign at the bottom of several papers and get the due date for the first payment. As I jotted down my payment date on a scrap of notebook paper, Brother Agee told me that he didn't like doing business with someone so young, but that he was certain I would get the bill paid because I had a social security check coming in each month, and because I seemed very determined. "I would be very worried about most teenagers being able to pay this bill in a few months, but I get a sense that you're a special girl, and will keep your word. I know that you'll get this paid off in a timely manner."

"I will," I said, getting up from the sofa and shaking his hand. "It's my responsibility and I'll handle it."

"I'm sure you will, but I do need to tell you anyway that a debt like this can cause you all kinds of trouble if you don't pay it."

"What kind of trouble?"

"The type that stays with you for a very long time, but you don't need to worry about that. You're a smart girl and good mother, and I know that you'll get everything paid off. Don't you worry about it one bit, you just give me a ring if you run into any problems," he said with a reassuring grin. 'There's always a way that we can work something out."

"Okay," I said, and left the back office. On the way out I wondered what the something was that we could work out, but I didn't let it get to me. Uncle said that it was my decision to make and I had made it. The insurance company would pay them the three thousand, and I would come up with the rest. It sounded simple enough to me, but so had having sex with Trip that rainy afternoon two years ago. *Amina, Perfect Daughter, Perfect Child, I think I have just pulled myself into a perfect mess.*

CHAPTER 3

I was startled awake this morning by the noisy creak of my rusty bedroom door hinges. I pulled my tie-dyed bedspread up to my neck and turned over groggily, hoping to see Uncle Simon smiling down at me, but instead I was greeted by the sight of little Eboni tiptoeing through my doorway with her tiny hands wrapped around a jelly jar glass filled to the brim with orange juice. She looked like she could spill it all over the place at any moment, and I cringed when I imagined myself and my bed clothing drenched in the cold, sticky, orange liquid. I sat up immediately and yawned a "Hi, Eboni." She walked over as carefully as she could, and held the glass out to me. I reached over to take it from her. Her nose was all snotty again, so I decided to pass.

"No thank you, Eboni," I said. "You go on and have it." She sat down at the foot of my bed and started taking little sips from the juice. Only a few drops of it spilled onto her plaid sundress and my bedspread, so I didn't even bother telling her to take it back in the kitchen to finish up. I crawled to the foot of the bed and flipped the switch on my small nine-inch TV. The screen flickered on, filling the tube with the sounds and images of two talking bears who looked like they were made out of Play-Doh. I shook my head and crawled back under my covers.

"Girl, you better hurry up and get out of that bed," I heard Yolanda say as my head hit the pillow. I looked up to see her standing in the doorway with an open pastry box of MK's best buttermilk doughnuts, the kind that made you search the box for crumbs after you had polished off all the pastry. I gotta lay it down straight, my mouth did water when I saw those goodies, but I waved them away too.

"I'm not hungry, girlfriend," I said to Yolanda. "You and Eboni eat 'em."

"Me and Eboni already ate five on our way over here, these are for you, girlfriend," she said, walking over to the bed and placing the box next to my pillow. "You gotta have something to eat. You haven't been eating much of anything."

"Girl, I'm not hungry. You can give them to Uncle. They're his favorite kind," I said.

"I already gave him a half dozen of his own. Like I told you, these are for you," she said. She sat down on the bed beside the box and picked up one of the delicious treats. I waved it away again.

"Thanks, but no thanks. I'm just gonna have some water this morning."

"Just water, girl, what's wrong with you? Just because your baby gone don't mean you can't eat. Look, I know how you feel," she said, dropping the doughnut back into the box. "I swear I do, but not eating anything ain't gonna bring you nothing but more trouble."

I turned over in my bed. I didn't want to hear Yolanda tell me how I should feel about losing a child. What did Yolanda know about it? She hadn't lost any children, not really. When I first met her at the clinic she told me that she had gotten rid of two babies, but that was something very different. I didn't get rid of Amina. I never could have. Instead I carried her for nine months and felt I would tear apart from labor pains with her. I rocked her to sleep while I studied for my math test, and dressed her in a gown of white satin, while a minister sprinkled water on her sleeping face. She was imprinted in me, her name written in each chamber of my heart. "A mother who buries a child, buries herself." I read that once in a ladies' magazine. It was in an article about a lady who had recently lost her oldest daughter. The girl was twenty, did cocaine, ran with a gang, and liked to go after other chicks with a razor. One day she got into a fight with a girl from a rival gang and the other girl smoked her. The mother was brokenhearted, and at the time I thought she should just get over it. She had twenty years with her daughter; they weren't good years, but she still had them. That's more than most parents of gang-member kids get, I said. Now I know better, because a part of your blood spills out too when you lose a child. It doesn't matter if your child was born with a halo or cloven hooves, she's still your child, and you'll never get over losing her. I turned back to Yolanda.

"I don't want anything, girl. So stop trying to make me eat before I throw your butt out."

"Okay, okay, damn. You ain't got to go there," Yolanda said. "I'll eat the freakin' doughnuts myself. Ain't nobody got to tell me not to pass up food."

"I know. You could bite a chunk outta a moving cow."

"That's so funny I forgot to laugh," she said. "Here I am trying to do something nice for your butt, and you giving me a lot of crap about it. I got a good mind to take my behind home," she said.

"You got a good mind. When did that happen?"

"Forget you, heifer," she said playfully, and started laying into the doughnuts, as if they were her last meal. I would have found it kind of funny, except I wasn't in any kind of a laughing mood.

Things have gone from bad to worse at the house, and it's all my fault. I didn't go to Amina's funeral, and Uncle is really upset with me about it. I wanted to, and should have, but I couldn't make myself do it. I didn't want to see my baby lying in a coffin, no matter how beautiful the coffin was. I never told anybody, but for weeks after Mama died I had nightmares of her in the casket. They were always the same. I could see her beneath the cold earth. She was furiously banging on the casket lid while up above three eerie-looking grave diggers shoveled on more dirt. Deep down I suspected the nightmares were probably being caused by some horror flick I saw with Trip, but they always terrified me. I woke up each time shaking and covered with sweat. I didn't want to go through that with Amina, too. I couldn't. It would have completely destroyed me.

On the morning Amina was buried I helped Uncle get into his black suit and placed a new roll of two-ply toilet tissue in the bathroom for all of the mourners that would be coming over later. When I was through with that, I ironed grandma's best linen tablecloth and placed it on the table, tacked all the sympathy cards to the wall in the living room, and left the house. I didn't even say goodbye to Uncle. I didn't call the funeral home and confirm the time the limo would be coming to our house. I fled and wandered the neighborhood. I stopped at Diamond's new meat market and checked the price of pork chops with mean ole King Red, and I peeked in the window at Brenda's Nail Studio, and checked out the snazzy new fingernail polishes. I got a soda at Diego's Taco Stand, and I stood at the counter in Campo's Bakery and watched as Carmen, a pretty brown-skinned girl with crescent eyes and Snicker Bar–colored hair, squeezed red rosettes onto an elegant white wedding cake. I went and saw Alejandra's cousin Michael and asked him to show me sketches of his tattoos. I did all of those things, and then I did the ultimate, and went job hunting.

I stopped at The Princess and the Pea Bookshop and asked Mrs. Waltrip if she could use my help. I had worked for her last summer, reshelving and selling used volumes of books like *Aesop's Fables; Grimm's Fairy Tales; The Lion, the Witch, and the Wardrobe; The Lord of the Rings;* and *Through the Looking Glass.* I loved the job. It was wonderful getting to read some of my all-time favorite books, and Mrs. Waltrip was nice to work with. She had tea time each afternoon, where she served lemon tea with fresh peppermint from her own garden. While we drank tea and ate lace cookies, she would tell me humorous stories that her husband, Albert, had told her that morning. I always laughed at the really funny parts, though I knew Albert couldn't have told her anything, because four years ago an aneurysm burst in his brain and he fell into a coma. I felt bad about that. I knew how hard it was on Mrs. Waltrip having a husband who would never again walk or talk. At times she seemed as decayed and worn out as the dusty boxes of books she kept in her small storeroom.

When I worked with her I had no problem going along with the only thing that seemed to take away her pain. It seemed like the normal thing for me to do. Unfortunately, on the day I went to see her I wasn't normal. When I went in the shop she was sitting on a stool behind her counter, reading a dog-eared copy of a book called *The People Could Fly*. On the cover was an intriguing picture of what looked like a group of black slaves rising up into a soft blue sky. I pondered the picture for a moment, then I cut straight to the point and asked her for a job.

"I need work," I said. She put down the book and peered at me over her bifocals. "I need work," I repeated. "I thought maybe I could come back and help you out like I did this summer. You got anything I could do, ma'am?"

"Oh China Cup, I'm sorry," she said. "You know folks around here ain't that big on buying books anyway, and with the economy so messed up people are hanging on to their money tighter than a bride-to-be hangs on to a discounted wedding dress. I'm sorry. I wish I could help you out, but I can't."

"Are you sure you don't have anything I could do?" I pleaded. "I really need to make some extra cash."

"I wish I did, China. I wish I could help you out. I enjoyed having you work here so much. It's good to see you again, though. I'm a little lonely around here without you, and I know Albert misses you too. How's your baby girl?" she asked, with a grin that almost lighted up her thin, withered face. I wasn't prepared for the question. I couldn't believe that she hadn't heard about my daughter.

"She's fine, ma'am," I lied and rushed out of the door. Later, I felt sorry that I hadn't stayed longer and let her tell me one of Albert's tales. Perhaps one of Albert's jokes would have cheered me up some, and I really needed some cheer. When I finally made it home several hours later, I found Uncle sitting at the kitchen table with a bag in his hand, surrounded by empty casserole dishes. He didn't even look up at me when I entered the room. He placed the bag on the table and slowly rolled to his own room. I opened the bag and looked in. Inside were beautiful pieces of broken china that some of the elderly sisters in my neighborhood had gathered to place on Amina's grave. My grandma used to tell me that in the olden days it was tradition for poor folks to decorate a grave with crushed pieces of their best servingware. The sacrifices showed love and appreciation. I poured some of the china out on the table, and wondered if it had been broken with a rock or a hammer. I studied it for a few seconds, then decided that it didn't really make a difference. It was shattered, like me, and like Uncle and the funeral guests must have been when I didn't show up. I'm sure they didn't understand at all.

"I'm sorry, Uncle," I said softly to myself. After that, I got up and cleared away the casserole dishes. That was a week ago, and things are still strained between us.

"I wish I could stop eating," Yolanda said, reaching into the doughnut box for a third time. "But you know how I get when something is working me hard."

"What's working you?"

"Jamal and his family."

"What about them?" I sleepily asked.

"To begin with, it looks like Jamal is gonna go down for about fifteen years for jacking that Jetta. It looks like his next place of residence is gonna be 90210 Huntsville Prison," she said.

"I'm sorry, girlfriend."

"I know, and I still think it ain't fair, but I can deal with it. It's the other thing that I have a problem with."

"What other thing?" I asked. She sighed.

It turns out that for the past two weeks Jamal's mother and father been coming over to Yolanda's house saying that Eboni would be better off living with them. In a way I can see where they're coming from. Jamal's father is only about forty-five and owns three auto-repair shops. I heard people say that he got money to roll up and light his cigarettes with. I sometimes pass his home when I take a shortcut to school. It's a big house, with *mucho* rooms and a spacious yard that a bad-ass kid like Eboni could run around in. I have to admit my first thought was that Eboni would be pretty happy there. She wouldn't be all scrunched up in the house with Yolanda and the rest of the wild bunch. I could see myself telling Yolanda to pack Eboni's puppy-dog PJ's and take her over there right away, only Yolanda is my friend. She lacks a lot in the mothering department, but she loves those little knotty-head kids, and everybody in the neighborhood is hip to that fact, especially Jamal's folks. They told Yolanda that she was a tramp and tried to get Yolanda to get rid of Eboni. They offered her lots of cash and a car to do it. Yolanda said no. I never asked her what she told them, but I heard around the hood it was something about them taking their money, putting it in the car, and driving it into the bayou. I think Yolanda was right to tell them that. Jamal's not worth the time it takes his father to pull the cash out of his wallet. He's only about twenty-two, but Yolanda once told me that he's been in trouble with the law since the fourth grade. I guess that's why his parents are now trying to get their hands on Eboni. Maybe they figure they can raise her to avoid all the crap that her father keeps getting stuck in.

"They want to take Eboni?" I asked. "How can they be so mean? I can't believe it."

"I can't either. They not as bad as Shronda Faye. They will buy some things for her if I need them to, but they still ain't never been really interested. Now they all over her. Jamal's daddy sent Eboni a bunch of presents last week, and the week before that he showed up outside her day care and told her he and his wife wanted her to come stay with them. He even showed Eboni a photo of her new room, told her that they was gonna paint it all yellow. Ask Eboni, she don't even like yellow," Yolanda said, wiping the glazed sugar off her hands and into the box. "And anyway, it don't matter, 'cause I'm gonna tell you right now, ain't nobody but me gonna raise my child. I'm not gonna let anybody take her from me."

"I hear you. Shoot, I sure wouldn't give them my child. That's just plain stupid. Why she got to live with them? They ain't nobody special. Tell them to go jump in the lake," I groggily said.

"That's just what I'm gonna do," she said, getting up from my bed. "I'm not gonna waste any time doing that." She tossed the doughnut box into the Scooby-Doo wastebasket underneath my night stand. "Now you get your sad butt up and start the day. Whatever you're feeling ain't gonna get no better with you just lay-ing around in the bed. Get over it, try to deal, girl," she said, gently tugging at Eboni's arm. "Let's go, Eboni."

"'Bye, big head," Eboni said to me.

I smiled weakly as she and Yolanda left the room.

I lay in bed for a while longer shocked by what Yolanda had told me about Jamal's parents. I knew they didn't think much of Yolanda, but why would they want to take her little girl? I crawled from underneath the covers and dabbed at a wet juice stain with a bunch of napkins Yolanda left. They turned bright orange, and I tossed the sticky mess into the trash can. The napkins fell on top of the empty pastry box. At the site of the box I did grow a little hungry. I pushed it to the back of my mind. Instead I walked to the full-length mirror attached to my closet door and twirled around slowly in the floral bikini panties and tank top that I crashed in the night before. I inspected every inch of my thighs and butt, running my hands over them, making sure that my body was really as tight as I thought it was. It was kind of important. Losing Amina wasn't the only reason why I didn't feel like eating. I was trying to keep in pretty decent shape. I was going to apply for a job where a lot more than my customer-service skills was going to be looked at.

Nobody knew it, but I was going down to Obsidian Queens to hunt for work. It was the only place that I knew was willing to pay the big bucks. I had walked all over the neighborhood and downtown looking for work, but it soon dawned on me that I wasn't going to pay Amina's bill by selling books at the local bookstore or spreading ketchup on burgers at the McDonald's on Main. I needed cash, real cash, and while I was at the dollar store the day before, one of my homegirls, Rani, told me that Obsidian Queens could hook a sister up. "That's where my cousin Toni worked for a bit, but she had to quit when she started showing. Toni told me they pay crazy money each week, and she woulda stayed there permanently if it wasn't for the baby. She said the only thing you have to do is work up at the counter, and learn to put up with a bunch of stuff," Rani told me, throwing a bottle of Ultra dishwashing liquid into her shopping cart.

"That sounds good to me, girl," I said, tossing two bottles of the same liquid into my own cart. I didn't ask her what "a bunch of stuff" was. I had heard enough about Obsidian Queens to know that it was definitely not something I wanted to ask.

Obsidian Queens was one of those places in our neighborhood that everybody was aware of, but didn't like to bring up in polite conversation. It was a new guy's club that had sprung up awhile back in ole Joe Lima Bean's place down by the Negro Union Tracks. One hot afternoon three brothers from Fort Worth rolled into town and said that they were looking for a place to get something started. They said that they had won a lottery a little while ago and ever since then they had been looking for a town or neighborhood where they could give something back. They talked about opening a new rec center for the senior citizens or starting a neighborhood food bank for folks who couldn't bring home enough bacon to feed their families. It was a wonderful idea and a super, kind gesture. Some people in the neighborhood wanted to do as much as they could to help the brothers get started. They hipped them to Joe Lima Bean's place, and let them know that it hadn't been occupied in forever. I heard the brothers seemed happy about that. They did whatever they had to do to secure the boarded-up property and got down to remodeling it, but remodeling it into what? The brothers never really said. Folks just assumed that because they had mentioned a food bank and a rec center they were actually building one of those things.

Anyway, I don't need to tell you that it wasn't true. Obsidian Queens speaks for itself. When it opened many folks in our hood threw a fit when they found out what it really was, especially the women. For weeks a lady named Sister Ashada from some church down the street led a group of faithful sisters down to the club to protest what she called "the corruption of God's beauty." By "beauty" she meant the shapely, buxom sisters that the guys hired to dance and waitress at the place. I'm not quite sure if she thought the girls were corrupting themselves by working there, or that the guys were corrupting them by paying them to do it. I guess we'll never really know, because it turns out girlfriend was seriously wasting her time. Guys *do* like to see good-looking chicks, and before long even some of the more respectable dudes in our hood were sneaking down there at night, trying to check out the girls. They would come back talking about how fine and hot the ladies were. The word quickly spread about the club, inside and out of our hood. It wasn't long before the club was pulling in mega bucks, and the brothers did start using some of the dough to help the community out in a positive way.

They started one program that bought school supplies and clothing for some of the really poor kids in our hood, and another program that helped the senior citizens buy their monthly prescriptions. With the kind of money that was flowing through the club they really weren't doing all that much for the community, but it was enough to get the people to back up off of the club and leave it alone. Who wanted to be responsible for Grandma Thelma not being able to get her heart pills last month, or little Lee not having a wide-margin notebook and new Nikes to start his third year at Madam C. J. Walker Elementary School? Nobody did, so the matter of the club just got squashed, and stayed squashed. That was fine with me, at least today it was. Rani had told me that Obsidian Queens had an opening, and I was going to go get it. Working there couldn't be any worse than having a baby at twelve. I had learned how to handle that. I could handle anything. I walked to the bathroom so I could take a hot bubble bath.

I washed quickly with Amina's Double Bubble bubble bath, and stood in the mirror for longer than I wanted to, piling on Rum Raisin eye shadow and super-shiny lip gloss that Yolanda let me borrow. When I was finished with that, I wiggled into a lace-trimmed cotton top and a khaki miniskirt. I glanced in the mirror. I looked hot on the outside. Inside was something different. Numbness had returned there. I felt dead inside, like I was the one buried in Peaceful Rest Cemetery beside Mama. I thought about Amina lying alone in her coffin, and shivered.

I remembered falling into a hole once. It was the summer Mama asked Joci, the teenage girl next door, to watch me. I was four at the time, and Joci hardly ever paid attention to what I was doing. One late evening she left me outside while she went to talk with her boyfriend on the phone. While she was gabbing, I left our yard and ended up tumbling into a drainage ditch that the city was digging three blocks away. The dirt in the hole was loose, so try as I might, there was no way I could get out. I screamed for a while, and cried for a whole lot longer. Finally, when I didn't have any tears left, I lay down on the cool dirt and curled up. I don't know how long I was in there, I just know that it was black-cat dark when Mama came and got me out. Weeks later I was still afraid to be by myself, or go into anyplace that wasn't lighted. Now I had put Amina in a place like that. I felt awful about it. And I knew that regardless of what Yolanda said, I would go on feeling awful about it until I was lying beside her. The only thing I could do was make sure that she had something beautiful to rest in until I got there. I had done that. It was what I was supposed to do as her mother, now I just had to pay for it.

I hurried from my room, and went to tell Uncle that I was taking off. He was sitting at his worktable shaping a piece of white clay into something that only he could see. "I'm going out for a bit, Uncle. Do you need me to do anything for you before I go?" I asked.

Refusing to look up from his work, he simply shook his head. "No, China Cup. Yolanda already helped me out this morning. Besides, I think you've already done enough," he said.

"Okay," I said softly, and started to leave to the room.

"China," he called out. "Remember just because we can do something doesn't always mean that we should. Problems we create during bad times sometimes take a very long time to clean up. You might have a paper that says you can make decisions like an adult, but you and I know you are far from being grown. You're a child, the only child I'll ever have, and there's nothing in this world that I care about more than you. I don't know what you think you're doing or why you didn't even go to your own daughter's funeral, especially after you fought everybody to have it exactly like you wanted it. Nonetheless, you are my baby, just like Amina was your baby. You come to me when you finally figure out what you've done to yourself, and Lord knows I'll do what I always do, try my best to make things better."

"I gotta go, Uncle Simon," I said, and I rushed from the house.

I ended up out on the front porch smothered with grief and guilt. I didn't want Uncle unhappy with me; nevertheless I had to do things the only way I knew how to do them. I didn't know how to explain that to him. Truth is, I didn't even know how to explain it to myself. I pulled my tank up to expose my midriff and looked down the street. To my delight I spotted Trip coming up the sidewalk and some of my gloom seemed to melt away. I wasn't actually sure that he would show up. Trip wasn't quite happy with me either, and since Amina's funeral things had been a little funky with us. He wasn't hurt and mad at me like Uncle Simon. Trip always supported me no matter what. Things were just off between us.

"I know you're hurt and all, China, but like your uncle Simon, I don't know what the heck you're doing. The day we came back from the funeral home Mama was bitchin' like crazy about your decision. I told her to back off. I told her that Amina was your daughter and that you were smart and always knew the right thing to do. Anyway, I'm not so sure about that anymore. It doesn't make any sense, you not going to see Amina off. I think maybe you got something really serious going on. Remember me talking about my cousin Siena in Miami? She lost her little boy two years ago, when he fell off a slide. It was hard on her for a long time, but somehow she got through. I talked to her myself the morning after everything happened and she helped me out in a big way. I think you should talk to her too. I told her about you, and she agreed that you might need some help," Trip told me over the phone a few days ago.

"Trip, the only help I need is the kind you can put in the bank," I said, and slammed down the receiver. I was angry at him for talking my business with a cousin that I never even met. I put the phone back on my nightstand, hopeful that I had pissed him off as much as he had pissed off me. Last night when I left a message at his house, telling him to come with me to find a job, I wasn't sure that he would even bother showing up. Now here he was, and I was thrilled about it. I hopped off the steps and ran down the sidewalk to apologize to him. He caught me in his arms and gave me a huge hug. "I'm sorry, China," he said. "I was only trying to help. I wasn't trying to put your business in the street. My cousin is a nice lady. I always talk to her about us. She really did want to help."

"I know," I said, pressing my face to his chest. "It's not your fault. I was trippin'. Uncle Simon is mad at me, and it's making me crazy. I won't hang up on you again. I just really needed to go to bed and not think about anything else."

"Me too. I turned in right after I got through talking to you. Don't sweat it," he said. "We cool, and we always gonna be cool. You're my best dark sister, and the mother of my only child. It's all right."

"Okay," I said, and pulled away from him. I noticed he was sporting his usual *Outer Realm* gear. He had on a cool black short set with two florescent green aliens in the center of the T-shirt and the words OUTER REALM written around each sleeve. His gleaming white sneaks were laced up with black laces that bore the letters *OTR*, but what really surprised me was his wristwatch. It had a photo of some red mountainous planet with the *Outer Realm* name written across a huge blue moon.

"Whoa, check you out, Mr. *Outer Realm* himself."

"I know, one of my aunts sent me some early birthday presents. They're pretty great, at least I think so. Shronda Faye was all trippin' over them, because she thought my aunt should have sent me some cash instead."

"Naw, she's wrong about that. Your aunt went out of her way to buy you all this stuff. It means she really cares about your interests. I think that's pretty cool. Anyway, we gotta go," I said. "I told the people at this place I would be down there before ten."

"Down where?"

"Uh, nowhere, just this place I need to find work. It's not too far. We don't even have to ride the bus."

"Really?"

"Really," I said, and started walking off.

"Hey, wait up, China," he said running after me. "I got something to run by you."

"Run it by me. What's up?"

A beautiful ghost who appears on a remote hiking trail and saves a co-ed from a would-be rapist, that's what was up. It's all Trip talked about on the way to Obsidian Queens. It was his new idea for an *Outer Realm* story that was going to take place in a small town in Colorado. I liked the story, but I didn't have enough mental energy to stay interested all the way through it. What did I care about the co-ed and her problems? Plus I knew that Trip was only avoiding talking about Amina. Any other time I would have loved hearing one of his tales. However, today it was like a piano concerto played in the wrong key. It was just noise, noise that kept him from expressing his feelings about his daughter. "Guess what else popped into my head that would make a great story idea?" he asked. I shrugged and kept walking.

If I had a dollar for every story idea Trip tossed at me on our walk to Obsidian Queens I wouldn't have had to go in the first place. He told me stories about guys giving birth to alien babies, soda that gave you the power to see through matter, another ghost tale where the ghost doesn't know he's dead and keeps going to work at a model airplane store, a West Coast rapper who sells his soul to the devil so he can win a rap war between himself and a new rapper on the East Coast, a hula doll that shakes her hips whenever her owner is about to be in danger, and many more stories that I didn't catch snippets of. The thoughts were flooding his brain quicker than the last rain flooded his front yard. It was a good thing too, because when we stopped in front of the orange neon hanging sign that advertised the entrance to the club, he barely noticed where we were until I was cutting across the lush green lawn. "Hey, what's up? What are we doing here?" he asked, looking around him. I kept walking until he caught my elbow.

"China, what's the deal? I thought you were going to look for some job. What are we—" he started to ask, then reality hit him. All the chocolaty goodness slid from his dark face. "Hell no, China, you have lost your mind!" he yelled.

"No I haven't," I snapped. "My friend Rani told me they were looking for some counter help here, and I thought I should check it out. She says they pay crazy digits, and we both know I need a whole lot of dead presidents."

"Not from here you don't, girl. This ain't no place for you to be. Mama got a brother who hangs out here. He's always talking about what goes on. He says he would disown one of his girls if he ever caught them working here."

"I'm glad. Good for him, but I'm not his daughter or yours, so quit trying to tell me what to do, and let me handle my stuff." I started across the lawn. He caught my arm again, this time harder, more insistent. I jerked away.

"Stop, Trip!"

"Okay, okay," he said letting my arm go. "Don't go all off on me."

"I'm not going off. I'm just trying to get some work."

"Okay, okay, true that. I totally understand," he said, taking me by the shoulders and gently turning me toward him. "I get it. I know you need the cash, and I also know that I'm not your father or even your boyfriend, but your uncle Simon would try to beat all the black off of my behind if I just stood back and let you walk in there without trying to set you straight. China, I think this is a bad idea."

"I knew you would. Nevertheless, I'm doing it anyway."

"Then why did you ask me to come with you?"

"You're my best friend. I need you to do this with me. Now quit trippin', Trip. I'm just trying to do something for our daughter. Emphasis on *our daughter*," I said. "You do remember her? She's the one that you and your mama couldn't pay jack to help bury."

"China, why you keep going there?" he asked in a pained voice. "My mama lost her job, and you know I didn't have any cash, so why you got to keep getting in my face about it?"

I took a deep breath and let it out.

"Trip, I'm not in your face," I said apologetically. "You're in mine. I'm sorry, but I'm going in to see about a job. If you wanna hang with me—hang. If not, you can just step off. I wouldn't have even asked you to come, if I knew you were going to go all altar boy over it. You're my homeboy. You're supposed to support me in everything."

"Not this. China, you know better than this. This ain't no place for you to work. Besides, I don't even think you're old enough to get in the door. Get a grip, girlfriend. They gonna kick your butt out of the door the minute they see what you look . . ." He dropped the "like" as his gaze traveled to my outfit. I could see his deep brown eyes going over me, checking out my body-hugging tank and miniskirt, and all that eye-catching makeup, that perhaps made me look just about old enough to ditch an ID check.

"Aw man, China Cup, when you have a bad-ass idea, you run all out with it, don't you, girlfriend?" he said.

"Come on, Trip. Don't get all over me about this. I'm just trying to look a little older so I can get paid. You know that. Stop sweating me about it."

"Okay, okay, fine. I'm through. I know better than to try and get you to see a lemon when you done already made up your mind that it's an orange. I don't wanna fight about it. Let's just go on up in there and let me see how many of these ignorant Negros I can keep off of you."

"Okay, but it's early, I doubt if there are any guys in there yet."

"Whatever, let's just go."

We walked up onto a deck surrounding the beautiful cedar building and rapped on the steel-plated door. "Wait a minute, wait a minute, we don't even open for another thirty damn minutes," a gruff voice yelled out. I jumped a little. Trip didn't.

"Okay dude, whatever, just let us in, man," he said turning to me with an annoyed look. Before I could tell him to chill, the door sprang open and the Angry Black Giant appeared, a bald-headed, mammoth brother with tree-stump limbs and a scowl that would make The Rock shudder.

"Say, why you beating on this door? What you want this early, little man?" he barked at Trip. Trip didn't even flinch.

"I don't want nothing," he said coolly. "My girl here is looking for a job. She heard ya'll was hiring for something, so she came to check it out."

"Oh, all right then, little miss. You can come in anytime," the Angry Black Giant said, glancing my way. I could feel the thin slits in his swollen face going all over me. His leering made me uncomfortable, and I could tell by the way Trip's hands suddenly clenched into fists that it really pissed him off. I wasn't worried, though. Trip wasn't a fool. There was no way he could check a brother that big. I touched one of his hands. It relaxed and settled into mine.

"My girl Rani told me that ya'll needed some counter help," I said gently, caressing Trip's palm with my thumb.

"Like I said, *mi casa es su casa*. I'll go get Miss Louisa," the Angry Black Giant said, peering into the top of my tank. I put my free hand up to block my cleavage. He winked at me and chuckled. Afterward, he backed away from the doorway and disappeared through another door in the hall. Me and Trip didn't know what to do. We walked inside to wait.

Surf's up, is all I could think when we strolled into the main club. A beach theme was definitely going on, right in the middle of the hood, right in a place where no surfer boy would dare come. It was amazing. All four walls surrounding the dance platform were covered from floor to ceiling with breathtaking ocean paintings. In front of us was a sandy white beach, surrounded by sea-green foamy waves, leaping up high underneath a mass of soft white clouds.

"Check out the realistic flock of seagulls flying over them palm trees on that island," Trip said, pointing to a scene on the adjacent wall. "Man, what's all the tropical-water stuff going on in here? What's that supposed to be all over the walls? Hawaii? The Caribbean? Shoot—South Padre?"

I shook my head. "I don't know. It's kinda pretty, though."

"And kinda weird. What are all these grown brothers doing hanging out in here with this Spring Break–looking crap?" Trip asked, pointing to a giant sandbox with a volleyball net resting beside the platform.

"Heck, I don't know. I guess somebody's been watching too many *Baywatch* reruns."

"Yeah right. Look, I can't get ready for all this. Check out those tables with all the fake crabs, starfish, and mess painted all over them. This place reminds me of some kind of twisted Red Lobster."

"Shut up, Trip. You're freakin' me, and I really don't need that. Besides, I think it's kind of cool to have something different like this in the neighborhood. It looks better than some of those skanky bars Mama's friends used to talk about hanging out in. And I know for certain, Perry's 24 and 7 is nothing like this. It's a straight-up joint. Ain't nothing in there but cheap liquor and drunk sweaty folks. This is different, kind of special," I said, pointing to the potted palms sitting between the round tables on the main floor.

"You think so? Don't kid yourself. This is what it is. If you fool these folks into hiring you, I guarantee you all this stuff you think is so attractive is gonna start looking really nasty pretty quick."

"Okay, Trip. You win. It's a strange place. Now just chill. I got enough crap to worry about," I said, wondering how long it was going to take the Angry Black Giant to come back with the lady who I hoped was going to hire me. I looked over at the spot that I might be working at. It was a horseshoe-shaped counter with a marble top, and behind it was a wide wooden cabinet with several box-shaped slots big enough to hold a hat, an umbrella, a backpack, or a small briefcase. I imagined myself behind the counter, smiling politely, and checking in items for a bunch of beer-soaked, rowdy brothers. I shuddered. I wouldn't tell him, but Trip was wrong. The place already didn't seem appealing to me. When I looked at the wall I didn't see a palatial scene. The waves didn't look calming to me, they looked choppy, as if a storm was about to roll in. I saw myself swept away in the waves, dragged deep underneath the painted ocean into a dark coldness where Trip and Uncle Simon could never find me.

"Be careful, China. It's very easy for a girl to fall and shatter in this world," Mama told me the night before she passed away. *"I did it without even knowing that I was standing on a ledge. Don't you do it too. Be a good, bright girl. Look down before you take a step. Always be sure of what you're walking into."*

"Yes, ma'am," I said. Now I was doing just the opposite. I wasn't sure of anything. I was walking blind, without even a cane to sort my way out. "I think working here won't be nearly as bad as you think," I lied to Trip.

"Good for you, I stopped thinking when I agreed to come in here, girlfriend. Now I'm just frontin' my way through it, 'cause I know it's what you want."

"Chill Trip, we'll be out of here soon enough."

"You're in a big hurry, sugar," a woman's voice rang out. Stepping out of a side door was a woman that made Trip's eyes nearly pop out. She was the most gorgeous woman I have ever seen. She was a work of art, firm black porcelain skin, with a kick-ass figure, slipped into a tiny white bikini that showed off *all* her assets.

"Damn," Trip said under his breath. "Baby got back, and everything else."

"She's old enough to be your mama," I whispered. "Quit acting so doggish."

"*Bow wow wow*," he said. I rolled my eyes. The sister came over to us. She really was something to see. She had one of those faces that a plastic surgeon might leave a photo of lying around his office, to make some insecure chick think she needed to have work done. Her nose and cheekbones were fabulous. She had shiny brown eyes that were clear and bright, like newly blown glass. I couldn't tell if her perfect half-moon eyebrows were artificially arched like Principal Nesby's, but the baby-smooth skin around them didn't look like it had ever had hair yanked out of it by the roots or ever been accidentally sliced by a disposable razor. To put it short, homegirl definitely *walked in beauty like the night*.

"Hi, I'm Louisa," she said, walking up and extending a hand with sparkling gold nails. I shook it without hesitation.

"Hello," I said.

"So I guess you're the one looking for a job, sugar?" she said with a thick Southern accent that reminded me of the time me and Mrs. Waltrip drank cool mint tea underneath the magnolia tree in her backyard.

"Yes, ma'am, my friend Rani told me that you all were looking for some counter help. She said her cousin used to work here before she had her baby."

"Yes, Toni. She was working here temporarily until she left to have her baby. Before her there was another girl, but she was forced to leave too. Anyway, sugar, we been looking for a new person ever since. We need somebody to check in personal items for the gentlemen. It's usually just hats and things, and not much else. Honey lamb, it's a fairly simple job. Do you think that it might be something you would want to do?"

I nodded. "Yes, ma'am, I worked behind a counter at my old job. I liked selling books and talking to people. It was really fun."

"I'm sure it was. Honey, it ain't nothing to this kind of work. Anybody can do it. I'm just looking for somebody special, somebody the gentlemen would like," she said, batting her silky lashes. She started walking around me nodding her head. She was checking me out like the Angry Black Giant, only I wasn't somebody she was hoping that she could get with, just somebody she was hoping she could sell to the guys. "You're a delicious little thing," she said, eyeing my figure. "You got a nice little top. What do you wear, about a double B cup? And the rest of you is fine too. You got good hips, and just the right size butt. It ain't too big or too flat. It's that in-between kind. That's the best one to have, sugar. It gives all the guys something to look at. Yes, you'll do perfect, even better than Toni. She was a little sparse in the chest. You look sorta young though. Honey, how old are you?"

"How old does she have to be?" Trip asked. Louisa grinned at him.

"She has to be at least eighteen to work behind the counter. And why should I be telling you that, sugar? Who are you, my handsome little brother?" she asked. Trip went all goofy in the face.

"I'm—I'm Trip, ma'am," he squawked, like a sixth-grader seeing his sexy choir teacher for the first time.

"Trip, that's a strange name. What does it stand for?" Louisa asked.

"I don't know, when I was little I was clumsy. I used to trip a lot. I guess that's how I got it."

"Oh, not you," Louisa said laughing. "You're a big strong boy, all muscled and pumped up. I'll bet you're very athletic. You look like you got it all together. I simply can't see you tripping and falling anywhere."

Trip grinned, and I grinned too. I had to give it to Louisa. She had him acting like he hadn't seen a woman before. She was good. Like Mama would say, she knew how to work a man. With her sexy figure and sultry voice I'll bet she was the kind of chick that never had to worry about paying her own bills. I had to admire her. She could turn a brother into chocolate pudding on the inside. There weren't many women that could do that, not even Yolanda, who I had seen work free stuff out of plenty of guys.

"You know what, I like you, Trip. You're sweet, a real nice young man," she said, slipping around him and placing her hands on his shoulders. Trip looked like he could turn into liquid and end up in a pool on the floor. I don't know why, but that suddenly bothered me. I shot him and Miss bikini-clad Louisa the meanest glance I could. Embarrassed, he wriggled out of Louisa's grasp. I thought she would look insulted. She giggled and turned back to me.

"Well, like I was saying, sugar," she said, "you have to be at least eighteen to work behind that counter. Now how old are you?" I thought about lying, and then decided to go with truth.

"I'm fourteen, but I got papers that say I'm just like an adult."

"Really?" she asked.

"Yes ma'am, they—they say I can do what I want."

"Do they?"

"Yes, ma'am. My Uncle got 'em for me. He's in a wheelchair and sometimes I have to look after things for both of us."

"Oh, that's too bad, honey," she said. "Well, I ain't never really hired nobody with papers like that, but I guess if you say you got 'em, and it means you as grown as I am, I surely ain't got no problems with them. Besides, I do like the look of you. You can start any time you want. We do a lunch crowd, but it don't get too busy during the day, so I guess I'll see you right around happy hour this evening."

"Yes ma'am, really?" I said, showing all my pearly whites.

"Really, and you got a pretty smile, too," she said. "You make sure that you keep it up. By the way, you know that we all wear swimsuits around here. It goes along with the whole beach theme that we have going on here. You don't have no problem with showing a little off?"

I shook my head. "No ma'am, I can wear anything."

"All right, honey. You got a lot of spunk. I didn't think you would mind. I'll send Big Robert to bring you out that cute little electric blue suit. It's all shiny and glittery. I wouldn't dare try to pull it off, but a young girl like you can make anything look good."

"Yes, ma'am," I said.

"Ooh, you're so polite. Honey, just call me Louisa. And one more thing. These uniforms, they cut kinda high, so make sure you take care of anything that might be trying to peep out," she said, looking down at my crotch.

"Yes, Louisa," I said, not even wanting to think about what might be peeping out.

"That's a little better. I'll see you later, sugar," she said. She started to walk off, but turned back. "Good-bye, Mr. Trip. I do hope I see you again too," she said, winking at Trip. Trip grinned all stupid, and looked like he could melt to the floor again. I cut him another look and his face went serious.

"Yes ma'am, I hope I see you again too," he said in a formal tone. Louisa disappeared through the side door. A few seconds later the Angry Black Giant, or Big Robert, reappeared with my electric blue suit.

"Here you go, young thing," he said, coming over and handing it to me, never taking his eyes away from my chest. Trip took the suit from him.

"Thanks bro," he said coldly. The Angry Black Giant didn't even bother looking at Trip. He licked one of his fat lips with a thick pink tongue. It made me sick and uncomfortable.

"I like 'em when they young and unspoiled," he said.

I swallowed hard, and held my nerves together. "Good for you," I said icily. Then I grabbed Trip by the arm and dragged him out of the club.

"Girl, what did you grab me for? I really wanted to check that triple-cheese-eating, double-wide bastard," Trip said as he slammed the door behind us.

"Let's go," I said. "I did what I needed to do."

"Fine with me. I'm all for getting out of here. It wasn't my idea to be over here anyway, girl. I told you I'm not down with this. That dude was looking at you like you was a plate of spaghetti that he wanted to gobble down. And you know that's the way all them messed up fools gonna be looking at you, strutting around with everything God gave you hanging out, don't you? It makes me wanna throw my breakfast up. I wish I could be there every evening," he said, walking down the deck steps. "I can't believe that Louisa chick hired you."

"Me either," I said to make him feel better. The truth is, neither one of us was shocked by my getting the job. Trip knew exactly why they hired me, and so did I. It was the same reason why Brother Agee had allowed me to make a contract with him for Amina's funeral. Nobody cared how old I was. It was all about what they thought I could do for them. Miss Louisa thought I could slip into her skanky suit and get more guys to hang out in the club, Brother Agee thought I could buy one of his overpriced coffins and get him a big fat commission. Nobody cared about my age. Money was money, even if you had to make it off a high-school kid.

I followed Trip across the lawn onto the sidewalk. Coming toward us were two fine sisters, in supershort shorts and clinging spandex tops that were little more than bras. Giggling loudly, they cut in front of us on their way to the club. They were a little older than me, and only a little. I could picture either one of them on the cover of *Teen Scene* magazine. I remembered a movie I saw one night with Uncle Simon. In the movie an old guy had a wife around his age and two younger women that he claimed to be married to also, but they were really nothing more than concubines. One day the old man decides to take on a new concubine-wife. The new girl looks like she's still into Britney Spears. Out of respect his servant brings the girl to meet the first wife. The older woman politely greets the girl, but when the young girl leaves, *"Such sins, such sins,"* is all she can say.

"How you gonna tell your uncle Simon that you took a job at that place?" Trip asked.

"What the willows don't know won't make them weep," I said.

"You using poetry on me again. Okay, let me use something on you. Imagine this, a pretty young girl is walking down the street and sees an ad posted on the door of a pet shop that says *Help wanted, great pay, start immediately*. It sounds good to the girl. She's been looking for a job, needs some extra cash to pay for them fancy human-hair weaves and braids she likes to wear down her back. She goes in, talks to a little round guy with glasses who tells her that all she has to do is make sure that his very special breed of dogs get fed."

"What's your point, Trip?" I snapped.

"Here it comes, girlfriend. Now listen up. Sister girl says okay. The job sounds simple to her. How hard could it be feeding some dogs in a cage everyday? She goes to work right on the spot. She follows the pet store owner past rows of cute, peppy puppies and playful kittens until they get to the back of the store. Behind a door she can hear whimpering, sniffing, and low barks.

'I'm glad you agreed to feed the dogs. They haven't eaten in a long time,' the man says. He opens the door just a little. The dogs start barking loud and growling. 'Supper's here, boys,' he says. He grabs the girl and hurls her through the door. A few seconds later it's all screams and 'Please help me! Oh God, please help me!'"

"Funny, Trip. I'll tell Uncle where I'm working," I said. He looked over at me and grinned. I stuck my tongue out at him. Then I looked straight ahead. I didn't want him to see that his story had freaked me out some. I couldn't afford to lose my cool. I would definitely need to look sincere when I told Uncle about my new job.

CHAPTER 4

"China, you are not going out of this house in that little thing!" Uncle Simon yelled as I brought in his box of clay from the front porch. I slammed the screen door and carried the package over to the sofa.

"Did anybody see you out there in that thing?" he asked.

"No, Uncle Simon, nobody saw me, but it's not a thing. It's my uniform, and we already had this conversation. It's what I have to wear at my job. Don't freak about it. I'm gonna put on my top and shorts in a minute. Man, give me a break. You've seen me in a swimsuit a zillion times before."

"Don't call me 'man,' and you keep telling yourself that thing is only swimwear, little girl," he said, wheeling his chair over to the sofa and starting to yank open the top of the cardboard box. "You keep telling yourself that outfit is something every young woman goes to work in. Keep saying it over and over, pretty soon you'll figure out fiction from the truth. You can still do that, can't you, China? I haven't failed you in that, too?" he said with sadness coming into his face.

"You haven't failed me in anything, Uncle," I said, leaning over to help him open the box. He moved his large hands and let me tear off the clear tape. I pulled it free and wadded it into a ball, while he reached around me and pulled out one of the cellophane-wrapped blocks of red clay.

"What are you going to make?" I asked.

"I guess I'm gonna make you a brain, China. Because it don't look like yours is working."

"My brain works fine, Uncle. I know what I'm doing. I'm just trying to take care of my child. I told you. I only want what's best for Amina. I ordered her all those things, now I have to pay for them. The insurance company paid for some, but I still got a long way to go. I'm just trying to handle what needs to be handled. That's the best thing for me to do."

"What's best? China, you don't even know what's best anymore, but when I went down to court and asked them to make you legal I certainly thought you did. The judge didn't want to give you those papers, but I made him see that we were living under unusual circumstances. '*I need her to be able to take care of everything if my next operation goes wrong. She's a bright girl. She's been through a lot, and always lands on her feet. I know she'll be okay on her own, if anything happens to me,*' I said before the bench. Yeah, I sure did think I was doing the right thing. I don't know what to think now. Sit down here, girl," he said pushing the box of clay out of the way. I flopped down on the sofa, ready to hear my second lecture in three days.

"What is it, Uncle?" I said, purposely focusing on the coarse gray-black hairs in his beard instead of his eyes.

"What is it? That's what I want to know. I've been trying to find out for weeks."

"What do you mean?"

"Just what I said," he said, throwing the package of clay back into the open box. "China, what's up with you? I raised you, and I've seen you make a mistake or two, but they've always been innocent, not deliberate. Now it seems like you're shaping and forming yourself a mess on purpose, and I just don't understand it, baby. That's all. I don't get it. I know you're upset, baby, but China, I just don't get what this is all about. Can you tell me?"

"Uncle, I don't know why we have to keep arguing over this.

I've already told you," I said, turning away. "I'm just trying to take care of my responsibilities. Obsidian Queens will help me do that. It pays more than any job around here, and I get big tips. It won't be long before I have Amina's bill paid off. The extra cash will help me do that, so don't be angry with me about it. I hate when you're mad at me."

"I'm not mad at you, China. And okay, fair enough," he said. "I can accept that working at Obsidian's will probably get the bill paid off, but I'll tell you what it won't do. It won't help you come to an understanding, and that's really your problem."

"I don't know what you mean."

"I think you do. In fact I know you do. China Cup, you're gonna have to open the door and look into the place you're afraid to see. It's what I had to do when the doctors told me that I wouldn't ever walk again. I didn't want to hear it or believe it. I sat in my room for years, wouldn't have anything to do with anybody that cared about me. I cut myself off from my family and all my school friends. I made things," he said, pointing to the clay. "I made all kinds of things with my hands. I formed people, houses, trees, streets, buses. China, I made a whole damn world that I could live in and hopefully never ever have to come out into the real one. My friends all grew up, and the neighborhood changed, but I didn't really see none of it. I didn't want to see none of it. China Cup, I missed everything. I got old and fat, and plain ole disappointed with my life. And I thought it was gonna be that way forever until you and Amina came into my life."

I looked back at him. "You are kind of old, but you're not that fat," I said, noticing that he was getting a little chubbier around his middle. I would have to pay a little more attention to his diet, make sure that he cut out that extra helping of pan sausage with his eggs each morning.

"Okay, I'm not that big, but that ain't my point," he said. "My point is, you haven't even gone to see where your child is buried. You keep talking about your responsibility. I'm not sure you even know what your responsibilities are."

"I do know what my responsibilities are. I know exactly what they are. I got a new list from Brother Agee the other day. He brought me over one that spelled everything out, down to the last penny."

"*'China, I know you'll get every one of these items checked off in no time. You're a good mother. I know you'll do what it takes to get your bill squared away'*—that's what he told me. He has confidence in me, Uncle. I won't let him or myself down."

"I have confidence in you too, China, but don't tell me nothing about a list," he said, irritated. "You know I'm not talking about any list."

"No—I don't. Look Uncle, stop sweatin' me about this. Don't be upset with me, please. I don't want you mad at me. Now I have to get to work," I said, getting up. "I'm gonna be late, and it's my first week."

"I wish it was your first and last. I won't stop you though," he said, shaking his head. "I've tried doing that before and I know that it never works out. My God! I was the one that put those papers in your hand. Lord knows I wish I had never done that. Well anyway, I only want you to think about this. Amina came out of you. You and she were molded from the same clay. Whatever you do she does. Don't you forget that. If you never ever listen to anything else that I tell you, you listen to that."

"Okay, Uncle Simon," I said. "I know that. Is this the end of the lecture? I gotta get to work. I'm gonna be late."

"It's the end. I know I can't change your mind on anything," he said, pushing his wheelchair away from the sofa to go back to his room.

"Not on this, because you're wrong. I know you're wrong. Now is there anything else, Uncle Simon?" I asked sarcastically. I didn't want him to know how much it hurt when he was upset with me.

He sighed and rolled past the used La-Z-Boy that one of Mama's clients gave her one Christmas. He went in the kitchen to heat up the green beans and fried chicken I cooked yesterday for dinner. I could have walked behind him and told him that he was wrong, and I did know what I was doing, only what was the point. Uncle and Trip were just alike. They thought they knew what I was feeling about Amina. They didn't. I wasn't feeling anything at all. It was still all dead inside, and I wanted it to stay that way. I didn't want to go down to the graveyard or even think about her in the ground. What was wrong with that? I turned my hands over and looked at the tiny brown scars on my fingers. I recalled how I broke the window the morning after she died, how I let the splinters pierce my flesh for four days until Uncle finally noticed them and dug them out. "China, you're lucky you didn't get a bad infection, letting your hands go on like this. Why didn't you try to get these things out?"

I couldn't tell him that after the first couple of days I didn't even feel the splinters. The feeling in my fingers was as numb as everything else inside me. A few months back our teacher read a poem about a man whose cheating wife cuts out on him one day. He comes home and all that's left in the house is a jar of canned pears. *"Our room, dark and empty, vacant as a bat cave at dusk,"* the man says. All the kids felt sorry when they heard that, even me. I don't think I'd feel sorry if I heard it now. Now I understand that darkness and emptiness is sometimes okay. Uncle said that I had to open the door to the place that I didn't want to see. I don't agree. Some places are better left closed. I walked to my room and found a cotton sundress lying over the back of the rocking chair where I used to rock my baby to sleep. Before I put it on I danced around in the mirror for a moment and made sure that I looked okay. Standing there in a suit with a bottom that wasn't much more than a thong, I did kind of understand how Uncle Simon felt seeing me in it. We weren't all uptight around the house, and he had seen me plenty of times in my underwear. But the suit was major revealing. It was smaller than even my skimpiest panties. Still, to me it was just a way to get what I wanted. I could put up with the consequences of wearing it, and whatever crap I had to deal with at the club. I had already started doing that.

The first evening I worked at the club was not a lot of fun. Trip walked me there, and I was a few minutes late because me and Uncle Simon had been going at it all afternoon about the job, and about what I intended to do about school. When I got to the club I was in a funky mood and not at all ready for Big Robert, the Angry Black Giant, to be in my face.

"You not dressed yet, pretty thing? I've been waiting on you," he said, looking like he would slobber all over me. Trip rolled his eyes at him, like he still wanted to lay him out. I wasn't in the mood for it, so I pushed Trip out of the door.

"All right, girl. Look, I'll be back at midnight to walk you home," he said.

"Thanks," I told him. "Where do the ladies change?" I asked Big Robert.

"Ooh baby girl, you don't need no special room to strip down in. You can do it right here. Go on and take it all off," he said.

"She's not taking anything off right here, and especially not for you. Go on and get out of here, Big Robert," Louisa's voice came from the main floor of the club. "I told you before to keep away from my girls. You go on, and find something else to do."

"All right, all right. I'm going. See you later, little Miss Tender Roni," Big Robert said, winking at me. I skipped the eye-roll. He was just a jerk, not even worth it. He walked away and Louisa came up. She was wearing a colorful Hawaiian string bikini. She looked like she had just swum in from the one of the islands in the painting on the wall.

"How you doing, sugar?" she asked. "I'm glad to see you made it here. Do you have your suit on under there?"

"No ma'am, I didn't get a chance to slip it on before I left the house. I'll have it on next time."

"It's okay, sugar. It's doesn't matter if you wear it here or put it on. Some girls like to put it on underneath their clothing, some girls don't. You just do what's easier for you. Now come on, honey. We're going to be open for our cocktail hour in just a few minutes, and I don't like the gentlemen coming in with nobody to greet them at the counter. Come on. Let me show you where you can put your suit on. I'll bet you gonna look real nice in it."

"I hope so," I said.

"I'm sure you will, honey. Let's fix you all up," she said, walking toward the side door in the main dance room. I followed her, all the while checking out her walk. It didn't surprise me that she had a wiggle walk. It was what all the guys would like. "*Shake it, but don't break it, cause Ben Taub Hospital won't take it*," we kids used to sing whenever we saw a woman walking like that. In her case it would have been a silly thing to say. I couldn't imagine any male doctors not being interested in her backside. I grew a little envious of her once more. Now that I had seen her again I figured her age had to be mid-to-late thirties. I was praying to look so good at her age.

"Come on, sugar, we want to get you changed as quickly as we can," she said, going through the door. I tried wiggling after her. It felt dumb, so I quickened my pace instead.

I closed the door to the dance room and followed her into a hallway with five doors. Three of the doors were partially opened, and I could hear muffled conversations and laughter wafting from them. It sounded like someone was having a good time. I hoped I was right, and somehow I would manage to have a nice time too. I walked behind Louisa to the third door in the hallway, and wondered about the fourth. It was shut, and all I could see was a sliver of darkness underneath. "That's Big Robert's little space. Don't you even pay it no mind, honey," Louisa said.

"Yes, ma'am," I said and put the room out of my mind. I didn't want to know anything about Big Robert's space. I didn't want to imagine him somewhere behind the door, possibly squeezing his huge jelly belly and bulging butt in and out of his black work suit or lounging on a sofa gobbling down a platter of buffalo wings and onion rings from the happy-hour menu.

"Gross," I said to myself.

"What?" Louisa asked.

"Nothing, ma'am."

"Just hold on, honey. Now here we are," she said, pushing open the door.

I was taken by surprise. The dressing room wasn't cheesy like all the beach stuff in the front of the club. It was kind of elegant. The walls were painted a lovely coral pink, and a plush rug of the same color was centered in the middle of the polished hardwood floor. I walked in wishing I could take my sandals off and sink my bare feet into it. It was exquisite and went well with the six white antique dressing tables with swinging gold-trim mirrors that were sitting against one of the walls.

"It's beautiful, isn't it?" Louisa said. "I saw a dressing room just like it years ago when my mama used to put me in all them silly beauty contests. It was the loveliest thing that I had ever seen. I told myself that if I ever had a dressing room of my own I would make mine look exactly like it. When the managers told me I could decorate this room any way that I liked, I searched all over creation until I found somebody who could reproduce the furniture for me."

"They're very nice. I don't have anything pretty like this in my room. I like them," I said.

"Me too," a woman shouted from behind a door in one of the walls. I heard the loud whoosh of a toilet. Afterward, the door opened and two ladies appeared. The first sister was a tall, busty chick with blue-gray eyes and shoulder-length frizzy hair the color of yellow broom straw. She was wearing a lavender bikini that blended well with her blanched-almond skin. Her button nose and thin lips told me that her father definitely couldn't trace his family roots back to Nigeria. She wasn't the finest sister I had ever seen, however she certainly wasn't somebody that you would want to leave your boyfriend alone with at the movies, while you went to get a juicy pickle or a package of Whoppers.

"I'm Star, and little schoolgirl, you're definitely gonna find out that I live up to my name," she said, walking over to me with her hands on her hips.

I didn't know what to make of the comment. I mumbled a "Hi," like a shy five-year-old.

She glanced at Louisa. "She gotta damn good figure, but she kinda green, ain't she? I thought there was a policy here about breaking 'em off before they even sprouted leaves."

"She's legal, Star honey," Louisa said. "She got papers and all. Only fourteen and the law say she can do whatever she want."

"I'll bet?" Star said nastily.

"Star, don't start that foolishness already. Miss Thing, go on and do what you get paid to do, and leave my new little girl alone."

"Whatever, I got no time for babies anyway," Star said. She sauntered off, giving me a mean look that was either anger or jealousy. I didn't know which, and I didn't care. I already knew I was going to stay out of her way.

"Aw, don't worry about Miss Wanna-Be-Somebody," the second lady said, walking toward us. "She ain't about nothing. She used to be out in Hollywood, trying to be an actress or something, till she found out that you had to have more than light eyes and good boobs to get a job. She can be venomous as a cottonmouth when she wants to be, but just like any old snake, all you got to do is bash her in the head, and she'll shut her mouth."

"Yes, ma'am," I said a little shocked, but not at what she had said. I was shocked at her. She was a mountainous sister too, as big as Big Robert, with a generous helping of everything. She was the kind of sister that I would expect to see in one of Grandma's old "Size 24 Plus" catalogs, yet I had to admit that she was a serious beauty. No woman ever looked better in a leopard swimsuit. With her tall brown fro and long curved nails she was both funky and exotic, obviously a ton of fun for the guys who liked to kick it with a heavier gal. Her face was well preserved with a lot of plumpness to keep everything mostly smoothed out. Except trouble had come her way, and I could see it in the few wrinkles around her lips and underneath her melancholy eyes. I figured she had to be about Louisa's age or maybe a little older. So far she was the most unique and unexpected thing I had seen in the club. I liked her. She seemed like a proud sister, and the type of chick that you would always want keeping tabs on your back.

"What's your name, gal?" she asked, coming and standing right in front of me.

"I'm China Cup Cameron," I answered politely.

She looked me over and smiled. "Your mama named you that? Is that your real name? Or is it just what you go by?" I shrugged my shoulders, not really understanding the question.

"It's my real name, and my mama didn't give it to me, but she learned to love it."

"I'll bet she did," she said, checking me out like Star. Her eyes went all over my chest and torso. "Well, little Miss China Cup, Star is right about one thing, you do look a little innocent and fragile. I'll have to make it my duty to see that you don't get too shattered," she said, reaching over and pinching my cheek lightly with her fat fingers.

"Yes, ma'am," I said, rubbing my face. She laughed.

"Well, I have to get on out there. The men will be here soon, and ain't no doubt they will be looking for a whole lot of Sweet Petite, that's my name," she said, walking around me and Louisa and heading for the doorway. "They call me Sweet Petite, and that's all I ever need to say about that."

"You got that right, sugar," Louisa said as Sweet Petite left the room. She walked over to the door where the two ladies had emerged from and opened it up. "The bathroom is in here. You can put your suit on in one of the stalls or in the dressing room. Just do it in a hurry, honey," she said.

I nodded. She wiggled back out of the door and I pulled it closed. When I heard the knob clang shut I ripped off my T-shirt and stepped out of my jean shorts. I was tugging at my nylon panties when I heard the knob clang again. A thin girl in a lively psychedelic swimsuit rushed in. I pulled my underwear back up.

"Ooh, I'm sorry," she said nervously, and quickly slammed the door closed. "I'm sorry, miss. Louisa didn't tell me that you were in here dressing. I wouldn't have flung the door open so wide. I know that some girls don't like that kind of thing."

"It's okay," I said.

"No, really, I'm really, really, sorry," she repeated.

"It's okay," I said again.

"I'm uh, uh, Onyx Moon," she said.

"Onyx Moon," I repeated.

"Yes," she said quickly. "And it's my real name too. My mama said that I was born one night while she was crawdad hunting with some friends, and that mostly all they had to deliver me by was the light of a big full moon."

"That's a nice story," I said. "Your mama must have really cared about you. She put a lot of thought into your name."

She shrugged her shoulders. "I guess. I live with my big brother. I haven't seen my mama in a long time. We don't speak too often."

"Oh," I said, wishing that I hadn't said so much. I tried to cover up the blunder. "I'm sorry. I have a big mouth sometimes. I'm China Cup," I offered without being asked. "My name is kind of different too."

"I like it. It makes me think of a fancy party, with cucumber sandwiches and lady fingers."

I giggled. "I guess it does."

She smiled, but I suspected that she didn't do it very often, at least not genuinely. She seemed sad, and she had incredibly sorrowful eyes, like the moon inside of her had stopped shining a long time ago. I wondered what *she* had been through? I checked out her flat stomach and thought I saw a faded stretchmark, though I couldn't imagine a baby popping out of her. She had one of those teen TV show bodies. Her dress size couldn't have been more than a zero.

"You got any children?" I blurted out, without even thinking that it was a nosy thing to ask.

"A couple. I got two little boys. They live with my ex-boyfriend and his mother, but I take them money every time I get paid," she said.

"Oh, that's good that you look out for them. A whole lot of people who don't live with their kids don't even pay them any mind," I said, trying to make her smile again. She didn't.

I looked her over some more. There were tiny black scars on her arms and legs. They were old scars, long healed over. She had to have been off of whatever she was on for while. That was good, only clearly not good enough for her to have her kids.

"What about you? You got any babies?" she asked, looking at my stretchmark-free belly.

I didn't know how to answer. I shook my head.

"Oh, that's good. It's better to wait to have them. You're really pretty. I hope when you do get some, they look just like you. That would be nice, wouldn't it?"

I didn't answer. I pulled my panties off and stepped into my swimsuit bottom. She watched me until I adjusted it and unhooked my bra.

"Okay, I better go out," she said as I started to put on my top. She turned to leave and I noticed that the back of her bathing suit *really* was a thong. The sight of her exposed bottom startled me and made me remember that no matter how many palm trees were painted on the walls of the club, I wasn't about to start a job at the beach. I took a deep breath and let it out as she left the dressing room, closing the door behind her. The second it closed, the Fat Boys' version of "Wipe Out" came blaring from the other side. I did a quick check in one of the mirrors and went back into the club.

When I opened the door to the main floor there were three middle-aged brothers in dark dress slacks and white shirts sitting at one of the tables drinking glasses of foamy beers. Sweet Petite and Onyx Moon were with them. Sweet Petite was sitting in a chair next to a short brother with a mostly white beard. She was hanging onto the guy's arm and laughing like crazy, as if the brother was a professional comedian or something. She looked like she was enjoying the hell out of herself, and I maybe would have gone over and asked her what was so funny, if I hadn't seen Onyx Moon's face. She wasn't nearly so happy. She was sitting on some slim, bald-headed brother's lap. He was whispering something to her, but whatever he was saying wasn't making her laugh. She still had that sorrowful look in her eyes, and a tight smile that looked like it was straining to stay in place. I walked past the group on my way to the counter, and of course before I got there, the third brother hopped up from his chair and got in my face. He was slim too, with a receding hairline, and a few crinkly gray hairs sticking out of his mustache. "Hey, little Miss Sexy," he said to me, with slightly slurred speech and stinky breath. "I'm the only one without a lady, why don't you come sit with me?"

"I have to work behind the counter," I said pleasantly, and tried to go around him. That was a mistake. He grabbed me by the back of my swimsuit top. I heard the material rip and to my horror the bra slid down my stomach and onto the floor. I put my arms up to shelter my breasts as quickly as I could, but not before everybody in the club got a good look at them.

"Ooh wee, those look real good to me," the drunk guy said. The other guys at the table laughed. I felt tears well up in the corners of my eyes, and I would have cried, except I knew I would probably be out of a job. I held my breasts with one arm and bent down to get the top. As I was retrieving it, Big Robert came out of nowhere and grabbed the guy by the arm.

"That kitten ain't ready to play yet," he said, escorting the guy back to his table. He sat him down in his chair roughly, and even drunk, the guy was smart enough to stay put. I walked swiftly back to the dressing room to see if I could fix my top. Halfway to the door, the Commodores' "Brick House" started up. Star came walking up the platform stairs in a silver G-string, with matching long silver boots, and a crown of sparkling yellow stars sitting on her head. The music turned up, and she began to dance slowly, gyrating her hips and pushing her pelvis out. All three men started clapping and hooting. I opened the door that led to the hallway and went back to the dressing room. A few moments later Onyx Moon came running after me.

"There's some safety pins in one of the dressing-table drawers," she said.

"Thanks," I mumbled. She nodded, and took a twenty-dollar bill out of her bosom.

"Here," she said, handing it to me. I looked at her, confused.

"It's from the guy who messed up your top."

I looked at the money and wanted to go throw it in the guy's face. Fortunately common sense got the best of me. I needed the money for Amina. I took it and mumbled thanks. She started to leave, but turned back again.

"Always take their money," she said. "Don't matter how ugly they treat you, or how much you want to smash your head against all them palm trees they got painted out there on the wall, you always make sure that you come away with the cash."

"Okay," I said quietly. I paused for a moment, just noticing that my heart was beating so hard it felt like a million hearts were stuck behind my rib cage. I sat down in one of the chairs and calmed myself for a moment. When I felt a little better I got up from the chair still squeezing the twenty-dollar bill tightly, and started looking for a pin for my top.

And that's what happened my first evening at Obsidian Queens. The crap came immediately, and I dealt with it. I kept my cool, and when Trip came to pick me up I was even able to manage a small lie.

"It went okay," I said, as we headed down the deck steps.

"Are you sure? Girl, don't fib."

"I'm not fibbing. I'd let you know if anything major happened. The guys there are just guys. I can handle the job. It's cool, and I made almost a hundred bucks in tips," I said, holding out the cash.

"Almost a hundred bucks? Just in tips!"

"Just in tips," I said, waving the bills at him again.

"What did you have to do for them?"

"I didn't do anything. I simply did my job."

"Only your job, that and nothing else."

"That and nothing else."

"Okay," he said. "I know you always tell me the truth," and after that he let the matter drop. I was glad for it. I didn't want him to pry any deeper. I didn't want to have to tell him about the guy who ripped my top off, or the one that offered me a fifty to do something that even my girlfriends don't admit to doing. It wasn't necessary for him to know about the guy who thought his hand should be attached to my behind, or the two weird brothers that asked me if I wanted to go home with them and spend the night. All I needed for him to know is that I appreciated him walking me home. He made sure that I got home safely that first evening, and has walked me home ever since. Trip is my rock. I don't think I could make it today without him.

I peered in the mirror a little longer, then grabbed a Bugs Bunny tank top and stretch shorts out of the drawer and put them on over my suit, so I could avoid the change at work. I looked decent, with absolutely nothing for Uncle to complain about. I reached for my backpack, sitting at the foot of my bed, and got ready to take off. I started for the door when Fatima, one of Yolanda's older girls, appeared at my door. Her warm brown face was wringing wet with sweat, and her frightened eyes made it look like the hound of the Baskervilles had chased her to my house. "China, you better come quick," she said, nearly out of breath. "It's a whole lot of mess going on at my house, and I think Mama is about to get into some serious trouble."

"What kind of trouble?"

"Just come quick. Please come," she said. I flung my backpack down and followed her. She went Superman fast out of my front door, with me working hard to catch up. One, two, three, four, five blocks we ran down to her mom's house, with her racing like there was a prize waiting for her at the finish line, and me wondering what in the world the so-called mess was all about. When we reached her yard, she ran to the side of the fence, and took the shortcut through the huge hole between the wooden slats. I raced behind her, tearing my tank on one of the splintered boards. As soon as we hit the back steps I could hear loud shouting. It was Yolanda. She was yelling back and forth with some man whose voice I couldn't recognize.

"Who is that, Fatima?" I asked as we went quickly up the steps.

"It's Eboni's grandfather. He and Mama been going at it for a long time."

"Aw shoot," I said. Fatima pulled open the back screen door and we went in through Yolanda's untidy kitchen, and right into her living room. When we got there it looked like hell was about to come up clean through the floor. Yolanda and Jamal's pops, Mr. Paulquinn, a pint-sized brother who never appeared without a business suit, were squared off like Holyfield and Tyson, just waiting for the bell to ring. I didn't like Mr. Paulquinn, and I felt like yelling at Yolanda to *get him*, except Eboni was there. She was standing right next to Yolanda with her thumb in her mouth. My heart fell into my knees when I saw all the fear in her face.

"Fatima, get your sister and take her to the bedroom," I said.

"Better for who?" Yolanda yelled out, before the girls even made it out of the room. "Who is it better for? You and that sorry wife? Hell, ya'll didn't do nothing with ya'll own child."

"We did the best we could, a lot better than you're doing for our granddaughter. We would never have thought it was okay to raise our child in a rat hole den of sin like this. You have to be pure ridiculous to think that Eboni should be growing up here," Mr. Paulquinn fired back loudly.

"A rat hole den of sin? Look, you uppity, need-to-get-his-own-damn-life bastard, my house is as good as your house or better. Just because I don't have all those overdecorated rooms and a big fat yard don't mean my home is any less presentable," Yolanda said, shaking her finger madly in Mr. Paulquinn's face. I noticed that her long braids were being held back with a large barrette, and she had on a nice mauve blouse that covered up "the Road Map" on her belly. Her Daisy Duke shorts were nowhere to be seen. Believe it or not she had on a plain brown skirt that came down below her knees. For once she looked like a pretty respectable mother, even if Mr. Paulquinn didn't think she actually was.

"Please, girl, don't be as simple as you look. The truth is you have nothing, and you are nothing. You're a five-dollar tramp who doesn't even have sense enough to get her own husband," Mr. Paulquinn said. "Go on and tell me I'm a lie. Tell me that you don't live your life off of other women's scraps."

"Excuse me! I date who I wanna date. You ain't my father or my mother, and even if you were, you wouldn't be telling me what to do. I packed my bags and got out of my parents' house when I was sixteen, because I didn't like them all up in my business," Yolanda said, getting right into Mr. Paulquinn's face, as if she were ready to start swinging.

"That figures," Mr. Paulquinn spat. "I figured you for the type of hardheaded girl that would rather make a disaster out of her life than listen to some good ole fashion common sense. Well, it doesn't matter to me if you listened to your parents or not. This is about Jamal's child, and I suspect she's the only decent thing that Jamal will ever do with his life. Now my wife and I want her to come live with us. We are still young enough to make a difference. We can make sure that Eboni has everything she's lacking here, everything you couldn't possibly give her."

"Get the hell out of my house," Yolanda said through clenched teeth. "I love Jamal, but he ain't nothing, and as far as I know Eboni will end up the same way, if you have anything to do with it. Anyway, she's not yours to do a damn thing with, she's mine. You don't get to tell me what I can and can't do with her."

"Fine, fine, I thought I could reason with your ignorant behind, but I see I'm just trying to put cream on spoiled fruit. You listen to me," Mr. Paulquinn said with blazing eyes. "Eboni deserves a lot better than you. Tomorrow I'm going to see a lawyer and make sure that she gets just that. I'm going to tell him about all the married men you've been with, and how you've forced your children to live your miserable life."

"You tell whoever you like, but you tell them the hell out of this house." I was surprised to hear Trip say that. I looked around, shocked, as he walked up to Mr. Paulquinn.

"Get out of here, man. You don't have a right to be in here harassing this lady," he said.

"And who the heck are you to tell me what I have a right to do, boy?" Mr. Paulquinn said glaring at Trip.

"I got your boy, old man, and I'm the one that's gonna put you through that screen door behind you, if you don't find somewhere else to be."

"Yeah, like right now," Yolanda said. "You get on out of my house."

"All right, all right, don't worry," Mr. Paulquinn said, taking in Trip's muscular physique. "I didn't even want to be here this long. I might catch something."

"Look, catch a cab, catch a Greyhound, catch a damn covered wagon if you want, just catch it far away from here," Trip said. He walked over to the screen door and opened it. Mr. Paulquinn shot daggers at him, before he played it smart and hurried out of the house.

"Don't think this is the last of this!" he yelled out on the porch.

"Maybe, but for today it is most definitely squashed," I yelled back. I shook my head at Yolanda. I expected her to go off on what Mr. Paulquinn had just told her. She latched the front screen door and ran to her room.

"Where did you come from?" I asked Trip.

"I was on my way to your house when I saw you and Fatima running over here. I followed so I could see what was up."

"I'm glad you did. I gotta go see what's up with Yolanda. Do me a favor and check on the girls," I said.

"Okay," he said, and took off down the hall.

I went to Yolanda's room. She was lying on her water bed staring up at the ceiling. I went over and lay down next to her. She was crying silently. Tears were running onto her cougar-print comforter.

"You ever read them classic romance novels, China?" she asked.

"Uh, no," I answered, wondering where the question was coming from. I didn't know that Yolanda was interested in any kind of novels.

"I do. I been reading them since I was a little girl. I don't know why. I just always been interested in them. In those books there's always some woman penned in."

"Penned in?"

"Yeah, in those books the women can't ever be nothing they wanna be. They can't dress the way they want, keep company with who they want, and they sho' can't marry who they want."

"Sounds like women back then had a bad life," I said.

"They did. It's all messed up in those books, but to tell you the truth it's screwed up today. Women still get treated like they ain't nothing but property, and they can't do what they want to do with their lives. I'm telling you it ain't fair. For instance, men can do whatever they want. Don't nobody ever call a man a slut 'cause he have a lot of girlfriends. They just call him a player, and when he leaves a bunch of big bellies all over town, they say he's a stud."

"Ain't that the truth. Guys get away with everything."

"For real, and it's not fair. Hell, ain't nothing equal for women. You ever seen that Moses movie, where one of them enslaved Jewish men say, 'Beauty is but a curse to our women' or something like that?"

"It's from *The Ten Commandments*, I think."

"That's right, except I think he got it wrong. Being born female is a curse to women. It ain't got nothing at all to do with what you look like."

"I suppose," I said. I reached over and took her hand and held it.

"I'm not gonna let them take my child, China. I know I'm not the best mother in the world, but I'm all God gave her, and that ought to be enough for anybody."

"It's enough for me," I said.

"I know, and I'm glad that Fatima ran and got you or I don't know how things would have went down." She pointed to the digital clock on her dresser. "You better go. You gonna be late for your job."

"Yeah, and I don't want to do that my first week."

"Naw you don't. By the way, how long you planning on keeping that job?"

"Until I pay off Amina's funeral."

"Okay, but don't you work it for even one day after that. Don't you let them men keep taking advantage of you."

"I can take care of myself."

"Not at Obsidian Queens you can't, and trust me on that. The minute you settle up your bill with the funeral home you get out of there. I'm older than you, and I been around some. Take my word for it. Don't hang around there any longer than you have to."

"I won't. Now I gotta get to work. I'm gonna be late," I said. "Trip is out there with the girls. Do you want him to stay?"

"Naw, I know he walks you to work. Just tell him to stop at the park on the way back and tell the rest of my kids to come home. They down there on them swings and slides."

"I'll tell him to run 'em back. I'll see you later," I said. I got up from her bed and walked into the living room. A second later Trip joined me there.

"Them girls about to talk me to death," he said, laughing. "They done told me about every doll they ever even thought about owning."

I smiled weakly at him.

"Is she gonna be okay?" he asked, nodding toward Yolanda's room.

"Not really, I don't think so."

"You want me to stay here with her?"

"Naw, she told me to ask you to make sure her other kids got back from the park. She wants you to holler at them on your way home."

"I can do that."

"Good," I said. "I'm gonna call Uncle and tell him to roll down here and stay with her awhile. She likes hanging out with him. Sometimes I come home from school or work and find them in the kitchen laughing and gossiping like two old ladies."

"Really?"

"Yeah. I don't know what to do, and she's cool with Uncle. I'll tell him to come down and keep her company. She can go out to the porch and tell him what's going on."

"I think I saw the phone in the girls' room," Trip said.

"Okay, I'll run and go get it."

"Wait a minute. I have a question. China, do you think Eboni is better off with them stuck-up grandparents?" he whispered.

"No, I don't think so. It doesn't seem right, since they didn't even want Yolanda to be with their son, but what the heck do I know?" I whispered back. "I don't even have a kid anymore. Yolanda has been raggedy to all her kids, but I know she loves them. Anyway, Uncle Simon will come talk to her. I don't know what to do, and he's better with problems than I am. I need to get to work. Right now that's all I know how to do."

"If working at Obsidian's is all you know how to do, you got a problem. But it's your world, and I'm still just trying to figure out how to live it."

"Lay off me, Trip. Don't even start. I just had a conversation with Yolanda about women not being able to do what they want to do."

"Working at that club is not really what you want to do, is it?"

"I already told you it isn't about want, so quit sweatin' me about it. I'm gonna go call Uncle. You still gonna walk me to work?"

"Always and forever. I'll walk you anywhere, even if it's someplace that you shouldn't be."

"And where should I be, Trip? Should I be off in there with Yolanda all sad because everything I know is screwed up?"

"There's nothing wrong with sadness, China. In my history class the books always say that from misery can come great strength. It's how people sometimes get through wars and stuff like that."

"I don't need to get through a war, Trip. I've already lost the battle. I'm just trying to take care of a casualty."

"What battle did you lose?"

"The same battle that Yolanda is losing—motherhood," I said. Then I went to the girls' room to find the phone.

CHAPTER 5

My mother was the daughter of a wealthy king. Each morning she would take a walk near the lily pond behind our castle. My father, a strong and brave warrior, would watch her from a hill overlooking the castle. He thought she was beauty itself. He loved her, but he was poor and had no money, so he had no hope of ever making her his wife. One day my grandfather, the king, joined my mother for a walk. While they were strolling, two assassins with daggers scaled the castle walls and attacked my grandfather. From the distance my father saw the incident. He flew over the wall and killed the two assassins. My grandfather was so grateful for his help that he gave him my mother's hand in marriage. They were married that same day. They didn't have much, but they were very happy. Soon they gave birth to a wonderful, sweet daughter, and that was me.

I wished that story was true, but it's not. It's just a fairy tale that I put myself in when I was very little. When I was younger I hated knowing that my father was some sorry janitor my mother slept with when she was in high school. I just didn't want to think about it. Today I still wish that my mother had never told me. I was pretty young, and I didn't really know what to do with the info. Trip told me we should look the janitor up on the Internet and send him a letter. We went to Mama's old school site on the Web and found out the janitor still worked at the district, so I wrote him a letter and

Trip put it in the mail. It was nearly six weeks before we got a response, and it wasn't at all what I was expecting. One afternoon when I got home from school the phone was ringing. I picked it up and a male voice was on the other end. I was excited because I thought it was my father. The excitement didn't last. The person on the phone wasn't my father at all. It was his grown son. The son told me that his dad had worked at his job for over twenty-five years, and just got promoted. It was his father's job to oversee janitorial departments at several schools.

"My dad is a good guy. He doesn't need a lot of stress in his life. I don't know who you are, little girl, but there's nothing for you here. You can tell your mother that's she's not going to get anything out of my dad by having you write here. My dad doesn't have any place in his life for bastard kids. Do yourself a favor, and don't send him any more letters. I guarantee you that he doesn't want to hear from you."

"Yes sir," I said, and hung up the phone. After that, I didn't send any more letters. The son made me feel like dirt. He made me feel like the crud that I scrub from underneath the rim of the toilet every month. I was down in the dumps about it for days until I finally told Mama about it. When I did she found the guy's number on our caller ID and called him back. She cursed him out. Then she told me she would never ever let another man treat me like filth, but last night Mama was nowhere around when another guy made me feel the same way.

It happened at Obsidian Queens, during the busiest part of the evening. A big crowd was there, and Sweet Petite was displaying everything in 3D. She was down to nothing but a red G-string that was mostly hidden by her hanging belly, and the guys were loving it. Some of them were standing in front of their chairs clapping and whistling, while others were going up to the stage and trying to shove dollar bills into the string they could hardly see. Sweet was fine with that. She had the biggest grin you ever wanted to see. She looked like she had just finished dancing at Lincoln Center or Carnegie Hall, and that made me feel a little less bad about being at the club. Out of the ten women who danced there Sweet Petite was probably the one who enjoyed it the most. She wasn't trying to be a star. She just liked being seen, and it didn't make any difference that it was only by a group of half-drunk guys who only wanted to know if they could touch her goodies. I liked that. I admired that she somehow found a way to enjoy what she had to do to pay her bills. I was grinning myself when some goofy looking brother with a shiny green suit and a drippy way-over curl came to the counter.

"What you grinning at, sweet thing?" he asked, leaning on the glass. With the amount of liquor on his breath he could have lit up every cigarette for the next three blocks, simply by blowing on them. I backed away from the counter and tried to be as polite as I could.

"Can I get something for you, sir?" I replied.

"Just your sweet self," he said. I resisted rolling my eyes, and asked the question again.

"Can I get something for you?"

"Aw baby, you can get me a whole lot of stuff," he drooled. I shook my head.

"Did you check a hat or something, sir?" I asked with a sigh.

"Hell naw, little Miss Lovely. I ain't got no ticket, and I don't need one."

"Have a good evening, sir," I said. I turned away from the counter, like I usually did when some idiot came over and gave me grief. It was standard procedure for me; back away and turn, pretend to do something else. Generally the guys just got tired of talking to air and moved on. Wouldn't you know this fool didn't. To my surprise he wasn't as drunk as I thought. He scrambled over the counter and grabbed me.

"Who do you think you are, turning your back on me?" he

yelled, holding my arms roughly. I struggled hard to get free. "What, you think you something special?" he asked. "I spent good money in this club. Hell, you ain't nobody to be turning your back on me."

"No, no sir. I don't think I'm anything."

"You got that, damn straight!" he yelled, and shoved me into the shelves. They shook and some of the items fell to the floor.

"I have to pick those up," I cried.

"Shut up, bitch. You ain't picking up nothing. You gonna stand right here with me. Yeah, that's right. You gonna stand here until I say you can go, trying to act like you too good to talk to. I ought to slap your teeth clean down your throat!" he yelled viciously. "What makes you think you too good to even talk to me," he said. He grabbed me again, digging his short nails deep into my flesh.

"That's not what I think. Please let me go!" I screamed from the pain.

"Hey, let that girl go, fool. Can't you see you're hurting her?" I heard another guy yell.

"You shut up. I'm trying to teach her how she s'pose to act when a man come in here. Hell, I ain't paid no high-ass cover charge just so some little five-dollar bitch can turn her back to me."

"Let me go, somebody please help me! I'm not a bitch," I said.

"Is that right. Well, you look like one to me," he said. He pressed me harder against the shelves and started kissing me on the neck. The feel of his lips made me wish I could shed my skin like the grass snakes that crawl through our backyard do. I mustered all my strength and shot my elbow into his belly. He fell sideways into the counter, holding his stomach.

"Damn, I'ma kill you, you little tramp!" he shouted. I dashed from behind the counter and found Big Robert and Louisa standing there, so I stopped. The drunk ran behind me and stopped too.

"Now, Mr. Bouton, sugar, is that any way to act with a nice young girl?" Louisa asked.

"That little cow hurt me," the drunk raged.

"Is that so?" Louisa said calmly. She walked up to the guy and put her arms around his neck. "Now, Mr. Bouton," she purred in her extraskimpy swimsuit, "I'm sure it was just a little accident because you frightened her so. She's new here, and a little young. I'm certain she didn't do anything on purpose. It was just a little mistake. Wasn't it, China Cup?" she asked me. "You didn't mean to make Mr. Bouton upset?"

"No ma'am, it was just a mistake," I said.

"See there. It was only a little error, so don't you even worry about being mad over it. You go on over there and get you another drink. Then Big Robert will find somebody to take you home." Louisa continued to purr, while lightly tracing the guy's ear with her long fingers. The drunk guy broke into a stupid grin. Louisa stepped out of his way and he followed Big Robert back to a table. A second later Christina, a shapely Latina sister in a royal blue thong, brought him another shot glass of liquor.

"Mr. Bouton is one of our best customers," Louisa said. "He comes all the way from Fourth Ward to be with us. He owns a butcher shop over there. Last month he must have spent five hundred bucks in here. He can be a little obnoxious at times, so next time you have a little problem with him you come and get Big Robert right away."

"A little problem? What he did—you call that a little problem? I didn't do anything wrong, ma'am. It wasn't even my fault. I swear. You gonna let him treat me like that?" I asked, doing everything I could to hold back the tears.

"I sure am," she said. "Honey, dealing with men like that is part of the job. It's the nature of the work, and you better get used to it, China. I know you want to keep working here. I know you want to keep making all this extra cash for your daughter."

"For my daughter?" I asked, rubbing my wrists.

"That's right, for your daughter, sugar," she said, turning nice again. "Now, you go on outside. Get some fresh air for a little while and come on back."

"Yes, ma'am," I said.

I marched outside of the club and stood on the front porch shaking from anger or fear. I couldn't tell which, but deep down I felt it was anger. I wanted to go back in and spit in Mr. Bouton's face. It was exactly what he deserved, and I wished I could give it to him, but I couldn't. I didn't like the fact that Louisa had somehow found out about my daughter and was using it to get me to shut up and dance to her tune. I didn't like it at all. Yet, I needed the money. The tips were amazing, and I had already taken lots of cash down to Brother Agee and put it on my account. In not too long I would have the entire amount. That is, if I could hang in there long enough to get it.

I couldn't go back and spit in Mr. Bouton's face, and I certainly couldn't go home crying to Uncle Simon, which is the second thing I wanted to do. Uncle would advise me to tell Louisa where she could stick her stupid counter job, then we would have soda and barbecue-flavor potato chips while we watched TV, and that would be the end of it—the end of all of it. I sighed. Even though I really wanted that to happen, it was better for me to leave things as they were.

I walked the yard for a few minutes and fantasized about the professional people working in the looming skyscrapers in nearby downtown. I wondered what it would be like to sit at a desk and make good money by landing some huge account. Some of my old girlfriends worked in offices after school. They wore high heels and suits, and knew how many tablespoons of coffee a coffeemaker takes. I calmed myself down, and ten minutes later returned to my job. A friendly older brother was there. I handed him his straw hat, and he gave me a ten-buck tip. I stuck it in my swimsuit top.

"Have a good evening, sir," I said.

"You too, baby," he told me.

I tried to. The rest of the night went well, so I mellowed out. The guy who had made me feel awful finished his free drink, and Big Robert got one of the busboys to drive him home. Everything was okay. I spent my free time chatting with Onyx Moon, who had a sore foot so she couldn't dance. It was nice. She told me about her two sons and how she was getting a new place of her own, so she could get custody of them. "My boyfriend started me on drugs, but then he got off of 'em and went straight. I wasn't that lucky. I got heavy into them, so he and his mama took the boys. I'm clean now, though, so I think I deserve to have them back," she told me as we wrote numbers on my item tickets.

"Good for you, girlfriend," I said, pleased with her for being brave enough to admit she had screwed up. It also impressed me that she would share so much personal info with me. In fact, I was so impressed I agreed to go and see her new apartment with her. She told me she was going to go and put down the rest of her deposit money, and asked me if I wanted to tag along. It sounded good to me. I told her that we should do it today because it was Saturday.

I knew that Trip was spending the morning writing new story ideas, and Uncle and Yolanda were going to see a free lawyer Trip located for them on the Internet at school. It was a good day to go out and not think too much about anything that was giving me trouble, like school, which I had quit going to. It was too hard to work all night and get up early to go listen to Robert Frost and Denise Levertov in my English class. I didn't have time to think about the War of 1812 or what DNA was composed of. I only had time to think about Amina. She was supposed to go to school, too. She was supposed to become a teenager, get a smart boyfriend who would treat her right, and apply for the same college after high school. She was supposed to get a medical degree, discover a way to make Uncle Simon walk again, and finally marry that high school boyfriend and settle down. That's what my Amina was supposed to do. Now she didn't even have a future. How could I be worried about mine? I knew Uncle didn't like it, but I wasn't going to feel guilty about missing a few classes. Amina was missing her whole life. I ate a banana and drank a glass of nonfat chocolate milk for breakfast. After that, I washed the breakfast dishes with liquid soap and lemon juice. I threw them in the dish drainer so they could dry naturally and left the house.

The Princess and the Pea is where I ended up a little while later. I wanted to say hello to Mrs. Waltrip, so I had asked Onyx Moon to meet me out in front. The bus stop was only a block and a half from the bookstore. It seemed like the perfect place to get together.

When I yanked open the door the delicious smell of orange blossom mint tea hit me. Mrs. Waltrip was making her best blend. I imagined the pot simmering on the stove in the back, filled with peppermint candies and orange peels.

"Come for some refreshment, China?" she asked, stepping from behind the cluttered counter in her much-loved denim dress with Tweety Bird and Sylvester printed on the skirt. I gave her a hug, and when I let her go I checked out the new paperbacks on her counter. She had obviously just gotten in a new shipment of classic children's books. Copies of *Charlotte's Web*, *The Velveteen Rabbit*, *The Snowy Day*, and one of my childhood favorites, *Madeline*, were everywhere. I picked up a copy of *Madeline in London*.

"Ooh, I love this one," I said. "I wish I still had my old copy. My uncle Simon used to read me this series after Mama died. I like it because the little girl in it is just like me. She doesn't have any parents, either."

"You have your uncle," she said, fixing a bobby pin in the bun on top of her head.

"Yeah, I'm luckier than she is," I said, watching her push her nearly white hairs back into place.

"I think you are. Everybody needs somebody special to be in their life. Your uncle is like my Albert. I don't know what I would do if he wasn't here for me. He sure knows how to cheer me up when I get down. Just last night he told me the silliest joke he heard somewhere."

"What was it?" I asked, playing along.

"He said that two pretzels were walking down the street and one of them was assaulted. Assaulted, do you get it?"

"I get it." I laughed. "It is a silly joke, kinda babyish."

"Yes, it is. You know my husband. He's like me. He likes all those things for kids. That's why we decided to open up this bookstore years ago. Anyway, come on back and have some tea so we can chat."

"No, I just thought I'd run in real quick and say hello. I don't have time. I'm going to go hang out with a friend soon. Oh, here she comes," I said, seeing Onyx Moon coming up the street in a white micromini that showed off her slim little legs. I waved at her through the glass window but I don't think she saw me. She didn't wave back. She kept on walking and suddenly turned into Diamond's grocery store. I figured she was going to get a snack.

"Is that the girl you waiting for?" Mrs. Waltrip said.

"Yeah, we're hanging out today."

"With her? You're spending time with her?"

"Yeah, she's kinda nice."

"What do you know about her?"

"Not much. I just met her. She seems nice, got a few problems though. She told me her boyfriend got her on drugs a while back, but she cleaned herself up. Now she's trying to get her two little boys back to come and live with her again."

"Is that what she told you?"

"Yes, ma'am."

"China, I know that child. She used to date one of my cousin's sons out in Third Ward, and he didn't get her on drugs. When he met her she was already that way, only he didn't know it. He fell crazy in love with her and they moved in together. I met her once at a family reunion, and guess what? That girl ain't never had no babies. She was pregnant once, but she lost that baby 'cause she was too messed up. The boys she's talking about belong to my cousin's son from a previous marriage, and when they were living together she was supposed to be watching them while he went to work. They were around three and four then. Anyhow, he came home one day and she was sprawled out on the sofa too high to move. The front door was open and the kids were nowhere to be found. It took their daddy hours to locate them. He searched all over their neighbor-hood, and was about to call the police when some old man called and said that he had found them trying to play with some rabbits he had in a cage in his backyard. They daddy went and got 'em. After that, he packed up his stuff and theirs and moved back home with his mama. I suspect she found out later that she was pregnant, but I already told you, there was a sad ending to that story."

"Apparently, but why did she lie to me about the boys?"

"Well, maybe she didn't, not really. While she was with them she was the only mother they had, and I suspect that if she would have kept herself clean my cousin's son would really have married her," she said, going back to the counter.

"She would have been their stepmother for real then," I said, walking after her.

"Yeah, I guess so. Besides, people like to color their life the way they want to. You see how I am," she said, thumbing through a copy of *Madeline's Rescue*. "Folks around here think I'm crazy because I tell them that my husband talks to me. They think I'm loony tunes, but I'm not. I just like to remember Mr. Waltrip the way he was before he got sick. My way of doing that is by talking to him the way

I used to, and pretending that he still talks and jokes around with me. It may not be real to anybody else, but it's real to me. I'm not lying when I tell folks about Albert. It's not my fault that they can't see and hear him the way I do. I guess it's the same with your friend. She's not really telling a story. She's just laying it out the way she sees it."

"I see what you mean, and she didn't exactly tell me that she gave birth to those boys. She just said that she had them. It's kind of sad, though."

"Yeah, but maybe she is about to get everything together. I haven't talked to my cousin in a good while. Maybe her son and your friend is about to be reunited, and she'll really take care of his kids."

"Maybe."

I looked through the glass and saw Onyx Moon emerging from the store with a small brown bag in her hands. "I gotta run," I said, heading for the door.

"Oh wait, China. Some guy been's coming around here looking for you!" she hollered.

"What guy?"

"He said his name was Brother Agee. He told me that he heard you used to work here, wanted to know if you were planning on coming back to work. I didn't tell him nothing."

"It's okay. I know who he is. You can talk to him. He's a nice guy. He probably just wants to know how I'm getting along."

"Okay, now you come back for tea anytime you want, China. We'll tell stories and read from our favorite books."

"Really? Then I'll be back real soon," I said. I opened the door and hurried out. As soon as I hit the sidewalk I glanced down and saw the Number 11 bus roaring toward us. I yelled at Onyx across the street. "Here comes the bus," I said. She raced across the street and together we ran to the crowded bus stop. We boarded the bus behind an elderly gentleman wearing overalls and carrying a huge red toolbox.

There was standing room only on the bus. We held on to the metal poles and chatted about the club a bit. I found out that Star's real name was Sarah Teal Robertson, and she actually was a professional dancer. One of the club owners had met her in New York, where she was dancing at another gentlemen's club, and auditioning for parts in off-Broadway productions. Most of the time she just got played by guys who told her they would give her a part in some production if she gave them a little somethin' on the side. By the time the owner brought her to Texas she was fed up with chasing the theater life, but she still had her need-to-be-seen attitude. She renamed herself and decided that she would become the main attraction at Obsidian Queens. Sales jumped about 30 percent the month she started, so Louisa, who really didn't like Star at all, was forced to put up with her funky attitude.

It was easy for Louisa, she had learned to deal with ugly attitudes early. Like me, she had lost her mother when she was young. She was raised by her stepfather, on a farm in, of all places, Pennsylvania. She lived there happily with him until she was about sixteen. That's when he died in a farming accident. He went away and left her alone in the house with her grown stepbrother and no will. Her stepbrother took over everything, and treated her like dirt until she left the farm almost two years later. Onyx says Louisa left with nothing but a few dresses and some underwear. She kicked around for a few years, got a job at a local movie theater, a farm, a cafeteria in a private Lutheran school, just about anywhere that she could. But without any real education she could never find a well-paying, respectable job. Soon she tired of living hand-to-mouth, and looked for any type of occupation that would pay her rent and buy her a car to get around in. Somebody in the low-income housing she lived in suggested she go seek work at an exotic dance club. She went there, got hired on the spot, and the next thing you know she was starting what would turn out to be a long career at clubs that catered to gentlemen only. She would turn out to be exactly like Sweet Petite.

Sweet had been in men's clubs for years too. She started when she was a little older than me. According to Onyx, Sweet told her that she used to be a really shy fat girl, who didn't even have a boyfriend. She had two older sisters that did nothing but rag on her all the time about her weight. One night she went to a club with her older cousin. It was amateur night and her cousin dared her to get up and shake her groove thing. She did, and the guys loved her, because she was young and different. They clapped and whistled, really showed their appreciation. She adored the praise, so she kept it up. It was funny, I didn't feel real sorry for Sweet Petite. She definitely lived for the guys' praise. I felt bad about Louisa and Star, though. I imagined that neither one of them had ever really gotten to do what they wanted to do with their lives. What would they have become if, like Trip says, all the planets had aligned themselves in their favor? I wondered about the owners who had brought them and the rest of the women into the club. I hadn't met any of them, but I wondered what they thought they were doing for the ladies. Were they trying to make things better in their lives, or just trying to make cash off them? I didn't know. Maybe it was a little of both.

"When I get my apartment I'm gonna pay my rent up for a few months and find a new job. I think that'll be the best thing to do for my kids," Onyx told me, as the bus swung sharply around a corner. I grabbed a second pole and hung on like a weather reporter suddenly caught in a hurricane.

"Good, I hope you find something else," I said.

"You too. I think you should be working somewhere else too."

"Where?"

"I don't know," she said, getting that sad look on her face again. "I think everyone should be working somewhere else. When I was little I wanted to work at Sea World."

"Really?"

"Yeah, but it was only a dream. I'll probably just end up at the pastry shop where I used to work. I made all the cookies. It was fun, though. Hey, what do you do for fun when you're not working?"

"I used to like to go with my friend Trip to Playland."

"Oh, I been there before. They have all those video games and a movie theater."

"Yeah, my friend Trip likes the sci-fi and slasher movies they show there. I kinda like them too, but mostly I just like chillin' with him and my girl Alejandra. She's always doing something crazy. The last time we were there she ran out of quarters, so she waded her butt right into that wishing fountain they have out in front of the building. She was picking up change like crazy until the security guard told her to get out."

"For real?"

"Yeah, girl."

"Man, she *is* crazy."

"Yeah, but I like hanging with her. We have serious fun. I can always act myself around her, Trip, and my best girlfriend, Yolanda."

"There used to be a girl at the club that I liked to hang with. She wasn't crazy, but she was really sweet and I could always keep it real around her."

"Oh yeah? What happened to her?"

"Her mama didn't like her working there, so her mama forced her to quit on one of the busiest nights of the club. It really pissed Louisa off. She liked my friend 'cause all the dudes were into her."

"Oh really."

"Yeah. Louisa thought my friend was going to be a big deal, 'cause she was really young and had a kick-ass figure like you. She threw a big fit on one of the owners when things didn't work out, but there was nothing at all she could do about it. She just had to deal. Now nobody will even mention my friend at the club."

"Why not?"

"'Cause each time they do it just sets Miss Louisa off again."

"Oh, I guess I'll leave that alone then," I said. "I don't want to piss nobody off. I just want to get paid."

"That's the best thing to do. I miss my friend, though. It was fun working with her."

"Yeah, I know what you mean. I miss all my girlfriends from school, especially Alejandra. She's called my house a couple of times, wanting to go places. But I didn't return her phone calls. I don't want to answer a whole lot of questions about what I'm doing or where I'm working at."

"Oh for real, girl," she said. "I can definitely understand that!"

I nodded and peered out the bus window.

The rest of the way we rode in silence, with Onyx Moon periodically peering out the bus window searching for our stop, and me wondering how Uncle and Yolanda were doing at the lawyer's office. I was glad that Uncle had volunteered to take Yolanda there. He knew how to make things right, and he was a good influence on Yolanda. She was now dressing a lot more motherly, and was paying more attention to what her kids were doing. Last week she and Uncle took all the kids to the new dollar-movie complex across town. They had a great time, and Uncle and the boys came back and gabbed about the action in the movie until it was time for the boys to go home and go to bed.

"See ya later. Can you come play with us tomorrow, please, Mr. Cameron?" the boys had asked as Yolanda ushered them out of the house.

"I'll be there," Uncle had called after them.

Yeah, if anybody could help Yolanda figure out how to keep

Eboni, it was Uncle. He knew what to do, and that was really a comforting thought.

"I like Yolanda's kids," he told me yesterday evening as I stood in front of the kitchen sink smoothing relaxer cream into my hair. "They can be trying sometimes, even hardheaded, like you say they are, but I think they just need somebody to treat 'em nice and pay some attention to them. Ain't none of them really got no father in their lives. That's got to be awful for a child."

"It is," I said.

"And Yolanda, she's nice too," he continued. "I know she's done some dumb and messy things in her short life, but I think she could pull it all together. She only needs somebody to teach her how to care more about herself and make her understand that she can't do anything that doesn't affect her children. What do you think, China?"

"I think this relaxer cream is burning my head up, and I think it's great that you're trying to help Yolanda," I said. Then I turned on the water and stuck my head under the faucet. I didn't need to talk anymore about Yolanda. I knew that Uncle had it covered.

The bus rolled through a pothole and we jiggled every which way we could. I looked out the window too. It was still several blocks to Onyx Moon's new apartment. I hoped it was worth the long ride and all the standing up.

A second bus ride later I determined that Onyx's apartment was worth it. When we pulled up to the stop I saw that the complex was nothing like the low-rent places in my hood. It was clean—not even a candy wrapper could be found on the splendid green lawns. A beautiful iron gate with lion-headed posts surrounded the rows of pink stucco buildings. We exited the bus and made our way up a lovely walkway that was inlaid with colorful rocks and minerals.

"It's wonderful, isn't it?" Onyx Moon asked. I spotted a large playground on the side of one of the buildings.

"Yeah, it will be a good place for your kids," I said. She ran over to the swing set and I ran after her. We sat down on one of the wooden swings and began swinging softly back and forth.

"This is fun, isn't it, girl? I always did like to swing. My little boys will love this!" she said with glee.

"Me too. I love to swing." *And my little girl would like this too*, I almost blurted, but I caught myself. "I'll bet any kid would like it," I said instead.

She smiled. "We better go up," she said. We left the swings and hurried to one of the buildings.

When we got to the second floor I was surprised to see that Onyx already had a key to the apartment. She pulled it out of her skirt pocket and opened the door. I turned all green as we stepped inside. It was wonderful. There were hardwood floors and there was even a fireplace. The skylight lit up a set of brand-new kitchen appliances, and she walked me around to see the three spacious bedrooms.

"Check this out, girlfriend," she said. She opened a narrow cabinet near the guest bathroom and standing in the corner was a slammin' washer and dryer set.

"Man, this is the bomb, seriously large," I said. "I can't believe you're going to be living here."

"Me either. The place that I'm living in now is pure crap. I'll be glad to get out of there, and did you see how much space there was in those rooms?"

"I saw," I said. She smiled again, and for a moment I couldn't see any sorrow in her. I didn't exactly know what was going to happen with her and her boyfriend, but it did look like they were going to give it another try for the kids. I envied her chance to start over from scratch.

"It's great," I said, twirling around on the hardwood floor. I wished me and my uncle Simon lived in something like this.

She actually grinned. "Hey, I'm kind of hungry. Do you wanna go get something to eat? There's a restaurant down the street. They sell all kinds of junk."

"It sounds good to me," I said. "I didn't eat too much for breakfast." She started for the door, and I walked after her.

"Hey Onyx, Onyx, where you at, girl?" Some brother's voice rang out. I thought it must be her boyfriend, until she started to get nervous.

"Hey Onyx, what you doing up there, girl?" the brother called. "You up there? Answer me, girl."

"I'm here," Onyx said in her timid voice.

"Who is that?" I whispered. She didn't answer me. Heavy footsteps sounded on the outside steps, then a tall bald brother with a thick black mustache appeared in the doorway. I knew right away he wasn't her boyfriend. The dude had been at the club several times since I started. He was the dude whose lap she was sitting on the first day I started work. I didn't get it. She always looked like she wanted to cry when she was with him. What the heck was he doing at her new place?

"Hey Onyx girl, what gives?" he said, grabbing Onyx around the waist. He kissed her on the lips. She didn't pull away, but I could see her narrow body go all tense.

"How did you know I was here?" she asked when he let her go.

"I went by your place. Your landlady told me you were coming over here. I figure this was the place to be," he said with a sly grin.

"No, it's not the place for you to be," Onyx said. "Skinner, I told you not to come around here. Brandon and the boys coulda been here. You coulda screwed everything up."

"Aw girl, I ain't screwing nothing up," Skinner said. "That dude ain't even here. I looked for his car and everything."

"He takes his mama's car sometimes," Onyx said. "He still coulda been in this apartment."

"All right, all right, keep your G-string on, girl. Like I said, he ain't here. Just let me take a look around." Onyx moved to block the door.

"Girl, you better let me in this damn apartment," he said, pushing her aside. "I'm the one who paid the first and last month's rent on this place. I ought to at least be able to check it out." He brushed past me. "Hey, brown sugar, sugar," he said. I rolled my eyes.

"Aw pretty girl, don't be that way," he said, and started walking around the place, checking it out. I glanced at Onyx. She looked like she wanted to run in the laundry closet and shut the door.

"Man, this is phat," Skinner said. "Girl, you spent my money well. A brother could get real good at spending time here."

"Skinner, you can't come here. I told you that. My family is gonna move in here soon," Onyx said, walking over to him.

"Yeah, yeah. I got that, girl. You told me, and I'm not trying to move in. I'm just checking the place out, being all nice. We friends, ain't we? I'm just trying to make sure the place you live in is all right."

"It's fine, Skinner, and I appreciate you helping me out, "Onyx said, taking his hand. "I promise I'll pay you back as soon as I can save up the cash."

"Aw, girl. Don't worry about that, you just keep on being your sweet self," Skinner said. He leaned over and kissed her again.

"You better go," she said, when he pulled away.

"All right, that's cool, girl, but you come on and go with me." Onyx shook her head and put on her club face, all willing and eager to please.

"Skinner, I can't right now," she cooed, rubbing his arm. "I want to, but I just can't. Me and China came together. We were just about to go get something to eat."

"Aw girl, now don't be like that. You know I'm all lonely. Don't make me spend the day by myself. Besides, I got a little somethin' in my car for you," Skinner said, placing his arms around her waist again. "You know I got just the kind of stuff you like." Onyx shook her head again.

"Skinner, you know I don't do that junk no more. I don't want whatever you got."

"Okay, okay, I hear you, but come on and spend the day with me, girl. Don't leave me all by myself. Come on now." Onyx glanced over at me with a pitiful look.

"I gotta go, China," she said. "I'm sorry. We can hang out together some other time. Can't we?"

"Aw, girl. Little Miss brown sugar, sugar, will be all right. Of course you can come too, if you want," Skinner said, winking at me. I rolled my eyes and folded my arms across my chest.

"I'll see you later, Onyx," I said. I moved aside and Skinner dragged her by the hand out of the door. I walked out behind them. I turned the lock on the door and closed it. Afterward, I watched them hurrying down the stairs. As they hit the bottom step Onyx turned back to me. Her face was full of intense emotions. There was a little of everything in it—fear, embarrassment, anger, regret, confusion. It was all in there, all in Onyx Moon. She and Skinner cleared the steps and went back down the walkway. As I saw him dragging her off I thought about what would happen in her life. Would she get her kids and lover back? I believed she would. She would get them to trust her again. They would move into that great apartment and live happily ever after, until her man discovered that there were several big bad wolves still in her life. The whole thing was depressing. It made me sad to think what those kids would go through when their father had to take them away again. I walked down the stairs and spotted a pay phone underneath the stairwell. I went over to it and gave Trip a call.

"What's the deal, China?" he asked when he picked up the phone.

"I'm feeling kind of abandoned. I was out here with Onyx from the club, and she cut out on me with some sorry dude that she met there. We were supposed to go get something to eat.

"I'm catching the bus right now," he said. "I'll be there in a bit."

"Naw, it's okay. I just wanted to see what you were up to."

"I'll be there, China. You can have lunch with me."

"Naw, I don't want you to come all the way out here. It's two bus rides."

"I'll be there in a little bit."

"Okay," I said. I hung the phone up and started up the walkway back toward the gate. As I passed the playground I realized that I hadn't even told Trip where I was. I smiled. I wouldn't bother calling him again. He could find me in a blizzard, if we ever had one in Houston—that was Trip. He was my faithful Saint Bernard in a world full of ferocious dogs like Skinner. I looked back at the playground. I could see Onyx's little boys swinging back and forth on the swings. I imagined my Amina swinging beside them. Three pairs of sneakers, two pairs of cotton shorts, one ruffled bunny-print dress, and two long pigtails, climbing toward the sky, descending toward the earth, in bliss, in peace. It would have been a wonderful sight to see.

CHAPTER 6

"Look, I know I'm good, but even I ain't no dancing machine. My battery runs down just like everybody else's. You got to find some other chick to get up here and wear her feet out. Anyway, you know I'm the person everyone comes to see. It wouldn't do this place any good at all if I couldn't get up there on the stage," Star said, coming over to me and Louisa with her hands on her hips. As usual she was being way more dramatic than she needed to be, strutting around with her imaginary white-hot spotlight hanging overhead, in a red lace bikini that looked more like lingerie than a swimsuit. Perhaps it was. The policy at the club stressed that the girls wore swimwear to go along with the beach theme, but in the time I had been working at the club I had seen girls dressed in just about anything. Incredibly sheer or completely see-through suits meant fatter tips. It allowed some of the girls to rake in the dough before they even got up on stage. I could excuse Star's peekaboo suit; what I couldn't excuse was her light bright behind thinking that she was the only dancer that was having to spend extra time entertaining the men. All the ladies had been doing it for the past two weeks, ever since Onyx Moon stopped coming to work.

The day Onyx took off with Skinner was the last day anybody saw her. She didn't show up for her shift that evening, so Star, Sweet, and believe it or not, Louisa took her dances. By the end of the evening all three ladies were tired and cranky, and Louisa said if

Onyx didn't call or come in the next day she might have to find a new place to work, but Sweet Petite didn't like that at all.

"Naw, Louisa, don't do that," she said, sitting down at one of the tables and rubbing her size twelve feet. "Don't fire her. You know that girl been trying to get her life back together. She probably just forgot she was supposed to work this evening. I'll bet she dead asleep with the phone off the hook. I'll get Mr. Sturges to run me by her place tomorrow evening and I'll tell her she better get her tail to work on time tomorrow night."

"I'll go too," I added. Later I wished I had kept my mouth shut. I didn't have a clue how dreadful I would feel the next afternoon when I met Sweet Petite and Mr. Sturges, her boyfriend-customer. On the drive to Onyx's place I imagined that I would say hi to her again, and me and Sweet Petite would see if she had overslept or was a little under the weather. All we were going to do was tell Onyx that Louisa didn't like taking her place, so she had better get herself back to the club pronto. Sweet and I didn't get a chance to do that. When we got to the old falling-down building where Onyx lived, she wasn't in her tiny one-bedroom apartment, and neither was her brother. The door to her place was ajar. As we crossed the threshold we could immediately see that there was practically nothing in the place, and I do mean nothing. There was no furniture at all, just a small old-fashioned microwave on the filthy kitchen counter and a pallet made of dirty quilts on the floor. Around the quilts were needles, like the kind Mama's old boss used to use for her diabetes. A stale smell of berry incense in the air was trying to cover up the lingering smell of weed.

"My Lord, what has this girl gotten herself into this time? I thought she was all through with this craziness," Sweet Petite said, shaking her head. In her low-heeled pumps and ordinary beige dress she hardly looked like somebody who danced at a club. She looked more like a concerned aunt coming to check on a niece.

"Look around, China," she said. "Maybe she wrote her brother's number or something somewhere, and we can get in touch with him."

"I thought she lived with him. That's what she told me," I said.

"Oh yeah, she does. She lives with him, but I thought I mighta heard her saying something about him spending most of his time at his girlfriend's. Onyx been by herself for a while. Go on and look for his number, baby. He might have some idea where she likes to hang out at when she gets like this."

"Okay," I said. I walked into the bathroom. The regular bathroom crap was there. I saw a plastic shower curtain with butterflies on it, and a matching tumbler and toothbrush holder. The bathmat was worn, but mostly clean, and the toilet looked like it had been wiped down at least in the last month or so. I opened the door to the medicine cabinet. More regular stuff, a capless bottle of Midol, an open bag of cotton balls, a box of ultrathin sanitary pads, some vapor rub, all things you would expect to find. I closed the door and glanced at the sink. There were a couple of nearly smoked blunts in it. I turned on the hot water faucet and splashed the butts down the drain. There was nothing else to do after that. I returned to the living room. I found Sweet Petite frantically looking through the cabinets.

"Nothing. I can't find one thing in this house with any kind of number on it. I looked in the bedroom, but all I saw was some boxes of clothes, and some new toys that I guess are for them children that used to live with her. You see anything?" she asked.

I shook my head. "No, just some normal bathroom items in the cabinets."

She sighed and leaned against the counter. Her huge frame caused the wood to creak. "Let me get off this rickety thing before it falls apart," she said.

"What do we do now?" I asked.

"Ain't nothing we can do. We just have to tell Louisa th
don't know where she at, or when or if she gonna come back.'

"What if she's hurt?" I said. "What if that Skinner guy got her all
jammed up again, but she doesn't want to be wherever she is, doing
whatever she's doing. What if she's trying to get home? Shouldn't
we call the police or somebody? Shouldn't we tell somebody what's
going on?"

"No, we ain't gonna do nothing of the kind."

"But why not? I don't understand."

"I know you don't—you still young. But think about it, who we
gone tell, China?" Sweet asked. "You think the police care about
some girl that gets high, and takes her clothes off at a club for men?
China, it don't work that way. Don't nobody ever come looking for
girls like Onyx and me. We mostly on our own. Sometimes we can
find a halfway decent guy like Mr. Sturges, who pays attention to us
for a little while, and treats us sorta nice, but usually the men that
want to hang with us are like Skinner. We ain't nothing but a slot
machine to them. They just want to see how much money they have
to put into us until they hit the jackpot. And that Skinner is the
worst. Ain't no telling what kinda game he done run down on poor
little Onyx, but I can't blame it all on him. Onyx is young, but she
ain't no baby. She knew what she was getting into, fooling around
with trash like Skinner. Damn, just when it looked like she was
gonna get back on her feet. I can't believe she would be so dumb."

"Me either."

Sweet Petite looked around the room and frowned. "Lord, I wish
I *could* call the law, only everything in me tells me that that would be
a gigantic mistake. Besides, ain't nobody kidnapped her or nothing.
She'll probably turn up soon, unfortunately a lot worse for whatever
she done got herself into. Come on, China. We better get to work,"
she said.

We left Onyx's place and walked to Mr. Sturges's new Lexus. I held the door until Sweet Petite got inside, then I slammed it shut and crawled in the back. The seats had that new car smell, and the leather was soft. I wished I could have been comfortable in it. I was too busy thinking about Onyx Moon. There was nothing we could do for her, nobody we could call, because she was grown, but mostly because nobody cared about girls like her. Why? How could you not care about people just because of what they did with their lives? I didn't understand. When Mama used to take me to Sunday school the teachers there were always talking about how we had to treat everybody the same way because God made all of us. Didn't he make Onyx, too? And yet deep down I knew that Onyx really hadn't been forced to go with Skinner that day. She wasn't dragged. She went willingly. I was devastated by that. A huge part of me was really hoping she could move in with her old family and live that happily-ever-after-thing.

"I guess ya'll gonna be a little short for a while," Mr. Sturges said from the front of the car.

"For a while. Onyx will be back in a few," Sweet Petite said.

"Yeah, she will, in a few," I echoed. Of course, now "a few" has turned into two weeks.

"Sugar, I already gave Swedish Lane a call and asked her if she can come in early a few nights. She's going to start doing that this weekend. Now that's the best I can do until I can find another girl. I'm sorry your feet are tired, but so is mine and everybody else's. Honey child, just get over it, and quit acting like you raised your hand and the universe was formed," Louisa yelled at Star.

"Okay, fine, whatever," Star said. She stormed through the club and went back to the dressing room, slamming the back-room door so hard I thought the coconuts would fall off the fake trees in the murals.

"Man, why she always got to make things worse?" I asked.

"That girl really needs to get over herself," Louisa said with a frown. "She thinks she's the world's eighth, ninth, and tenth wonder. I'd let her behind go today, if she wasn't dating one of the managers. But don't you let it worry your sweet face none, honey. Star is working my nerves, but she's right. I'm going to have to find somebody to take Onyx's place. I do hope she comes back, but this is a dance club, and I can't keep it going without girls to dance." She looked down at her watch. "Go get yourself something to eat before it gets too busy, China. I'll keep an eye on the counter."

"Yes, ma'am," I said.

I left the counter and followed Star through the side door of the club. When I got inside I walked down the hallway and through another door, which led to the kitchen and bar shelter out back. It was a structure where everything consumed in the club was prepared. Drinks, appetizers, desserts, full-meal deals, party platters, whatever you wanted, it was all created in that one place. It was fixed up real nice by four grandmotherly-type ladies who looked like they should be preparing food at Uncle Simon's favorite diner. They were lovely ladies. They were like Mrs. Waltrip, and always made me feel right at home. They treated me like I was one of the many grandkids they loved to brag about. That was really comforting. When I was with them I could pretend that I hadn't gone through so many changes in my life. "You ain't nothing but a baby. You ain't got no business at all working in that place. You need to be out here with us, instead of in there with that pack of heathens. All of 'em need to be on they knees praying to Jesus," the ladies say to me.

"They're not that bad," I tell them.

"Yeah, they are. You just too young to know it. You don't know all what goes on in there."

"I guess I don't," I say, and it's only an itty bitty lie. I really do know some of the uglier things that go on at the club. I've seen the Triple X lap dances, and the part-time dancers who purchase condoms from the bathroom dispenser. Every other Friday you can catch them on the side of the club with the nearby chemical plant workers, and that's not the only thing I've witnessed. My third week at the club I walked into the dressing room and saw Star giving what she later claimed was just a private dance to one of the special guests. Neither one of them had on a stitch, and what they were doing I guarantee you wouldn't be on anybody's stage.

"Schoolgirl, get your young butt out of here and lock the door behind you," Star shouted. I slammed the door closed and left. I have to tell you, I was shocked and disgusted by what I saw. I wanted to quit. But the next day I got a call from Brother Agee at the funeral parlor. It was the third time he had personally gotten in touch with me since I signed Amina's papers. The first time was when I came home to find him on my doorstep in his colorful dashiki, with an itemized list of what I owed in his hand. He gave it to me and told me to circle the deadline date at the bottom of the list, so I didn't forget it. "You don't want to make a mistake and miss the last day to pay for all of these," he said.

"No sir, I don't," I said.

"No, of course not. You're a very responsible girl. You won't open yourself up to a lot of trouble by forgetting. I know you won't do that."

"Don't worry. I won't. I know what I'm doing. I'm not gonna mess up," I told him. Then I said it again a few weeks later, when he turned up again with a stack of sympathy cards and two shoe boxes of lovely broken dishes that some older ladies had sent to the funeral home. "It's wonderful when a child is loved as much as your daughter was. I can see why you would want to do all that you can to ensure that she truly rests in peace. And I know that you would never do anything that tarnishes her memory, like not paying your bills. You won't dishonor her like that."

"No, I won't. I'll make sure that I do everything I'm supposed to do," I said defensively.

"Of course, and I'm sorry for the way that sounded. I only meant to say that I have absolute faith in you."

"I know, sir."

"Okay, I'll talk to you at a later date," he said. Less than two weeks later he was on the line again.

"Hello China, I know it's late, but I was just thinking about you and wanted to know how you're getting along."

"I'm doing okay, sir. I'm going to come down and make another payment on Amina's funeral soon," I said, as I opened my dresser drawer and searched for my nightshirt.

"Good, I knew that my faith wasn't misplaced in you. I knew from the moment I saw you, you wouldn't be like some of the other customers I've had to hand over to the collection agency. That's a bad deal, you know, it's part of the trouble I was talking about. It can wreck your life well into your adult years. It can make it virtually impossible for you to purchase a car or even get a loan for college, and both of those things will eventually be important to you, especially college. You're still young, China. Someday you may want to further your education. I would hate to see anything keep you from doing that."

"Me too. Someday I might really want to go to a university. My mama would like that."

"Of course she would. She would love to know that you are taking care of your responsibilities. Mothers are always proud of things like that, but they're not very proud when their children mess up. You don't want her to look down and become disappointed with you."

"No, no sir, I don't. I don't want to make my mama unhappy. Anyway, it's all okay. I've got a good job. You don't have to worry about me. I'll have all the money on time."

"I know you will, and I really wasn't calling about that. I just wanted to see how everything was."

"I know. Mrs. Waltrip said you had asked about me at her shop."

"Yes, of course. That was a while back. I just stopped by to say hello, but you weren't there. Well, have a good night, and you give me a call if you need anything."

"I will," I said, and hung up the phone. Then I put on my night-shirt and went into the living room to watch late-night TV with Uncle. I sat on the sofa next to his wheelchair and rested my head against his shoulder.

"What's wrong, China?" Uncle asked me.

"Nothing," I whispered. "I'm fine. I'm just tired." He leaned his head against mine.

"What are you tired from, China?" he asked. I hunched my shoulders.

"It's been a long night."

"The night is only as long as we make it, China."

"I don't know what that means."

"Well, let me explain it to you. Sometimes I dream all night. I lay back comfortable on my pillow and I allow myself to be taken away by images of me, back when I was younger. I see myself hanging out with my friends after school. I'm standing in the courtyard, holler-ing at all the fine sisters as they walk by in them thigh-showing dresses you girls like to wear. It's back in the day, I'm shooting hoops at the court down the street from my house, or running laps around the gym, fast, super, superfast, while a bunch of jealous dudes look on. China, all night long I'm who I used to be—who I sometimes still wish I was."

"Sometimes?"

"Yeah, sometimes. Like I said, that's when I allow myself to dream all night."

"Allow yourself?"

"Yeah, I do that sometimes, and so do a lot of people. You do it when you're barely asleep, and you know that whatever you're seeing or feeling isn't real. You know that all you have to do is turn over and it will go away, but you don't do it. You know what I mean?"

"I guess so," I said.

"Sure you do. We both do, and sometimes it's okay being there. It feels good when your life is exactly what you want it to be. But it's not real. It's as fake as them clay figurines you threw out the day after Amina died."

"Uncle Simon, I don't know what you're talking about. What kind of strange stuff you been reading?"

"I ain't been reading nothing. I'm just trying to say, whatever place you've put yourself in, you can get out of it. All you have to do is turn over and wake up."

"I'm tired, Uncle," I said.

"I know, baby girl. I'm tired too."

"I'm going to bed," I said. I kissed him on the cheek above his scruffy beard and went back to my room. I didn't sleep at all that night, and the next afternoon I returned back to the club, back to my counter.

"How you like working here?" a buff brother with a mile-high fro asked me as I handed him a heavy backpack.

"Everybody here is really cool. It's great," I lied.

"It seems like a good place to work," he said. "I used to date a girl that danced in one of these places. It was a nasty place, but here, they keep it good for everybody."

"Yeah, they keep it real good for everybody," I said.

If only that were true. I walked up the path to the food shelter. The delicious smell of barbecue chicken wings floated through the open kitchen window. The scent reminded me of some of the barbecues that me and Yolanda had in her backyard. I giggled when I remembered her sprawled out in the lawn chair while her kids made me pull my hair out. They were crazy but nice memories. For a little while I forgot all about the things that

I didn't like about the club. I headed for the door of the shelter.

"China, China Cup Cameron," a man's voice called. I glanced toward the fence. A large white guy with a clean-shaven face and a church haircut was standing on the other side in a light gray business suit.

"Excuse me?" I said.

"Are you China Cup?" he asked, all friendly.

"Who are you?"

"I just want to talk to you a minute, Miss Cameron. Can you come over for a second," he said.

"I don't talk to people I don't know," I said.

"Oh, uh, you can talk to me. I'm working for your friend Yolanda. She told me to come and speak with you."

"She did," I said, walking over to the fence. "You must be the lawyer that she and Uncle have been going to see."

"Can you tell me a little about her?" he asked. "I heard you're her best friend."

"I am, what do you want to know?" He looked at my swimsuit.

"You're a little young to be working at a place like this, aren't you?"

"I'm legal," I said. "I got some papers that say so. What do you want to know about Yolanda?" I asked again.

"Well, I know she fighting real hard to keep her little girl Eboni, but what about her other kids? What kind of mother is she to the rest of her kids?"

"What kind of mother is she to her other kids? I don't know. It's hard being a mama. I guess she could do better sometimes," I said honestly, assuming that Yolanda had been honest too. She wasn't big on intentionally stretching the truth.

"She could, how so?"

"I don't know," I repeated. "Sometimes she's not so good at making them mind her. They can be really hardheaded and sassy sometimes."

"Really?"

"Yeah, it ain't no big deal, though. She only needs to get a hold of them a little more."

"She doesn't spank them?"

"Not really. I only seen her hit 'em a couple of times. One time she gave Vonda a few licks with a belt. Vonda threw a shoe and conked Eboni bad on the forehead. Everything was okay, but Eboni hollered like she had gotten a serious beatdown, so Yolanda spanked Vonda. That turned out to be a big mistake."

"How so?"

"You know, I guess she told you that Vonda's teacher called social services on her because Vonda had a few bruises."

"Yeah, sure, she told me," he said nodding his head. "She told me they threatened to take all her kids or something like that."

"Naw, that's not what happened. They just sent a dude to check her out. Yolanda told him she hardly ever spanked the kids and why she had hit Vonda. She showed him the bump on Eboni's head, and the man said that he understood why she went off, but that she didn't need to discipline her kids that way. He suggested some parenting classes, and said he would come back in about six weeks to see how things were going. I don't think he did, but it don't matter. I know Yolanda never hit any of her kids again."

"Oh, good for her. It's a bad thing hitting a child, or sitting back and letting one get hit."

"She didn't sit back," I said defensively. "What happened, just happened."

"Oh of course," he said with an apologetic smile. "Of course, I didn't mean it the way it came out. I'm just trying to find out more about Yolanda's relationship with her kids, and the people in her life."

Then he said, "What about you? I hear you just lost your little girl a few months back. I'm sorry."

"Thanks," I whispered. "I don't think I want to talk about that."

"Oh yes, of course. I wouldn't want you to. I heard it was a tragedy. You left her at some old lady's house. She got sick there, and before you could make the time to get over there she was gone."

"What?"

"How long have you been working here?"

"A little while."

"Are you a dancer?"

"No sir, I just check in things. I work behind the counter."

"Well, you look like a dancer," he said. "You're sure not wearing much." I looked down at my electric blue bikini and suddenly felt like I needed a robe or big beach towel to cover it.

"It's just a uniform. All the women have to wear them," I said, even more defensively.

"But you're not a woman. You talk old enough, but you're just a little girl. What does your mama think of a little girl like you working in a place like this?"

"My mama isn't alive anymore."

"Oh yes, that's right, you live with your Uncle Simon. He seems like a nice man, moved in to help take care of you after your mother passed. I can't imagine that he likes you working in a place like this."

"He doesn't, but what does that have to do with anything? I thought you wanted to know about Yolanda. What does my uncle's opinion of me working here have to do with that?"

"Oh, uh, nothing of course. I'm just trying to get a feel for who Yolanda spends her time with. It will help me better understand how to proceed with her case."

"Yes sir," I said. "I really hope you can help her. I know she doesn't want to lose Eboni."

"Of course she doesn't. Well, thank you for your time, Miss Cameron. My talk with you has been beneficial."

"I hope so."

"It has. It's just what I needed to hear and see," he said. With that he left the fence and walked back to the street. He waved casually at me and disappeared into a black, late-model convertible. I watched him pull off down the road, and before he even reached the busy stoplight a crater formed beneath my feet. I turned to go to the food shelter and fell right into it, a pit of my own stupidity. It suddenly dawned on me that I hadn't asked the lawyer his name or anything. Did I really know who he was? If he was Yolanda's lawyer, why didn't he know what I did at the club? If she told him where I worked she would certainly have told him what I did for a living. Oh man, I got a really bad feeling, like the time when Uncle had his operation and fell into a coma. I remember sitting in the hall by myself waiting for someone to come and give me some details. It was two and a half hours after the operation before the surgeon showed up, and when he did I knew right away that something wasn't right. I can't describe what I felt like when I saw homeboy's face, but right now I was feeling it again. It was like I didn't know exactly what the heck was going on, but I sure as hell knew that it wasn't good.

I raced back to the club to make a phone call. I walked quickly into the hallway and found, of all things, Sweet Petite and Star loitering there, along with Louisa and a leggy Vietnamese girl that calls herself Jasmine Tea. They were standing with their heads pressed to Big Robert's door. "What's going on?" I asked, walking over to them.

"Shhh, be quiet, stupid girl," Star whispered icily. I rolled my eyes.

"You don't tell me what to do," I whispered back.

"Both of you keep your mouths still," Louisa said. I rolled my eyes at Star again, and shut up.

"Say man, let go of me! Who you think you are?" I heard Skinner's voice yell out from the other side of the door. I caught my breath.

"You don't need to worry about who I am. You just answer the question!" Big Robert, the Angry Black Giant, yelled back.

"Say, man, screw you. You don't run nothing I do," Skinner said.

"Oh, I don't!" Big Robert said. Then I heard a smack, a big one, like a fist against flesh, and a huge thud. Skinner hollered in pain.

"Stop it, man, stop it! Why you tripping so hard on this. That girl ain't nothing. Why you acting like this?"

"Answer my question or I'm gone really jack your ass up!" Big Robert warned. "Do you hear me? I ain't playing. I'll put you down for a long time. You don't want to play with me, fool. You gonna end up really messed up."

"Forget you, man. You big double-belly, mean bastard. Screw you!"

"Oh screw me," Big Robert said. "Oh screw me!" I heard another smack and a huge crash, like somebody had fallen into glass. It was followed by a loud groan.

"Stop it, Big Robert. You done knocked my teeth out, you done knocked my teeth out. Don't hit me no more," Skinner whimpered. "I'll tell you what you want to know."

"Get to talking," Big Robert said.

"All right, all right, man, I swear. I swear, I haven't seen that girl. She took off on me after the well ran dry. I don't know where she went. I thought she went home, or over to her new place. I don't know, man. She could be anywhere. You know how folks get when they can't stay away from that stuff. They take off sometimes, hit the streets. Hell man, she could be anywhere, but she'll turn up soon. You'll see her as soon as she runs outta places to get some cash. You gotta believe me, dude. I don't know. Ain't nobody done nothing to Onyx. She'll be back when she needs to bum something off of you."

"Are you sure you don't know?"

"Look, man, I'm sitting here bleeding all over my new shirt. I would tell you if I did. But hey man. Onyx is a big girl. She was messing around with that stuff long before she met me. I ain't responsible for her."

"All right, all right," Big Robert said. "Now you get the hell outta here, and don't come back. I mean it, Skinner. If I see you anywhere around any girl here I'm gonna bust you up."

"I got you man. I got you. I ain't coming back," Skinner said. I heard the shuffling of feet on the floor, as if somebody was getting up.

"I guess he really doesn't know anything. Let's go, ladies," Louisa whispered. We all scattered like sewer rats into the dressing room.

"Damn, I really did think that low-down fool could help. I thought him bringing his sorry behind in here was some kind of blessing," Sweet Petite said.

"I gotta go home. There's an emergency with my uncle Simon," I blurted out.

"Right now?" Louisa asked.

"Yes ma'am, I have to go and see about him."

"Okay, okay, sugar, I know. You run on home. Me and Jasmine Tea will look after things while you're gone. We're already a girl short. I guess it won't matter if we're down two. Go see what's going on with your uncle, then give me a ring and let me know when you're coming back," Louisa said in a motherly tone.

"I'll be back as soon as I can," I said. I didn't have time to comprehend what had just gone on with Skinner and Big Robert. I was in a major jam of my own.

A while later when I jogged into my front yard I didn't have a clue what in the world I was going to say to Uncle. To make things even more friggin' terrible, he and Yolanda were both there, along with Eboni and Yolanda's twin boys, Peter and Percy. It was a wonderful windy day. All three of the kids were standing in the yard flying kites made of white string and empty hotdog-bun bags. It looked like a bunch of fun. I walked up on the porch, where Yolanda and Uncle were playing a game of dominoes, and sat down in a lounge chair beside Uncle.

"What are you doing home, China? Are you sick?" Uncle Simon asked, reaching over and feeling my forehead.

"No, I'm fine. I just needed to come home."

"Needed to, what does that mean? Did somebody hurt you?" He turned to me, concerned.

"Naw, it's not like that. It's nothing like that," I said, noticing his graying beard was completely gone. He looked a lot younger without it, almost handsome. He looked like the kind of guy a girl might actually give a second and third glance. I forgot what I was going to say and laughed out loud.

"What's up with you?" I asked. "What are you trying to be, a player?"

Yolanda laughed. "That's what I told him," she said before he could answer the question. "I asked him, was he trying to be the real Mac daddy?"

"Aw, naw, forget ya'll," Uncle said in a surprisingly boyish voice. "I just thought I needed a change. I was beginning to look like somebody's grandfather."

"Is that right?" I giggled. "Well, now you look like you trying to be somebody's boyfriend. Have you been slipping around with Mrs. Waltrip, trying to make a move on her while her old man is in a coma?"

"Of course not," he said, giggling. "That lady is way too old for me. I need somebody with a little juice still left in them, somebody to give me a reason to get up outta this chair."

"Please, what would you do when you got out of it?" I asked.

"Go down there messing with one of the fast heifers at Perry's 24 and 7 joint, and get himself shot up by one of they boyfriends."

"Yeah, that's about right, girlfriend," I said, giving Yolanda a high five. "Next thing you know some fool will be bringing him back here full of holes."

"Okay, okay," Uncle Simon said, laughing. It made me feel good. It had been a long while since we all just sat down and laughed. I wanted the moment to last forever. I missed it. I missed just loving my life and the people in it. I rested my head on his shoulder. He reached up and patted my forehead again.

"Are you sure you're not sick?" he asked, turning all serious again.

"No, I'm not sick. I just . . ." I hesitated.

"Just what?"

"I'm not sure. I think I may have done something stupid," I said, in a small voice.

"Stupid how? Come on now, just tell me. I'm sure it's no big deal," he said.

"Yeah, girl, spit it out. We trying to play a game here. We ain't got no time to hand out no sugar tits."

"Yolanda, quiet," Uncle said—and snap, she did exactly what he asked. She didn't even roll her eyes or flip her long braids, like she did whenever a guy asked her to chill.

"Talk, China," Uncle said.

"I think I might have said something to somebody that I shouldn't."

"Who?"

"Some guy, this white guy came around to work a little while ago. He was asking some questions about Yolanda and her kids," I said.

"What white guy? And what kind of questions?" Yolanda spoke up.

"Just some stuff, not too much. He wanted to know how you treat the kids. I didn't tell him hardly anything."

"Hardly what? Oh Lord, oh Lord," Yolanda said, rising out of her chair. "I don't know no white man. He probably somebody Jamal's daddy sent over there. What did you tell him?"

"Like I said, barely anything. He asked about the kids. I told him that you didn't discipline them much, that you barely ever hit them."

"If that's what you said, that's great," Uncle told me. "What are you upset about?"

"Yeah, what are you upset about?" Yolanda asked. I started wringing my hands in my lap.

"Just spit it out, China Cup," Uncle said.

"I thought he was the lawyer you guys have been going to see. I told him that Yolanda hardly ever hit her kids, but there was that one time with Vonda."

"Oh Lord!" Yolanda cried again. "China, you told that guy about that? What the hell were you thinking? How could you be so damn stupid?"

"Watch your mouth, Yolanda," Uncle said. "Your kids are just a few feet away. Remember what the lawyer said. There's more to being a good mother than just dressing like one."

"Well, what difference does it make how I dress?" Yolanda said tugging at her white blouse and flower-print skirt. "How the heck can it matter what I say, or how I dress, when my best girlfriend is handing my kids over to social services. China, I can't believe you would be that dumb. I thought you were way smarter than this. How can you act so friggin' immature!"

"What's the matter, Mama? What's up, Mama?" Percy asked from the yard. He walked over to the porch.

"Boy, don't ask me about nothing right now!" Yolanda snapped. "Just keep playing. This ain't the time."

"Don't yell at the boy. What's going on ain't his fault, Yolanda," Uncle said.

"I know. It's China's fault. I can't believe you. How can you be so plain stupid? Why would you do something so clearly babyish?"

"It's not, I didn't, and I'm not stupid. I didn't know that guy wasn't your lawyer. It's not my fault—and don't call me a baby."

"You are a baby, a big stupid baby who don't know what to do and say when they around grown folks."

"Yes, I do. It was an accident. I didn't mean to do it. It's not my fault," I repeated, like a ten-year-old trying to stop his mother from whipping him because he broke her favorite lamp.

"Oh it's not, well whose is it? I didn't open my big mouth!" Yolanda flamed at me. "I didn't go around telling my best girl-friend's business."

"Okay, okay, just hold up. Yolanda, this isn't China's fault. She couldn't have known that the man who showed up at her job wasn't your lawyer. We didn't fill her in on the details," Uncle said, in his usual fatherly tone.

"She didn't have to know no details. All she had to do is keep her mouth closed," Yolanda said. "I wouldn't have ever told anybody all her personal things."

"I don't think it was like that. It looks like this guy could have purposely deceived her, taken advantage of her youthfulness," Uncle said.

"Yeah right. I shoulda known you would take her side. But I don't care what you say. If it was me, I woulda backed my best homegirl up. Come on kids, let's go home," Yolanda said, beckoning to her children. "I'm done with all this mess." She walked off the front porch, and the kids joined her.

"Aw come on, Yolanda. Don't take this someplace where none of us wants it to go. China was just trying to help, like me," Uncle said, rolling down the ramp after her.

"Aw, just forget it. She ain't gonna listen to nobody," I told him.

"Just hang tight for a little bit, China," Uncle said. "Let me go talk to her and make this right. We can call her lawyer and figure out some way to do some damage control. I'll be right back. I'm drying out some pieces in the oven. Do me a favor, baby, and go check on them."

"Yes sir," I said. I left the porch and walked into the kitchen. When I got to the kitchen I sat down at the table and cried. Tears went everywhere, as I thought about what I had just done to Yolanda, and what I didn't do for Onyx. Poor Onyx, what would have happened if I had tried to stop her from leaving with Skinner that day? Maybe Yolanda was right. Maybe I was just a stupid baby who didn't know what to do in a grown folks' world. But I wasn't grown. The bus pass in my purse confirmed that. It said *student*. That's what I was—or used to be. Before Amina, Yolanda, and Onyx I was just a regular kid.

I wiped tears from my eyes and remembered when Mama first got sick. I begged her to let me help her out in the beauty shop. I was still little, but I already knew how to do hair. At home I would stand on a stool and braid Mama's thick hair for a short, natural look or weave in some human pieces for a fancier style. I knew how to use a hot comb to straighten out kinks, and a curling iron to make crisp tight curls. On the days when Mama felt too tired or sick from the chemo I knew I would have been a help, but Mama said no when I asked her. She said that you needed a license to work in the shop, and that I was way too small to handle the work anyway. "China, I appreciate your wanting to make things better for me, but you're not ready for a real job yet," she told me as I gave her some pain pills. "You act like a big girl, but you're still way too young for most things." Was she right? Of course she was back then. Now it had all changed. Now it seemed like I wasn't too young for anything. At least *I* thought I wasn't. I dried my tears and tried to think of the cherubs, the way I normally did when I was dealing with something awful, but they wouldn't come. I couldn't even conjure up a scorched wing or a chubby body. I got up and opened the oven for a peek. No cherubs, just little figurines of Yolanda's six kids: droopy-eyed Peter and Percy, her three other ashy-feet little girls, and Eboni. Six children, perhaps soon to be five because of something I said. I slammed the oven door closed and decided to go to Trip's while Uncle tried to help Yolanda out of the chaos I put her in. When he came back, he could find me at Trip's, if he still wanted to talk to me.

CHAPTER 7

"A young father takes his only son, who's about four years old, on a trip to the zoo."

"What zoo?"

"Any zoo, but it has to be big, with lots of cats."

"What kind of cats?"

"Can you let me get the story out, China?" Trip said.

"Okay, okay, go ahead, you're taking too long," I said, reaching over him to grab a ranch potato chip from the plastic bowl on the other side of the bed.

"All right, here it is—a young father takes his son to the zoo. While they're there they see a lot of animals—monkeys, elephants, snakes, bears, aardvarks, zebras, and finally stopping in front of the cat cages—lions and tigers."

"Big cats."

"Yeah, big cats," he said, taking a chip from my hand. "Anyway, when they get in front of the cat cage the cats go crazy. They start roaring and snarling."

"Why?"

"Just let me tell it, girl. Hold up a minute. Okay, while the cats are snarling and roaring the father has a strange look in his eyes, like he knows why they're snarling, even wants to join them. Then he looks down at his son and his eyes get even stranger."

"How?"

"It's hard to explain. He looks kind of aware and alarmed at the same time."

"So what happens?"

"The father takes his son home. The mother is there, pretty and sweet, and of course they have all this nice family time."

"Okay."

"Okay cut to that same night—late. The mother is asleep, and the daddy tiptoes into his son's room. He stands there just watching him. Slowly the kid wakes up. He looks up at the father, and then everything goes black and we hear lots of snarling or growling, and the sound of something being eaten—devoured."

"Oooh, gross."

"Yeah, and the next thing we see is the father in the bathroom washing blood from his hands."

"Oooh, that's even grosser. What kind of story idea is this?"

"Just wait, it's not what you think. It's really, really cool. You see, the next day the mother goes into the bedroom and there's no little boy. She goes around the house calling his name and looking for him, and when she doesn't find him she runs and tells the father and they call the police."

"But the father ate the kid," I said.

"No, not at all. Here's the truth. The father doesn't eat the kid, the kid tries to eat the father. It turns out that the father comes from some kind of weird cat-person family."

"Cat-person family?"

"Yeah, every spring some strange hormones inside them kind of turn on, and when they do—*bam*, they morph into dangerous wild cats."

"So the father is really a big cat?"

"No, here's the thing. The father inherited the genes, but for some reason the hormones never turned on in him. He figured that whatever ran in the family's blood, he didn't get it. He was able to lead a regular life, get married, have a kid, get a fantastic house in a great neighborhood. Homeboy had it all until he went to the zoo and realized that his son had inherited those ugly hormones."

"Are hormones inherited? I thought only genes were inherited and that everybody just had hormones."

"We do, I guess. Look, whatever, that's not important. What's important is that something goes really wrong with the son. Because his mom is human, things go all screwy. He turns into a cat-person long before his father's people usually do it. He attacks his dad and jumps out of the window."

"His father doesn't know what to do about it. He doesn't want to expose his heritage to his wife . . ."

"So he pretends the kid was kidnapped or something like that," I interrupted.

"Yeah, cool, right?"

"It works. I like it, but it's really gross—and you're gonna have to change the sound of the father being devoured, if the kid only bites him."

"I like the devoured sound better."

"But it doesn't work."

"I think it does. But okay, I'll change it, but only if you do something for me."

"What's that?" I said, reaching for another chip.

"Go to see Amina," he said. I sat up on the bed.

"Don't go there again, Trip. Just leave it alone."

"China, I went there last week. I took her some flowers, and a story idea that I was writing just for her. It was about a little girl who can feel whenever somebody is hurting inside. She feels their pain. When she does, all she has to do is go over and kiss them on the cheek, and all their troubles go away."

"That's nice."

"Yeah, I liked that story for my little Bunny Face. I taped it to her headstone. Mama said that it would probably just blow away, but I don't care. My Bunny Face knows I put it there."

"Yeah, she knows."

"She also knows that you haven't even been there. I know she does, because I would. I don't care how deep I was buried, I would know if you never came to see me."

"Give it a rest, Trip," I said. "I can't go there. I don't even want to know that she's there. I just don't want to know it."

"Well she is there, and there's nothing that either one of us can do about it. China, you're just gonna have to deal. Amina wasn't a doll. She wasn't a Barbie that got broken, and you just threw her away."

"I know she wasn't a doll, Trip. You know I know she wasn't something I was just playing with."

"Yeah, I know. I'm sorry, my bad. I didn't mean to say it like that. I know you didn't think Amina was a doll."

"You know what?" I said, changing the subject. "The last time I was over at Yolanda's house, the girls were having a Kool-Aid and cookie party for their stuffed animals. I sat down and played with them. It was fun. I wish I was still little sometimes."

"You wanna be a kid again, like Yolanda's crew?"

"No, not like them," I said, getting up from the bed. The movement made the bowl of chips tumble off the other side. Trip got up to retrieve them.

"You don't want to be like Yolanda's kids? Kids are kids, my dark sister. I guess what you're saying is you're still on Miss Thing's list," Trip said, throwing the chips back in the bowl. He must have missed a couple. When he walked back to the bed crunches sounded everywhere.

"Yeah, Yolanda's not talking to me, and I mean not at all."

"I haven't seen Yolanda in a good while. Why is she still so pissed at you? Break it down for me."

I told Trip that since the day I talked to the guy at the fence

Yolanda won't even say hi to me. She's been over to the house four or five times to see Uncle, but she always avoids me. Uncle says that Yolanda is still in too much shock to deal with our friendship. I guess it's true. She has something bigger to worry about.

Eboni is gone, and so are Peter and Percy. Three days after I spoke to the guy, the social worker that came to Yolanda's before suddenly popped up again on a Saturday morning. One of the kids let him in, and it wasn't a good thing. Yolanda had had an old boyfriend come over and spend the night. He and Yolanda slept in late. When the social worker got there it was around twelve o'clock. The house was a mess. Vonda and Fatima were in the kitchen burning the hell out of some eggs, and cracked eggshells were all over the stove. Keisha and the boys were sitting in front of the TV eating stale cereal out of the box. Nobody had bothered to get Eboni dressed. She had another cold, and she was walking through the house in only her panties, leaving a trail of snotty tissue wherever she went. I honestly think the social worker could have forgiven all that, but he couldn't forgive Yolanda's old boyfriend strutting around in front of the girls in nothing but his BVDs. He also had a problem with the dime bag and open bottles of whiskey and rum that her boyfriend left sitting in the middle of the coffee table. The worker was livid about that. While Yolanda stood there clutching her bathrobe, he told her that he knew he should have come back and checked on her and the kids, and that as far as he was concerned she still needed a lot of help figuring out what she was supposed to do as a mother. "Miss Kemp, I'm extremely sorry that I didn't follow up with you. I warned you the last time I was here that you needed to do a lot better with your children. Judging from what I see today, and all the reports I've been reading, I don't think you've done that at all. In fact, at this point, I can positively say you haven't done anything. You are still taking your pleasures at the expense of your children. As far as I'm concerned you are definitely not an adequate parent for them, especially the younger three. They are still at an age where they are completely dependent on your total parental care."

"I know that," Yolanda told him. "It usually ain't this bad around here. I just got a late start. I had a little trouble this morning."

"Not *had*, Miss Kemp, still *have*. And it's not just a little trouble, you have a lot. More trouble than I'm willing to let you pass on to your kids," the social worker said. After that, he went over the house with a microscope. He questioned all of the children and decided to take the younger ones into protective custody until Yolanda improved her living arrangements.

Everybody is still shocked by it. We were all afraid that Jamal's parents would take Eboni away, now it looks like Yolanda could lose her boys as well. It seems crazy to me. I know Yolanda's ways. I know that even though she had gotten a little better lately, her house wasn't nearly as clean as it should be, and I also know that she could do better with her boyfriends. She should never be putting them over her kids. Still, I don't think it was fair to take her children away. When she came over crying about it to Uncle I wished I was on the other side of the world. I never saw her so unhappy. She wasn't the strong kick-ass sister I know her to be, the kind of sister that told guys to get out of her face whenever she wanted to, and let their wives know if they were taking care of business at home their husbands wouldn't be fooling with her. She was devastated, sobbing hysterically in our living room.

"I'm sorry, Yolanda. I wasn't trying to get you in trouble. I was only trying to help," I said to her.

"Yeah, you helped all right! You helped me right out of my kids. I trusted you, China. You my girl. You supposed to get my back. I can't believe you did this!" she screamed. And that was all she said to me the whole time she was there. I didn't know what to do. I went into the kitchen and closed the door. I took out a tray of chicken breast strips and a bottle of teriyaki sauce and started to make some teriyaki chicken for Uncle while he calmed her down. Later, when he had made her feel a little better, he came to the kitchen and we talked.

"That smells good. What you making?" he asked, as I moved the sizzling meat around in a skillet with a metal spatula.

"Some Japanese chicken. My teacher taught us how to make it last year in Home Development and Personal Growth. I've been wanting to make it for a while. It's pretty good, sweet," I said, trying to hold back my tears.

"I like sweet," he said, rolling his chair over to the stove.

"I know, that's why I'm making it for you," I said, going back to the refrigerator to find a cabbage. I brought out half of an already-washed head. I got a knife from the drawer and cut it into strips. I ate a few of them raw, and tossed the rest into the skillet along with the meat.

"That does smell good," he said, then he sighed. "Look, China Cup, what's going on with Yolanda is ninety-nine percent about her and one percent about you. No matter how much she wants to blame you, you didn't create the situation that got her children taken away, she did."

"I got a big mouth. She should be able to do what she wants, Uncle. That's what our teachers always say in school. They say that when you get grown you can do whatever you feel like doing. Isn't that right? Doesn't that mean that Yolanda has the right to do whatever she wants?" I said, taking out some of the chicken for him to taste. I held it over the skillet and shook the grease off for a second, so it wouldn't drop on his favorite eggplant-colored shirt. It used to belong to my great grandfather, along with the blanket on his bed that he never takes off, not even in the hottest days of summer.

"Yes it does. I know it does," he said, watching me shake the meat. He held out his hand to take it from the fork.

I blew on it and gave it to him.

He gobbled it up and nodded his head with approval. "It sure does. It means Yolanda got a right to play her game however she wants to play it," he continued after he had finished chewing the meat up. "But honey, it isn't that simple. What your teachers told you is mostly true, but the real world doesn't really work like that. Do you remember when Amina was born, and we talked about how your life no longer belonged just to you?"

"I remember."

"Of course you do. You remember when I told you that whatever you did would affect her, too. I don't think anybody ever told Yolanda that. I don't think she ever figured out that she and her children are attached."

"I guess so," I said.

"China, it is so. Look honey, I'm not just trying to dump on Yolanda. I like her. She has a great deal of faults, but she makes me laugh a whole lot, and she always talks plain to me, never treats me like I'm half of a person just because I can't use my legs."

"Yolanda is like that."

"Yes, she is, but she's also like a woman who doesn't know what to do with herself, and more importantly, her kids. She thinks that flying in the face of what she calls *a world run by brothers* is the way to gain her independence and make a life for her kids. It's not."

"She doesn't like rules," I said, opening the bottle of teriyaki sauce and pouring a little more over the meat.

"Nobody does. Why do you think people complain so much when tax time comes along, drive sixty when the speed limit sign says forty-five, and try to get three sale items when the store flyer says that you can only have two? China, nobody likes being told what to do or how to do it, but there's a reason why sometimes you need to do things the way other folks do them."

"For instance if you don't pay your taxes you maybe go to jail, and if you drive too fast down the street you can have a bad accident," I said.

"Exactly, and to use one of them clichés they always use on TV, Yolanda was one bad accident waiting to happen. When we went to see the lawyer he told her to keep them trifling guys out of her bedroom and make sure that her house and children were always pulled together. She was supposed to start a training program, one that would help her get a good job and take care of her kids, without counting on whatever she could scrape up from their fathers. It wasn't gonna be easy, but it was gonna be doable—that is, if she wanted to do it."

"Maybe she wanted to, but I just ruined everything when I talked to that guy," I said, turning the fire off underneath the skillet. I took a bowl out of the dish drainer and threw the mixture in.

"China, come sit down near me," Uncle said. I put the bowl down on the counter and sat down in one of the dining-table chairs across from him.

"Look, China, Yolanda is a great deal older than you," he said, leaning over and looking into my eyes. "She's young, but she's still had plenty of years to screw up her life. The state took her kids because of a mistake she made, not because of anything you did. If there wasn't anything to tell, you couldn't have told it, and even if you did you're not responsible for the social worker showing up to her house."

"I guess, but what if she doesn't get her kids back?" I said. "I'm sure Jamal's parents have Eboni's room all fixed up with expensive stuffed animals and that furniture from those baby boutiques you have to send away for."

"Probably, but I never say that a piece of work is finished until it's all painted and completely fired," Uncle said. He reached over and squeezed my hand like he always did when he wanted me to cheer up. "China, what I want is for you to work through you own problems and not take on Yolanda's or mine or anybody else's."

"I don't know how to do that," I said. "Yolanda isn't even talking to me. We get mad sometimes, but she never pushes the mute button on me. It's never been that way with us."

"I know, baby. I know, this is a difficult time for everybody," Uncle said, running his hand through his short, coarse fro. "I understand, and I'll talk to Yolanda and try to make this right. For now, just handle your own and take care of yourself. Can you do that, China? Can you really take care of yourself?"

"I can take care of myself."

"I wish that were true," he said with another sigh. "I wish you could, only I think you're on the same wrong train that Yolanda got on."

"I'm not Yolanda, Uncle Simon," I said, getting up from the chair.

"No, you're a lot more fragile than she is," he said. "You're a whole lot more breakable."

"Put the chicken in the fridge. You can make some rice to go with it, if you like. That's the way my teacher served it at school," I said, and walked away from the kitchen. I didn't want to hear his lecture about me, but on that afternoon I kind of understood what he was saying about Yolanda. I got it then, only today I still wish I had kept my trap shut about her business.

"So Yolanda still has you off her speed dial, does she?" Trip asked, taking the bowl of chips and placing it on top of his desk.

"I'm not even the last number," I said. "She won't even speak to me on the phone. The only people that call me these days are you, Alejandra, and Brother Agee."

"Brother Agee, that dude down at the funeral home, he calls you?"

"Yeah, and comes by sometimes. He checks up on me and asks how things are going. He reminds me of what I'm working for.

'China, your little girl would be so happy if she could see how you've honored her. You're doing exactly what a good mother should do,' he says."

"Really?"

"Yeah, or something just like it."

"You're for real? He shows up, calls and says those things? What's up with that? Why is he on you so much?"

"He's not. He's just trying to help. I'm glad that he gives my case extra attention. It keeps me focused."

"Keeps you focused. Well, I wish you were focused on finding another job, but I'm not going to start ragging about that. Let's go catch some rays, and not even worry about Yolanda. It's almost three hours before you're due at the club."

Trip and I decided to walk back over to the high school and see if his cousin Rick was running laps on the track. Rick had borrowed one of Trip's sci-fi tapes and Trip wanted to get it back. I didn't say anything to Trip, but I would have enjoyed going anyplace other than the school. I didn't want to run into anyone I knew, and I didn't want to explain why I wasn't attending classes anymore. I also didn't want to see Principal Nesby. The last time I came up to see Trip she spotted me from her window, and came out to try and tell me what to do.

"Come back to school, China," she told me, standing in front of the gate in one of her dressy Oprah suits. "I can talk to your teachers, and together we'll get you caught up in your work. I can't believe that what you're doing now is what your uncle Simon or your daughter would want for you."

"I'm not doing anything," I lied.

"That's not what I heard," she said. "And I don't want to really force the issue, because something in me says I'll make things much worse."

"I don't know what you're talking about. My uncle Simon isn't having any problems with me, and my daughter is dead. She doesn't know anything at all anymore," I said.

"Then why are you doing what you're doing?" she asked. "Don't you miss being with your friends, China? Don't you miss some of the things you were able to do around here? I talked to your English teacher again. She said when you made it to class you were a great student. She said you genuinely liked poetry, and she thought she could get you interested in some of the classics, too."

"I guess," I said.

"I also spoke with your Home Development teacher this semester. She told me that you're an excellent cook. She says you have a natural way in the kitchen, like you were born to cook gourmet dishes and desserts. She said you would do wonderfully in our life-prep program. You could get a paying internship after school in a kitchen, and be well on your way to being a chef. Wouldn't you like to do that, China? Isn't that something you would be interested in doing?"

I shrugged my shoulders and didn't verbally answer. Instead I saw Trip coming out of the main school door and ran to meet him. I still felt a little bad about that. I did like cooking. It was one of my favorite things to do for Uncle. I liked whipping up new dishes for him, and also throwing together some of his old favorites. Perhaps my Home Development teacher was exaggerating a little, but maybe it wasn't too late for me to be a chef. Maybe I could be one of those folks who cooked delicious desserts on the PBS channel or spicy entrées at one of the Cajun restaurants in town. But what did Principal Nesby have to do with that? I still didn't think she had a right to be all up in my business. I wished she would just leave me alone.

"I hope Principal Nesby has already gone home. I really don't want to run into girlfriend again. She's just gonna ride me about not coming to school. It's already old," I said to Trip, as we cut through the backyard of Bobby's Rib Shack.

"I see your point. She's been stopping me every time she sees me, too, telling me that I need to talk to you about your choices. We been there. You ain't listening anyway."

"I'm listening. I just don't need to hear it right now."

"It's cool. It's cool, but there is one other thing. One of your girlfriends, I think her name is Takara. She's been asking about you. She stopped me at the park the other day. She wants to know why you haven't been coming around Soul Brother's Fried Ice Cream Shop."

"She asked you that?"

"Yeah."

"Dang, I wish I could. You remember Takara? I met her up at the maternity ward when I had Amina. She has a little boy, but he stays with her boyfriend half the time. Anyway, when it was her weekend to have him, we'd sometimes hang out together. We'd meet at the ice-cream shop. The kids would eat Vanilla Dream while we'd gossip. It was way cool. Takara knows *all* the football players and cheerleaders. She always got some good stuff to tell on them. She lets you know every bit of their business."

"Really, what kind of business?"

"Everything. She knows it all."

"Well, you should probably use the little free time you get off and see what she's up to."

"Yeah, I guess I should. I do miss her. But it wouldn't be the same without Amina there to play with her little boy, would it? Nothing is the same now. I probably wouldn't even like being there with her."

Trip sighed. "Naw, I guess you wouldn't," he said. "We'll go around to the side gate. We won't have to see anybody but the guys on the track."

"I can handle that," I said.

We walked over to the school and went around to the side gate. There were four boys still out there—a couple of skinny guys that I hadn't seen before, Tommy, the handsome Korean guy who likes to work out with Trip, and Trip's cousin, Rick. It was hot as Hades, but the burning heat wasn't stopping the guys from racing around the track like mad. I trudged up to the shaded part of the bleachers and sat on one of the wooden benches while Trip ran out to catch up with Rick. I checked him out as he ran across the grassy court-yard to the track. The weight-lifting was really keeping him in shape. That tight, beautiful, Hershey's Special Dark bod was hot enough to put in one of those Mr. Universe contests. Trip was really the man.

I wondered what he would look like when we got a little older? In fact, I wondered what we both would look—and feel—like? I don't know about Trip, but I felt tired these days, like Yolanda sometimes felt when she had all six of her kids. I sat back on the bench and frowned. Trip caught up with Rick, and they were now jogging slowly around the track, rapping about the tape that Trip probably wasn't going to get back. It made me feel all chocolate-dipped strawberries inside.

I liked that Trip always went after what he wanted. He was serious about his sci-fi, so serious that I would never let anything come between him and his goal—not me, not even our daughter. Trip had *vision*. When I imagined myself, I always saw me as a grasshopper in a jar, smashing my body against the metal lid, trying to hop away to places that I couldn't even see. Trip could see beyond the lid. He knew how to crash through it, all the way up to the stars, and I so wanted him to. With Amina gone all I had left was the little hope that Trip could do some of the things that our daughter would never do.

Go, Trip, get whatever you want, I said in my head.

"Those guys are crazy out there running in the hot sun, aren't they, China?" a girl's voice said. I looked down. Coming up the bleachers was a girl with a short blond fro, wearing a gold tank top and red bike shorts. On the tank in vivid letters was the name Tommy Hilfiger. It was my old girlfriend Kembra, who used to have a big crush on Trip. I couldn't believe it. She hadn't said one word to me or Trip since she found out I was carrying Trip's baby, yet here she was coming up the steps hollering at me like we were still best girlfriends.

"You know guys, they think it makes the sisters like them better, if they stupid enough to go running around in weather that even the devil wouldn't work out in. Guys are dumb sometimes."

"I guess. It sure is dumb to be doing that," she said. She made her way up to the bench right in front of me and stopped. I expected her to go back to her regular whispery voice. I expected wrong.

"Ooh girl, that ozone ain't giving off much protection today," she said in a loud clear voice.

"Naw, not today. I'm about to burn up, girlfriend."

She sat backward on the bench and lifted the tail of her tank to wipe her forehead. Her flat stomach was sporting two gold navel rings. I raised my brows. Back in the day she would never do something like that. She really had changed.

"What's up, girl?" I asked.

"I heard about your little girl. I'm really sorry," she said with sincerity.

"Thanks."

"I can't believe that happened," she said, shaking her head. "She was just a little baby. That don't seem right."

"It's not right. Kembra, what are you doing here?" I asked.

"I came for a friend."

"What does that mean? What friend?" She hesitated for a moment, then looked around, as if she was worried about something.

"What are you looking for?" I asked. She turned back to me.

"Onyx, I'm here for Onyx," she said.

"What? Onyx Moon, you know her?"

"I know her. You work over at Obsidian's with her, don't you?"

"How did you know that?"

"I know. I know you work with her," she said.

"I do, but she hasn't been to work for a long time. Everybody is wondering where she got off to. She's on that stuff."

"I know. She been on it for a while. She was off at one time, though. I thought she was still okay with it."

"You know her pretty good?"

"We hang, and she wants to talk to you."

"She does, well, why don't she come over to the club? Everybody there is looking for her. What is she trippin' like this for?"

"She got her reasons. Look, China. I'm just trying to help Onyx out. She back there behind the bleachers. She say she got something to say to you. I told her that I knew you, so I would come and get you. You wanna hear what she got to say, go listen to it. If you don't, that's your business," she said coldly, reminding me that we really were no longer girlfriends.

"Okay, thanks, I just didn't know why you were being all I-spy about it."

"Whatever, I'm just trying to run an errand." She glanced over at the track. Trip and his cousin had stopped running, and were standing underneath a tree near the track. She looked back at me. I could see the old hurt in her eyes. "Tell Trip I said hey," she said.

"You can tell him yourself in a few minutes. I'll run and get him," I offered.

"Naw, he don't want to talk to me. Just don't forget about Onyx. I'll see you at school sometimes," she said, getting up and walking off.

"Sure, I'll see you too," I said as she made her way back down the bleachers. As soon as she cleared the last bleacher she waved at me without turning to see if I was waving back. I knew it meant that she had no intention of ever having a conversation with me again. I hollered and beckoned for Trip to come back for several minutes. Finally I got his attention. I trotted down the bleachers to greet him.

"That fool must be crazy if he think I'ma forget about my tape," he said, coming up the steps.

"He can't find it?"

"Hell naw, he say he loaned it out to some dude he shoots hoops with. I told him he better get it back before I go all Terminator on both of them."

I giggled. "Yeah right," I said. "Come on. I need to go see about something."

"About what?"

"Nothing, just come on."

We went down below and walked to the back of the bleachers. The whole time Trip kept asking me what the heck I was up to. He shut his mouth when he saw Onyx Moon standing in the shadows beneath the bleachers. She looked like I expected her to look, all shaky with saucer pupils, and a face that looked like it had aged three years since the last time I saw her. She looked bad, but I had seen junkies hanging out behind Perry's 24 and 7 that looked much worse. She was definitely back on something again, but not so heavy that it was too late for her to find her way off.

"Where you been, Onyx?" I asked casually, walking up to her.

"Around," she said. "Is that your boyfriend?" she asked, pointing to Trip with a trembling finger.

"He's a boy, and he's my friend, fill it in any way that you like," I said with a smile. She tried to smile too.

"Where you been?" I asked again. "How come you quit coming to the club? Everybody been wondering where you at. Are you okay?"

"You got any money?" she blurted out. I shook my head.

"Nah, I'm pretty broke."

"How come? You been working steady for a while. What happened to all of them big tips? Where's your cash?"

"I've been saving it for something," I said, glancing over at Trip.

"Saving it for what? That baby you told me you didn't have?

176

Why did you lie about that?" she said in an accusing tone.

"She doesn't have a baby," Trip spoke up. "She died."

"A few months ago—not like your little boys," I said.

"What little boys? I don't have no kids."

"You were pregnant once. I saw some marks on your stomach."

"Oh, them things. Naw, I was just really fat once."

"Oh."

"Yeah, I was real heavy, almost as fat as Sweet Petite. My mama put me on some pills to slim me down, then I got extra skinny." She shrugged. "I guess it was better than being fat. China, you got any money or not?"

"I told you I don't, but why don't you come back to the club. I'm sure Louisa will help you out."

"I'm sure she will, but I ain't going back there."

"Why not, because of Skinner?"

"Skinner ain't nothing. He just likes to get what he can, but there's a whole lot of dudes around there like that. You get used to it. At least he was giving me something. Naw, Skinner ain't the reason."

"What is the reason?" I repeated.

"You don't wanna know. I'm just not going back there, that's all. Hell, even high I know better than that. It's too much mess going on there."

"Like what?"

"Like the kinda stuff that you don't even wanna know about."

"What kinda stuff?" Trip asked.

"China, you sure you ain't got no cash? Come on, girl, you gotta have something. I need some money real bad," she said, wrapping her arms around her body.

"For what, more drugs? What about your little boys? You gonna stay all messed up like this? I thought you were trying to get it together for them. What about that nice apartment you got? You gonna throw all that away? What's up with that?"

"Ain't nothing up with that. I told you them boys ain't really my kids, China," she said. "I can't do nothing for them."

I sighed. "Not like this, I guess you can't," I said.

"You're just a kid, China. You don't even know what you talking about. You just a baby like Kembra. You don't know nothing at all," she said, backing away.

"What? You know Kembra, how?" Trip asked.

"Yeah, she my friend. She used to have China's old job. She had it for a little while, before the other girl came."

"Kembra had China's job? I know it's a small neighborhood, but damn. Did you know about that?" Trip asked me.

"No, nobody said anything about it to me," I said, shocked.

"Yes, I did. I told you I had a friend that was working there."

"Kembra, you were talking about Kembra? She's the girl that sets Louisa off each time you bring her name up?"

"Yeah, it pissed Louisa off when Kembra's mama made her quit. The men liked Kembra. The young ones always bring in more cash."

"Aw, man," Trip said. "I didn't need to know all that. I never needed to know all of that."

"Sorry, too bad, didn't mean to freak you. Look, I gotta go. Ya'll can't do nothing for me," Onyx said, walking off.

"Damn. I changed my mind," Trip said. "China, let's go back to one of those you-finding-somewhere-else-to-work conversations," he said, as she headed across the street.

"Let's not," I said. "It's burning up out here. Go tell Rick he better get your tape back, so we can go."

"Okay, and by the way, you can keep changing the subject, but the subject ain't going away."

"Go get your tape, Trip. I'll be waiting here in the shade," I said.

"Fine," Trip said.

"Fine," I yelled at him as he took off. I strolled deeper into the shade. Across the street Onyx was holding herself as she went shakily down the sidewalk. I averted my eyes and looked at the back of the wooden bleacher stand. *"Such sins, such sins,"* is all I could think to say.

CHAPTER 8

I got up this morning and decided to go to church. I don't know why. It was Sunday, and as soon as I saw the stripes of bright orange cutting through the thick purple clouds I decided that I wanted to visit the old church that me and Mama used to go to. I helped Uncle get dressed in the suit that he wore to Amina's funeral, and put on an attractive, simple blue skirt set that Mama used to wear to services. It smelled like her favorite perfume, and when I was making our breakfast of leftover homemade applesauce and buttermilk biscuits, I remembered sitting next to her in the pew. I would listen to her say *Amen*, wondering what the minister's sermon was making her feel.

"Religion is hard. You either see Jonah in the belly of a whale or you don't. It's just the way it is, my dark sister. It's all on the inside," Trip said when I called him and told him to tag along with us.

"True, now be *inside* of my house at nine-thirty A.M.," I said, and hung up the phone.

Thirty minutes later Trip showed up in a pressed ivory shirt and khaki pants, dragging his mama with him. She wasn't in black anymore, but she somehow managed to make the occasion ridiculous as usual. She showed up in a blue-jean blouse and ankle-length skirt with Jersey and longhorn cows on it. Topping the outfit off was a black cowboy hat that made her look like she was on her way to the rodeo. "China Cup, you didn't tell me we were going on a cattle drive," Uncle Simon laughed when he saw her coming up the steps.

"Oh God, stampede!" everything in me wanted to yell, until I saw Trip's please-don't-start-up face.

"How you doing this morning? You look really nice," I said to Shronda Faye when she stepped up on the porch.

"I still ain't got no job, that's how I'm doing. You done went to see your baby yet? Trip told me you ain't even been out to her grave. It's a shame. I guess I'll have to do it. Having a grandmother visit is better than not having no maternal figure at all."

"I'm sure she'll be happy to know that you're looking in on her," I said through clenched teeth.

"We gonna be late," Trip said, taking her by the arm.

"Thanks," I whispered. I pushed Uncle down the ramp in his chair and we were off.

It was a fifth Sunday at the church. The youth group was running the services. Kids around our age were singing beautiful solos and giving moving prayers and scripture readings. Even the speaker was a kid, an impressive, towering young sister in a crimson-red robe. She was preaching a fiery hell-and-brimstone sermon that caused most of the church to continuously jump up from the benches. They clapped their hands and shouted loudly, "Tell the truth. Preach it right, girl. Preach it right!" until the whole sanctuary seemed to be rocking and shaking from the spirit-filled enthusiasm.

"Man, she's good, isn't she?" Trip asked beside me.

"Yeah," I mumbled. Truth is, I wasn't paying attention. I was thinking about the week before, thinking about Kembra.

I had Kembra's old job. Like Trip's Mr. Spock would say, *it wasn't logical*. Kembra wasn't me. Back when we used to hang out at the pool she would put on her sister's skimpy bikinis to impress Trip, but you could tell that she never felt comfortable in them. They were only to get Trip to like her, maybe take her to get a snow cone or something at the cart in front of the pool. I couldn't see her wanting to get a snow cone or anything else from those dudes at Obsidian Queens. Yuck, she wasn't even like that—the Kembra I remembered wasn't like that. She had changed, someone had changed her. That bothered me. Even when she wasn't speaking to me, Kembra was a constant, like Trip. I could always count on Kembra to be Kembra. Her new car and designer clothes never made her stop being the nice girl that everyone wanted to know, like me. I still wanted to know her. What I didn't want to know is that she had been working at Obsidian's. Why didn't my homegirl Rani tell me that? She had no reason to keep quiet about it like Onyx. She didn't work with Louisa. She could mention Kembra's name as much as she wanted. Man, it was strange, and even stranger that her new stepfather would think it was okay for Kembra to be strutting around half-naked in front of a bunch of grown men. I thought fathers were supposed to stop daughters from doing things like that. What kind of man was he? Why hadn't *he* stopped her from working at Obsidian's?

"You better get your house in order before it's too late! No man knows the day, the time, or the hour. Come to Jesus while you have time!" the girl preacher yelled down from the pulpit. She walked to the edge of the red carpet and started beckoning for people to come up.

"You heard what she said," Trip whispered to me. "You better get up there girl, before it's too late. Go on, get your house in order."

"Shut up," I whispered back. He giggled softly. In front of us a father and son combination heard the calling, and started up the aisle. The son was about thirteen, dressed casually in a T-shirt and jeans. The father was dressed a lot more formally. He was a policeman. He was sporting his uniform, badge and all. The two went up hand in hand. The sight of them made me misty-eyed, but I was mostly tearing up out of envy. I had never gotten to take my father's hand and go anywhere. What did it feel like, knowing you had a dad that cared what happened to you on earth and beyond? I imagined that when the father and son got home the rest of the family would help them celebrate their joining the family of Christ. There would probably be a big dinner. Cousins, uncles, and aunts would come over bearing tasty casseroles and homemade pies. They would sit around the supper table and share family news along with tips on the best Bible courses for the guys to take. It would be a great time for everybody, with all the love and sharing. I never had that. Mama's family was so fractured they hardly ever got together for anything, and I'm sure my father's family had plenty of get-togethers, but Lord knows the bastard daughter was never included, and according to his son never would be. There was an unfairness in that. When I thought about it, it actually made me really, really upset.

"I need to go to the restroom," I said to Trip. I got up and slid past him. The preacher was still telling folks to come up and meet Jesus before it was too late. I walked down the aisle feeling guilty about going the opposite way.

Inside the bathroom only the stall with the handicapped sign was open, so I went into it. I felt even guiltier as I sat down on the cool toilet seat. I did my business quick and popped up. When I exited the door Shronda Faye was standing in the oval bathroom mirror reapplying her lipstick. I went to the nearby sink and washed my hands.

"Well it took you long enough, but you finally managed to do it," she said as I cut off the water.

"Do what, ma'am?" I asked politely.

"Shame my son again, that's what. I knew you would get around to it directly."

"Shame him how?"

"You know how, running around at that club, taking your underpants off for them men."

"I'm not taking my underpants off for anyone," I snapped.

"Of course you are. It's a dance club, ain't it. One of them clubs where the hoochies wiggle all they got for a little extra change."

"There are some ladies that dance, but I'm not one of them. I just hand stuff out," I said, reaching for the paper-towel holder on the wall.

"Yeah well, I know what you handing out, and I'm sure it's the same thing that you handed my boy," she said, putting her lipstick back in her leather handbag. "I'm sure it's exactly what you gave Trip."

"What's that mean?"

"You know exactly what it means. Ever since my boy met you, you done had his head turned around on one damn thing or the other. First it was all that silly sci-fi crap, then next thing I know you come stepping in my house with a big belly, hanging his name on it."

"Excuse me. I never hung anything on Trip. We had a baby together. Both of us messed up, but as I recall I'm the one that got stuck with the problem. I never asked you and Trip to buy Amina so much as a pacifier."

"You didn't have to, just knowing that you hung that weight around my son's neck was enough. There he was having to play daddy and he wasn't nothing but a baby."

"Me too. How old do you think I was when Amina was born?" I said through gritted teeth. I wasn't going to let her get me upset enough to start hollering in church.

"Too old, that's your problem. You always been too old. Even when you was little you was never much like other little girls. You always did think you was grown, liked to hang out with your mama at the shop, instead of spending time with the other little girls. Your mama say you didn't really like playing with dolls or doing dress-up games. She said she had to make you do those things. That's fine, you a little too big for that mess now. But let me tell you something that my son and your uncle Simon won't tell you, you still ain't nothing but a little pigtail-wearing girl. You don't know nothing about life. All you know is how to screw up. That's what happened to your baby. If you had gone over there when that old lady asked you to, you probably coulda seen that something was really wrong with that child. You probably could have—"

"Shut up! Just shut up! I'm not gonna let you tell me anything about my baby. You don't know what you're talking about, and you sure as hell don't know nothing about Trip. If you did, you wouldn't be ragging on him about his story ideas. He's really good at writing those things," I said, much louder than I intended to.

"What he's good at is throwing away my money on a whole lot of stamps and paper, sending that junk off to all them places in Hollywood and everywhere else. He just wasting what little we got to live on."

"It's not junk."

"To them people out there in Hollywood it is, and they all that counts. I'm his mother. I love him, and I don't like him wasting his time, but no matter what I'm always gonna be on his side. I'm not the one sending him them no-thank-you notes. I'm not the one that's gonna end up breaking his heart."

"Trip can handle himself. He's not gonna get all down just because he gets a few letters and a couple of piss-off T-shirts. Just quit ragging on him about everything, and it'll be fine," I said, snatching a brown paper towel from the holder.

"I'm not ragging on my son," she said, wagging her finger at me. "I'm only trying to get him to understand that there are other things he can do with his life. He's smart in school. There's all kinds of academic things he can do, or maybe he can join the military like I did. He can give back to his country. I'm just trying to hip him to all the things he can be. That's what a parent is supposed to do. I know you don't really get that, without having a parent of your own and all."

"That was really mean. You know I have a parent," I said, throwing the towel into the plastic can under the sink. "My uncle Simon looks out for me."

"Yeah, I see how he looks out for you," she said, backing out of the door. "He ain't even got sense enough to tell you to quit that trashy job."

"I don't need him to tell me what to do. I know what I'm doing," I said.

"Yeah right. Whatever, little girl, you can talk grown, but I guarantee you, you ain't. Anyway, you just keep my son out of whatever cave you done stumbled blind into. He don't need to shoulder no more of your mistakes."

"He don't need to go to the military either. You just want him to do what you done."

"What if I do? The military is an honorable profession. It will do Trip a world of good to get out and see the country. He's strong and smart. He could probably be an officer in no time."

"He probably could, if he really wanted to. But Trip wants to go out to Hollywood. He wants to work on a show. You would know that if you really knew him."

"He's my son. I know all about him. I just don't want to see him get more hurt, and he won't, if you start letting him run his own life."

"Fine, I'll stay out of his business. And you can send him off to the military, where all he'll be is miserable."

"You don't know that."

"Yes ma'am I do, and I'm surprised you don't. Now just leave me alone," I said. I pushed past her and rushed out of the bathroom with her on my heels.

"I'm not finished, don't you walk away from me, little wanna-be-grown girl," she yelled after me.

"Go to the devil!" I shouted.

I rushed back into the main sanctuary. The girl minister was doing a laying on of hands. A crowd of people were lined up in front of the altar. I slipped in next to Trip.

"Do me a favor and go with Uncle back to the house," I said.

"Go with him, where you going?"

"I don't know, just out of here," I said.

"China, what's wrong?" Uncle asked, leaning over Trip.

"Nothing, I just need somewhere to chill," I said. "I'll be home in a bit." I started up the aisle and discovered Shronda Faye standing in my way with a scowl. I walked past her like she was a ghost, and went out of the church.

I thought about going to see my girl Alejandra, but Yolanda's place was really where I wanted to be. Yes, she was still pissed at me. Yolanda could milk a grudge forever. She was still mad at a girl who beat her out of a drill-team spot in junior high school. She was gonna give me hell when I saw her, but Trip's mom had made me see all kinds of red, first calling me a slut, then dissing what Trip wanted to do with his life. That was the thing that bothered me the most. All this time I never knew she blamed me for what Trip wanted to do.

When we were younger she used to talk about Trip being a soldier, and bought him a lot of action figurines of guys in fatigues and with guns. Trip played with them for a while, but he always went back to reading his fantasy comics and watching his favorite *Outer Realm* episodes. When he turned the TV off he would immediately start telling me his own stories. I would sit amazed at his ideas. No, it wasn't me who was keeping Trip from living his mother's dreams, it was Trip. It was always Trip. Shronda Faye had no reason to chomp my tail about it. It made me angry when I saw her standing in front of the mirror in that stupid cow suit, telling me how I had let down my child. I should have stuffed her head down the toilet for saying that. Who was she to tell me what happened that day? Did she know what seeing my child lying there not breathing at all had done to me?

"Come on, let's go on home," Uncle Simon said that awful afternoon. What home was he talking about? What home was there without my child playing with her rag dolls in the middle of my bedroom floor? There was no home without Amina. That's what they had taught me nearly two years before in Mother Care class. They told me what Uncle had really already told me the day she was born. "Always remember that as a mother everything in your home revolves around your child. Every decision that you make includes her, affects her life. Never forget that your house is her house too."

"I won't forget, ma'am," I told the helpful teacher, while folding a newborn diaper over Amina's torso. I took to heart everything she and Uncle Simon said. Amina was so tiny and light. She was like the stuffed baby panda that Mama had given me on my seventh birthday. She hardly seemed real, and I knew from looking at her soft crinkled face that protecting her would be a lot harder than changing her diapers and giving her a bottle. When I got home that afternoon I cleaned the house from top to bottom. I threw out anything that I thought would harm her. She wasn't able to reach for anything yet, but I put all my sharp pencils and pens into my pencil case. She couldn't crawl, but I moved all my old sneakers off the floor. She wasn't able to walk, and I still moved all of Uncle's figurines off the low shelf in the living room. I had Uncle buy an electric air filter to filter the air in my bedroom. I did everything my teacher suggested. I even stopped Alejandra from coming over and kissing her all over the face.

"Girl, a little spit ain't gone hurt her. My mama just had my little sister. I kiss her all the time, and she ain't dead yet. You trippin'," she told me.

Maybe I was, but I made sure that Amina was the most important person in my house. When she was alive it was truly her place.

Whose place was it now? Me and Uncle were there, but without Amina we were like Mama's cherry and rhubarb pies without the cherry or the rhubarb. There was nothing at all in us, nothing to fill the house up. Last week Uncle came in my room and asked me if I wanted to give Amina's things to the Salvation Army or the Goodwill. I hunched my shoulders. Did it really matter if her clothes stayed in my room or went to the needy? It wouldn't make me feel any different. It wouldn't make me feel alive again. What did Shronda Faye know about that? How dare she get in my face about my child? Trip might not be doing what she wanted him to do with his life, but at least he was still alive to make her upset with him for not doing it. She had to see the greatness in that. Didn't she?

I fumed about Shronda Faye until I got to Yolanda's house. When I reached there I didn't hesitate before going up the steps. Yolanda was my spirit girl in motherhood. We shared something that Trip and I could never share. I wasn't going to let her end our relationship simply because I had a big mouth. I rapped on the door and waited for her to answer it. A couple of minutes passed, and Keisha came bouncing to the door, wearing a pair of oversized sunglasses and one of Yolanda's big cotton shirts for a dress.

"Hey Chinaberry Tree, where you been? Law get cha?" she asked.

"My name's not Chinaberry Tree, and what do you know about the law?" I asked.

"I know a lot. I know they got Eboni's daddy and mine too last year. They both locked down for a long time."

"Your daddy's not locked down. He just went to jail for a couple of days for not paying some parking tickets. He's been home."

"No he's not. Mama say he in jail. That's why he don't come by no more. You don't know what you talking about, Chinaberry Tree."

"Okay, okay, my bad. I don't know jack. Just tell me where you mama is," I said.

"She in her skin, in her room. That's where she at," she said, rolling her eyes. Even through the shades I could see her dark brown pupils going up to the ceiling. I shook my head and went into the house.

Once in the door I freaked. Everything in the living room was gone. Yolanda's butt-worn paisley sofa and chair, her two dusty coffee tables, the imitation oriental throw rug that we got at a garage sale, the folding TV trays that usually stood up against the pink flamingo–colored wall, and all the wooden framed photos of the kids were missing. The only thing in the room was boxes, giant taped-up boxes with orange labels scribbled in Yolanda's miniscule handwriting.

"Hey, what's up with all the junk?" I said, hurrying to her room. I found her standing in the middle of a bunch of other boxes, folding the jet-black curtains that normally hung over her window.

"I'm moving, and not really moving, China," she said, not even looking around at me.

"What the heck does that mean?"

She sighed, and put the curtains into an open box. "What are you doing here, China?"

"I'm having a bad day. Anyway, I came to say that I'm really sorry."

"Don't sweat it. It's cool."

"You mean you're not still mad at me?" I asked, walking over to her.

"Hell yes, I'm as pissed as I ever was at you, but I can't dwell on it. That's all somewhere over the rainbow, or some corny mess like that."

"Okay, and what are we really talking about?" I asked.

"Nothing girl, I ain't got too much to say. I'm just talking, talking and moving."

"Moving where?" I asked. She hesitated, then sat down Indian-style on the floor. I joined her and tucked the tail of my skirt in between my legs while she adjusted her Oxford shirt over the Road Map.

"Moving where?" I repeated, pulling my braids back away from my face. She stalled again, pulled her braids back too.

"I'm just going down the road, not too far," she said after awhile.

"Not too far where?"

She sighed. "China, me and the girls are moving in with Eboni's grandparents."

My jaw dropped clean through her wooden floor and onto the cool dirt beneath the house. "What? Are you trippin'?"

She shook her head. "Naw, girlfriend, I'm not," she said. "Eboni's grandparents got that big house over there, with all them bedrooms, and we going to stay with them."

"What for?"

"To get my kids back. Jamal's dad said that he would talk to social services and help me get back my babies."

"But he's the reason they took them away!" I said.

"I know that. I know he hired that investigator to get in my business, and that's why they came here and took away my three youngest kids."

"Darn right. If he hadn't done that, that social worker would never have come back to your house. Can't you see he tugging the hell out of your strings, girlfriend. He making you dance around like them paper puppets you get at Diamond's grocery store."

"True, and I'm gonna dance too, if it's the only way I can get my family back together. China, I'm gonna dance until my feet ain't nothing but red mush," she said, beginning to shed tears.

Seeing them on her cheeks made me feel angrier. "Don't cry, fight," I said. "Go tell Jamal's parents what they can do with their house. Tell them that you can get the kids back on your own. My uncle will help you. I know that he won't give up no matter what they pull. I'll go call him right now and tell him to get over here."

"Naw, you don't need to do that," she blubbered. "I already talked to Simon. I told him what Jamal's parents asked me to do, and he told me that he thought I should do it, if only for a little bit. He told me that while I was living in their house rent-free I could go back to school, maybe night school, and get some kind of associate degree."

"Uncle Simon told you that? Why would he do that? I can't believe that he would tell you to give up."

"He didn't, 'cause I'm not. China, I been a bad mama," she said, wiping her face with her hands. "I know it and you know it. All that stuff about a woman living her own life, I meant that, and I believe it, except you shouldn't do it if it's gonna screw with your kids."

"You got a right to live your life any way you want," I said to make her feel better.

"Naw, I thought I did. But China, I started bathing in dirty water a long time ago, and I went and pulled my kids right into the tub with me. I ain't no fool. I know they wouldn't of taken my three youngest kids from me, if they hadn't found something really off in my house, really off in me."

"That's not true."

"Yes it is," she sobbed. "China, do you know why I have so many kids?"

I shrugged.

"When I was about twelve my mama got pregnant again, and I do mean again. I come from a really big family. There was already nine of us, and my mama couldn't afford anymore. She didn't want to do it, but she picked me up from school one afternoon and we went down to the women's clinic to take care of her little problem. I remembered how she looked when she came out of that office. I can't even describe it without hurting inside. I told myself that afternoon that I would never do that to myself or my child. Do you really want to know why I got rid of two of my kids?"

I nodded.

"The truth is there was something wrong with both of those babies. The doctor told me early, and there was no way I would purposely have a really messed-up kid. It wouldn't be fair to anybody."

"I guess not," I said, still trying to take everything in. "I wouldn't either."

"Yeah, I know," she said, getting up. "It's a mother's job to do the best thing for her child. That's what I'm trying to do, China. Didn't you ever do anything that you didn't really want to do just because it was right? You always tell me that you don't like going to them hospital appointments with your uncle. You tell me you hate it because you don't like knowing when he's going to need another operation or procedure. But you go anyway, because you know there's no way you can do anything else."

"I get your point," I said, getting up too. "Only I still don't see why you need to move in with Jamal's folks. They don't even respect you. I can't believe Uncle Simon would tell you that it was a good idea. I can't believe he did that. Why would he mess me up like that?"

"China, this ain't about you. Let's just stop going there. I'm gonna do what I need to do. Maybe it will be all right." She pulled me to her and gave me a big hug. "I'm sorry I won't be seeing you for a long time," she said. "I guess that's what I'm really unhappy about."

"What are you talking about?" I said, pushing her away.

"I guess Simon didn't tell you that, either. China, I can't be hanging out with you no more, at least not for a long time."

"Why not, what's up with that?" I said angrily.

"China, you know you my girl, but you working at Obsidian's now, and I can't have that around my children. If I'm gonna get Eboni and my twins back I got to be the perfect mama. That means I can't be messing around with them dudes I used to mess with, and it means I can't have no friends that work in a strip club."

"It's not a strip club. And you know all I do is check in things there."

"I know, I know, girlfriend," she said, patting my cheek. "I know, but you still there, still wearing one of the suits that barely cover your behind, and still letting them dudes drool over you for cash."

"They don't drool on me, and you know that I'm just working there to get cash for Amina. Yolanda, why you got to be like this? You know that I'm just trying to take care of my little girl just like you. I'm trying to do something good for her, that's all. It's not fair that everybody is treating me so mean because of it."

"Nobody is treating you mean, China. This is the real world. And honey, I get that you just handling your business. You looking out for your own, now you got to let me look out for mine. I can't hang with you, China. It's as simple as that. Jamal's daddy done already told me how it's got to go down. Simon told me to respect that. He told me to do what I can to get my family back together."

"Oh, he did. Okay, whatever, fine. Go on, live with Jamal's parents. Kick me to the curb. Do whatever you like!" I said. "I don't even care. I don't know how you and Uncle Simon can be so mean!"

"Come on, China Cup, don't be like that. Don't be so immature."

"I'm not immature, and you have a nice life," I told her, and stormed out of her room.

"China, damn, don't be that way. It's only until I can get everything back on track. Come back and help me pack, girl. Don't be so mad about it!"

"Enjoy living in the big house!" I yelled. I opened the screen door and slammed it hard before I raced down the steps and out of the front gate.

• • •

I don't know what I was feeling when I got back to my house a few minutes later. I had gone to Yolanda's place to try and get back a friend, only to find out that it wasn't possible. I guess I could have dealt with it if she had told me that she was moving a thousand miles away from the neighborhood, but she wasn't. The only thing she was moving away from was me. I wasn't good enough to hang around with her and her kids anymore. I couldn't believe it. It made me feel dirty, like my insides were garbage. Me, her best girlfriend. I wasn't good enough to spend time with anymore, that's what Jamal's father had told her, and Uncle Simon, my uncle, had backed him up. My uncle Simon, the person who waited up for me to come home each night. How could he do that to me? How could he tell my homegirl that it was okay to kick me to the curb and move in with folks she didn't care anything at all for? It was just plain ole mean. I would never do him like that. I flung open the front door and marched in the house to try and get him to explain himself to me. I got as far as the living room when the sight of Trip cut me off. He was sitting on the sofa with his hands in his lap, looking on the outside like I felt on the inside.

"What's wrong with you?" I asked.

"China, what did you say to my mama?" he said with his arms folded across his chest.

"What do you mean? I didn't say anything to her."

"In the bathroom at church, what did you say to her?" he asked in almost an accusatory tone.

"What does she say I said?" I asked back in the same tone.

"I don't know, but she's acting all funky. She says you really made her mad, and all she was trying to do was give you some advice. You really upset her, China. Now I'm just trying to figure out what's going on."

"That makes two of us, 'cause I don't have a clue what you're talking about. Shronda Faye got on my case, so I set her straight about some things."

"What things?"

"Look, nothing, okay. I just told her to stay out of my business. She was riding me about my job, and about you."

"What about me?"

"You know, the same ole crap. She doesn't like the fact that we had a kid, that's all. She's still in my face about it, blaming me for what happened to Amina, and for you not doing what she wants you to do. She says that she doesn't like you sending off your sci-fi and fantasy stories. She thinks you're wasting your time."

"She said that. I don't believe she said that," he said.

"Of course she did. She told me that she doesn't like you spending her money on stamps and typing paper. She says you're wasting money on something that is never going to happen."

"No she didn't. My mama likes to have things her way. She gets on me sometimes about spending too much time writing, but she would never say anything like that."

"Maybe she won't to your face, but behind your back she thinks that you would be better off in the military. She thinks being all Hollywood isn't for you."

"I don't believe that, China," he said. "You just don't like my mama. You never want to give her a chance."

"You mean she never wants to give me a chance. You know she doesn't even like me being on the planet with you."

"That's not true either. You just make it difficult for her," he said, way too nastily for my taste.

"I make it difficult for her. Okay, Trip, fine, I'm not going there with you this afternoon. Shronda Faye got all over me, so I kicked her off, it's as simple as that, so just quit sweating me about it. I've already had a bad day. Yolanda is moving, did you know that? She's moving in with Jamal's parents. She's going to live with them, and she says that I can't hang around with her anymore. She says we can't be friends and that Uncle told her it was okay. I can't believe he did that. It was so unfair and cruel. So right now I'm going to go get on him about it!" I snapped, walking off. He snatched the back of my jacket.

"No you're not, China Cup," he said, yanking me down next to him on the sofa. "You're not gonna go make him upset over this."

"Yes I am. Yolanda's my friend. He had no right to tell her not to be friends with me anymore. How could he hurt me like that? It's not fair. He had no right."

"He had every right. She's his friend too, and besides, you're the one that asked him to help her."

"I did ask him to help her, but I didn't ask him to tell her to toss me aside, like I was a carton of smelly sour milk. He should have known better than that. How could he be so dumb?"

"How could you?" he asked.

"What? Why are you taking his side?"

"I'm not taking anybody's side. Man, China, when you don't get things, you really don't get them. You don't get it at all. Yolanda isn't just leaving you—she's leaving your uncle Simon, too."

"So what, she's my friend. What does he care?"

"He cares. China, I guess you haven't noticed it, but your uncle Simon really likes Yolanda, I mean *really* likes her."

"What? Likes her how?"

"How do you think? Why do you think he was so eager to help her out? Why do you think he was going over to her house and spending time with her kids? He didn't shave his beard off to look younger for you. Why do you think he can sit around laughing with her for hours, about stuff that nobody else in the world could find funny? Think about it, China. How do you think he likes her?"

"Oh my God," I said, and placed my hand over my mouth.

"You know what?" Trip continued. "She likes him too. Why do you think she keeps bringing him those special boxes of doughnuts?

I come by some nights while you're at Obsidian's and she and her kids are always here. They are sitting right here in this room watching some silly family show."

"What? Be for real. Yolanda just got her kids taken away because they caught her with one of her old boyfriends."

"That may be true, but I am for real. Yolanda and your uncle Simon have been into each other for a long time. Anybody could see that, anybody but you. Because the only thing China can see is China. China thinks everything is always about her."

"Trip, you know what Uncle did wasn't right. So don't even start trippin' on me," I said.

"I'm not tripping. I'm being honest, and you know it's true. You haven't had time for your uncle Simon or anyone else since Amina died. You act like you're the only one that lost her. I guess you forgot that your uncle lost her too."

"I didn't forget anything, Trip. I know who lost what, but I'm the one who carried Amina for nine months. I'm the one who cleaned up her poop, and washed spit-up off of her dresses. I'm sorry I didn't know about Uncle and Yolanda, but I'm not gonna take any guff over it or anything else. I'm not gonna take it from you or your mama. And by the way, she really did say that you were just wasting your time writing story ideas, and I stood up for you. I got your back. It would be nice if you got mine sometimes."

"All I ever to do is get your back, China. Just do yourself a favor and don't go getting on your uncle's case for telling Yolanda to take care of her business. He doesn't deserve that, and in case you still don't get it, let me say it one more time, not everything is about you."

"Okay, fine. I'm tired of people telling me that. Nobody understands how I feel," I whined. Then I got all sarcastic again. "Go be with your mama, Trip. I'm sure you can help her get over whatever trauma I put her through."

"Fine, whatever. You should check on your uncle. He was okay this morning, but now he's all down. He's in his room. I asked him if he wanted some lunch, but he said he wasn't hungry."

"Me neither. Go home to your mommy," I said, getting up from the sofa.

"At least I have one to go home to," he shot back. "All you got is an uncle, and you won't even have him if you keep treating him like he don't even matter."

"I don't treat him like that, Trip," I said defensively.

"Him, me, and everybody else, my dark sister. Try getting over yourself for just a little while," he said, and walked to the front door. I waited for him to go out of it, then I ran and locked the latch behind him. After that, I went straight to Uncle's room and rapped on the door.

"You in there, Uncle?" I called out in a normal voice.

"I'm busy right now, China," he called back.

"I know. I only wanted to know if you would like some lunch."

"No, I'm not hungry. Go on and fix yourself something to eat, baby," he said.

"Are you sure? We can have breakfast again for lunch. I can make those pecan waffles that you like."

"I'm not hungry, China," he repeated. "I'm okay, you take care of yourself."

"Okay," I said, but I didn't want to leave it that way. I opened the door and went into his room anyway. What I saw disturbed me. He was at his small worktable holding the figurines of Yolanda and one of her twin boys. The rest of the kids were spread out among the red clay scraps on the table. I walked over and picked up Keisha's figurine.

"It looks just like that little, bad big-head girl, except there's no 'Devil Child' carved in the forehead," I said, hoping he would at least smile. I got nothing. He simply dropped Yolanda's figurine and picked up the one of little Eboni.

"You sure you don't want lunch?" I asked.

"I'm sure," he said.

"Are you certain?"

"I'm certain," he said, looking up at me. I noticed a few scraggly gray-black hairs jutting out from his chin and upper lip. He was changing back to his old self. I could tell he was grieving again, only this time it wasn't just for Amina. There was a sadness in his eyes that I hadn't seen since she died. I don't know how I could have missed what was going on.

"Where did you go?" he asked me.

"I went to see Yolanda. I wanted to make things right again. She's moving," I said.

"Yeah, I know. She's moving in with Jamal's parents, and she doesn't like it, but it's the right thing to do. They'll give her back her kids. She can hopefully start a brand-new life."

"What about the life she had? What about that life?" I asked.

"What about it?"

"I don't know. It just doesn't seem fair that she can't live the way she wants anymore. She told me that she can't even hang with me at all. I don't see how that's right."

"China, not everything is about being right, or even fair. I think I've said this to you many times before, that some things are just about accepting the inevitable and dealing with it. It's about figuring out how to reshape the messes we get ourselves into. That's what I told Yolanda that she needed to figure out—how to get herself out of the mess."

"Am I part of the mess?" I asked.

"No, baby," he said, grabbing me by the waist and pulling me to his side. "You're not a part of the problems Yolanda has, and I'm not either. But she's going to have to walk away from us and try and clear them up."

"You like her, don't you? Trip told me you liked her more than I thought you did."

"Trip's right. I like her, like I thought I would never be able to like anyone since I had my accident years ago. She makes me feel like I'm completely done on the outside, and not just halfway finished. Do you know what I'm talking about?"

"I think so," I said. "Mama used to say that love can sometimes come with some really funky complications—and I guess I'm the complication."

"No, not really. Like I said, Yolanda has had problems for a long time, and she just has to make some adjustments to work through them."

"I'm one of those adjustments."

"You and me. We're part of a whole—mixed in the same batch, poured into the same mold, and fired in the same kiln. Whatever adjustments she makes regarding you, she also has to make regarding me."

"That's not fair," I mumbled.

"It's not about being fair. It's about her holding her babies in her arms again. Now go on, girl. Go make yourself some lunch. I'm not hungry," he said, grabbing me and giving me a hug.

"Okay," I said, pulling away from him. I walked to the door.

"Oh yeah, you got a call from Brother Agee down at the funeral parlor. He says he needs you to come by and talk to him about your account."

"What about it?"

"I'm not sure, China, he didn't say. Just run by there when you get a chance."

"All right," I said. I left the room and went back to mine. When I got there I sat down on my bed, stunned. Yolanda and Uncle, more than friends, maybe on their way to being some kind of lovers. Why didn't I see it? Why didn't I see that the changes in Uncle, and his willingness to go over to Yolanda's house whenever she called, meant that a relationship was blooming between them? Now the relationship was over, because of my job at Obsidian Queens. It wasn't right. Yolanda wasn't being fair. She knew how much it was gonna hurt Uncle Simon to lose her. I hated her for it, and in truth hated myself even more. Who did Uncle have left? Because of me he had already lost Amina, now I had run off his girlfriend, too. Yolanda had issues, but she seemed to respect Uncle a lot. I think they could have been good together, if I hadn't ruined it.

I got up from the bed and pulled my old history book off the small bookshelf sitting against the wall. I opened it and pulled out some cash I had been saving for Amina's funeral. I rolled the dollar bills up and stuck them in my bra. "I'm going to the funeral home, Uncle," I hollered as I tossed the book on my bed. On my way out of the house I turned off all the emotions in me again. There was nothing I could do about Uncle, or about Yolanda changing her whole life because Eboni's grandparents said she had to. All I could do was take care of my daughter. There was nothing more important than that, nothing more important than making sure she got the best.

CHAPTER 9

Each year Uncle and I attend Bobby's Rib Shack's
annual "Eat Everything on the Table Night." It usually takes place
the day before Bobby's birthday. It's a time for the maids and jani-
tors, garbage men and street sweepers, hair dressers, yard men, and
shop owners to hang out together in fellowship. People make
friends, get tips on jobs, hear the latest church gossip, even sometimes find a future husband or wife. It's a big deal in our hood, and
usually everybody has a wonderful time enjoying the smoky meats
and delicious fixings. But every once in a while somebody does something dumb. Some brother gets jealous because another dude is
macking on his girl, and pulls out a blade, or some gang kids show up
and get into a squabble. On those occasions things go bad quickly.
Right away about a third of the people get disgusted at the violence
and leave, and when the incident is really terrible just about everybody takes off. Then the law comes around and hauls whoever is left
down to the police station. That's the worst. It makes the entire
neighborhood upset. For weeks afterward everyone is depressed.
We are all left wondering how just a few people can make things
unfair and ugly for everyone else. When I ask Uncle Simon about
it, all he ever says is evil happens. You can't make sense out of some
things that people do.

Of course I know he's right, and the afternoon that I went to see
Brother Agee about my funeral bill I was reminded how much. I

didn't know what Brother Agee had called me in for, but I was hoping he was going to tell me I was mostly paid up. Every dollar and tip I'd made at the club had gone toward Amina's bill. It wasn't unusual for me to work ten to twelve hours a night, trying to get the bill paid off. Lately I'd been too distracted to add up the exact amount I still owed, but the last time I looked I was pretty close to paying off the bill. When I went back into his business office and sat across from the painting of the Sudanese women carrying large cloth bundles on their heads, I was really excited—until the overhead ceiling fan broke loose and slammed into my head.

"China, I have really bad news," Brother Agee said, leaning over the desk in his colorful dashiki. "I was going to tell your uncle about it, but I thought that it would be better if we spoke face to face."

"What is it?" I asked.

"It's about the headstone that you bought for your little girl."

"What about it?"

"I don't know if you saw the *Neighborhood Times* paper a couple of days ago, but there was some vandalism down at Peaceful Rest Cemetery. Some of the graves were desecrated."

"I don't read that paper, sir. What do you mean by desecrated?"

"Well, some of the graves were bothered—headstones were run over and smashed, mausoleums were broken into, some of the in-ground markers were tagged with gang symbols, and even the monument that lists the names of the buried slaves was broken into pieces."

"Why would somebody do something terrible like that?"

"I'm not sure. It was probably some kids from another neighborhood. I refuse to believe that any children from this neighborhood would do it. Anyway, I'm sorry to tell you this, but your little girl's stone was one that was smashed."

"Amina's stone? Why, Amina never hurt anybody. Are you sure?" I asked.

"Yes, I'm sorry. Many of the stones that got knocked over were newer stones, ones that were simple to uproot. Your little girl's was only set a little while ago. I'm afraid it was an easy target."

"Easy target. I can't believe it," I said, shaking my head.

"Neither can I. There's no history of this kind of tragedy at Peaceful Rest. It's a neighborhood cemetery. Most people around here treat it like it's holy ground."

"Yeah, nobody around here would do something so ugly. It doesn't make sense. We have to get her another one right away."

"That's what I called you about," he said, reaching in his desk drawer and pulling out a manila folder with mine and Amina's names on it. "I called you because I was sure you would want to get another stone, and because this is so very unusual."

"What do you mean?"

"I mean the whole situation is unique. You see, because Peaceful Rest is an old neighborhood cemetery, I'm afraid it doesn't have insurance to cover an incident like this," he said with a pitiful face.

"Excuse me?"

"Well, they don't really have a way of reimbursing you for the stone. We can get you a replacement, special ordered, and as wonderful as the first one, but I'm afraid that you are going to have to pay the replacement cost."

"I have to pay it? Why do I have to pay it? That's not right. Why isn't it the cemetery's responsibility to take care of it?"

"It is, but like I said, Peaceful Rest is primarily a small neighborhood cemetery. Not very many folks get buried there anymore. They often operate on a miniscule budget, and have even been known to donate plots to folks who can't afford them. They simply don't have the money to replace all the damaged stones. You can sue them, but it would probably take a long time, and I'm not even sure what the outcome would be."

"I don't want to sue them. I don't know nothing about that. All I know is my mama told me the cemetery was the first thing that folks in the neighborhood created. She said they created it to rebury some of the slaves that they brought with them from the plantations. She told me that when the slaves were given freedom, some of them didn't want to leave their loved ones behind. They dug up the ones that were buried in caskets and brought them along."

"Exactly, the cemetery is a very historic place, and sometimes we have to sacrifice for history. I'm sure you've learned that in school, learned that we often have to give things up to get the things we want. That's just the way it is. Everything comes with a fee."

"Excuse me, sir. I don't . . ."

"Oh," he said, and broke into a comforting smile. "All I meant was it wouldn't be a good idea to try and get the cemetery to pay for a replacement."

"Oh, yes sir. I see that, but what about the people who made the stone? Don't they have to do something if it breaks? Isn't there some kind of guarantee on it?"

"Yes, they guarantee that it gets here safely, and that it will hold up for a certain amount of time, but there's no guarantee against intentional destruction."

"So I have to do it by myself," I said.

"Yes, I'm sorry, but that's the only sure way. If it helps any, I contacted the maker of the headstone. I informed them of your predicament. They have agreed to give you the replacement stone at a fifteen percent discount. When I worked the numbers out this morning I came up with roughly around fifteen hundred bucks. That's what it will cost to rush it here and get it back in the ground immediately. If you like, I can simply tack the figure on to our existing agreement. Is that okay with you?"

"Is it okay with me?" I said with a sigh. How could it not be? What choice did I have? The stone was gone. I had to purchase another one. Could I simply lay plastic flowers on Amina's grave, like some of the other folks did in our hood? Could I hope they didn't melt in the hot Texas sun, hope someone didn't come along and think they would look better on their little girl's grave? I had bought the best for my daughter, and I wanted her to have it, even if it meant I had to work from sunup until sundown to pay for it. That's what mothers do, work for the things their children have to have.

"Should I tack it on? Do you think you will still be able to fulfill our agreement, if I do? You have to let me know now, China. I have great faith in you, but I took a big risk in allowing you to take on this kind of debt in the first place. My boss, Ms. Aldrich, wasn't very happy when I told her about the deal we made. She thought it was foolish of me to make this contract with someone so young. My job is on the line here, China. You've done very well so far, but you have to let me know if you can handle this addition to your commitment."

"I can handle it. I won't let you get in trouble about it. It wouldn't be fair. You've been super to me."

He grinned again.

"Good, I trust you," he said, putting the folder away. "You're a good mother. I trust that you can get this paid. Besides, I believe that I told you before, you don't want to have any trouble with this. A debt like this can follow you around for a long time, if you don't pay it. You don't want it to mar any future plans you might have for your life. And suppose something happens to your uncle Simon. Insurance only goes so far. You might need to acquire a personal loan to help him out. It would be a shame if he couldn't get lifesaving medical care because you couldn't borrow the cash, wouldn't it?"

"I won't let that happen. I won't let my uncle suffer for me," I said, getting up from the chair. "I'll make sure everything is paid on time. You just replace the stone."

"As good as done. I'll tell them to hurry the job, and it will be here as quick as a flash, my little African Queen," he said, extending his hand. I shook it and left. When I returned home I called Louisa, and asked her if I could come to work. She said yes, and I slipped into my bikini uniform.

"You're going to work on a Sunday?" Uncle Simon asked, rolling into my room.

"Yeah, I'm gonna work the Sunday 'Surf's Up Brunch.' I'll be back later," I said.

"China, I wish you wouldn't go do that, but I know better than to try to get you to understand why you shouldn't."

"I'll see ya when I see ya, Uncle," I said.

"China, what did Brother Agee want to talk to you about?" he called as I left my room.

"Nothing much, he only wanted to tell me how happy he was that I was taking care of Amina's account," I lied. And with that said I went to work. I couldn't find the words to tell him what was going on. It hurt me too much to even think about somebody being cruel enough to break Amina's stone. I didn't want to hurt him, too. *What the willows don't know won't make them weep*. Uncle would find out about the stone soon enough. I already had enough to worry about. I didn't have time to stop and comfort him about Yolanda *and* Amina's problems. I went back to work that Sunday, and I've gone every Sunday since then. I've also added extra hours on to my shift. Last evening it was nearly 3 A.M. when I got in. Uncle was waiting up to jump on my case about it.

"China, you've got to tell those people to stop working you so late. It's ridiculous!" he shouted.

"I will," I said on my way to my room, and that was the farthest thing from the truth. I did the complete opposite. This evening when I got to work I went straight up to Louisa and asked her if she could give me even more extra work. I didn't know it was possible, but my request actually shocked her.

"More work, China honey? I don't see how you can possibly

handle more work. You've been working just about every hour this club is open," she said, stepping out of the bathroom in a white halter-top pantsuit. She closed the bathroom door and peeled off the pants, revealing a matching French-cut bikini bottom, that I knew all the dudes would have their eyes glued to the minute we opened the club door.

"I have been working a lot, but it ain't nothing but a thing. I can handle more," I said drowsily.

"Can you?" she said, setting down at one of the dressing tables to touch up her already flawless makeup. "China, I don't think you can. Sugar, I really appreciate your enthusiasm. You've done really good here for the past few months. You work hard, and I've never had to get on you about being late or missing a shift, but China, I got a rule here. I don't like my girls to work longer than they can handle. I know that we call this a gentlemen's club, but it should be obvious to you that not all the men who come here are gentlemen."

"I know that," I said, wriggling out of my cotton panties and slipping into my own swimsuit bottom.

"Good, sugar, and I want you to keep on knowing that. You can't, if you too tired from pulling too many hours. Sleepy girls aren't alert girls, and here I need you to always be alert because Big Robert is good, but he can't possibly watch every single girl when this place fills up."

"I know that, ma'am. I can look after myself. I really need the extra cash. I have to have it for my little girl," I said, shoving my panties into my backpack. I slipped my shirt off and put it there too.

"What kind of cash you need? 'Cause it's plenty of space for you up there on the dance stage, little high-school girl," Star said, coming in the door. I ignored her. She walked around and got in my face. As usual she was stretching the rules in one of her notice-me outfits. This time she had on a black leather thong, and her top was nothing more than two leather cups stuck to her breasts with some kind of adhesive. "What, you trying to play me off, high-school girl?" she asked.

"I'm not even talking to you. You weren't even part of this conversation," I said.

"I'm part of it now," she said, rolling her eyes. "So don't be getting all smart-assed with me. I'm just trying to help you out. You say you need some cash, I'm just trying to tell you how to make some."

"Go away," I said.

"I'm not going . . ."

"Star, honey, back off of that girl and leave her be. It's bad enough I got to get dressed in here because one of the clients is using my room. I don't need to listen to you being stupid as well."

"I'm not being stupid, Louisa. I'm just trying to help out the girl. She say she needs money to pay for her little girl. I'm just telling her how to make it. Hell, a sweet little high-school girl like her can make four hundred bucks a night dancing."

"I'm not a high-school girl, and I'm not interested in doing what *you* call dancing," I said.

"What *I* call dancing? Look, little grade-school heifer. I'll have you know I was dancing before you could even write your name. Don't even try to tear my stuff down. I'm a professional."

"A professional tramp," Sweet Petite said, coming into the dressing room with Swedish Lane, the only one hundrd percent white girl at the club, a curvaceous platinum blond chick with a ghetto accent and a Hollywood bod. "You got that straight, girlfriend," she said, walking around me in her hiphugging jeans and tank top. She stopped at a seat next to Louisa, and started stripping everything off. Underneath was a camouflage-print string bikini.

"Screw you, Sweet, and your Project Barbie friend," Star said, rolling her eyes at Swedish Lane. "I don't know why you trying to sweat me. All I'm doing is schooling the little girl on how to break off some cash around here. It's plenty of dirty ole dogs around that would love to see a little puppy like her up on that stage, and you know we could use somebody else up there with Onyx Moon gone."

"Shut up, Star," Sweet Petite said, pushing me aside. "Don't even open your mouth to bring that up. What makes you think you even have the right to complain about Onyx?"

"She don't. As far as I know she needs to quit flapping her big trap about it," Swedish Lane said, folding up her jeans and placing them in an open drawer of the dressing table.

"I'll shut my mouth when I feel like it. Besides, I got the right to complain about whatever I want to complain about. Hell, I didn't do nothing to that stupid girl," Star said.

"Naw, but you didn't do nothing for her either, you sorry tramp," Sweet Petite said, putting her hands on her hips. It was kind of hard to take her seriously with her yellow fur bathing suit and matching boa, but her body language was coming through loud and clear.

"Okay, okay, ladies, we been through this before," Louisa said, getting up from her chair. "Sweet Petite, just let it go, honey, and you," she said, pointing at Star, "you say you can dance, go dance. Take your tail out of here and stop telling my employees what to do. China already has a job, and if or when she wants to change it ain't your business."

"Whatever," Star said. She marched around me and went to do her thing. I scowled at her back, just wishing I had the nerve to take my shoe off and throw it at her.

"Later for that trashy cow," Swedish Lane said. She put her tank away in the drawer too.

"Shoot, I gotta go work it. I'm trying to get me a new car," she said.

"Go get that down payment, girlfriend," Sweet Petite told her.

"You know I will," Swedish Lane said. She sashayed past us in her camouflage suit, on her way to hunt down some of Star's big-tipping game.

"See ya'll later, girls," she hollered as she closed the door.

"Man, that girl is gonna make a lot of money tonight in that suit. She's going to take plenty of cash from Star. Them fishing dudes that's gonna come up later from the country, they love that kind of suit she got on," Sweet Petite said.

"So do I," Louisa said. "I'm always happy when my girls can please some of the out-of-town customers. Anyway, China darling, I know that you need money. I know that's why you're working here. I think that's great. You're a good mother, but Star is right. Sugar, this is a club for dancers. That's what it's about here. If you want to make the big bucks you have to be willing to get up and show more than your pretty face. You got a nice figure, and these guys really would go crazy over it. I'm willing to give you a shot, if you want it, but I know you don't. Honey, I understand that. I know that's not your thing. Anyway, I wish I could help you out by letting you work more hours, but I have to stand by what I said. I need all my girls on their toes. I can't have you coming in here so drowsy that you can't even watch out for yourself," she said, placing her hands on my shoulders. "Darling, I hope you can find a way to work your financial problems out."

"Yes ma'am," I said.

I finished dressing. After that, I exited the dressing room and went into the club. It was only around six, but a nice crowd of Hispanic brothers was already there. They were wearing the club's homemade birthday hats, cardboard crowns with a beach scene featuring all the dancers in the club. Salsa music was pumped up to full volume, and Star had wasted no time giving the guys the show they had come in for. She was already down to just the leather bottom of her suit, her ample boobs jiggling and bouncing with each of her sexy dance moves. The guys were loving it. They were yelling words at her in Spanish that I could barely understand, except for the words *"Más! Más!"*, which I was fairly certain meant "more." *"La chica es muy buena!*" they kept repeating along with it. I didn't know what that meant, but I figured it had to mean they liked what they were seeing. They would give generous tips before they left the club. I yawned and continued to my post, walking sleepily between the four tables they were occupying. As I did a big guy with shiny black hair trailing down his back grabbed me and pulled me into his lap.

"Hey! Look what I got, how much for this one?" he yelled in English while I struggled to get free. His friends all cracked up.

"*Muy* young and *bonita! Muy* expensive, sugar!" Louisa yelled, stepping out of the back room.

"How expensive?" the guy asked, pawing me and tugging at my suit strap.

"That's up to her, sugar! Do you see a price tag stapled to her behind?"

"Let me see," the guy said, and turned me over his knee. "Man, she got a nice one. Happy birthday to me," he said, laughing, and sticking some kind of bill into my suit bottom.

"Okay, be nice and let her go. She's got work to do," Louisa said, walking over to him. He laughed heartily and turned me loose. Before I could get out of reach he swatted me hard on the rump. I walked to my counter rubbing my tailbone.

"Hey pretty girl! You want to make some real money? Meet me out by my car in the back when you get off!" the Hispanic guy yelled at me. "A sexy little *niña* like you. I'll pay whatever price you charge." I smiled and took the money out of my suit, like I had done so many times after some fool grabbed me. That seemed to be a big thing with guys, grabbing a girl and copping a feel. It still freaked me out some, but I liked the money that came with it. As I stood there I was beginning to think that Star and Louisa were correct. What I could get out of the club was only limited by what I was willing to put into it. I watched Star dancing her moneymaker around a new pole that Louisa had recently put in because some of the guys wanted it. They were howling like crazy. When she left for the evening she would be taking off with the cash I desperately needed.

"*Más! Más!*" all the guys screamed, and started throwing crumpled twenties at the stage. I took a rag from underneath the counter and started cleaning dust from the shelves.

It was around one A.M. The club was overflowing with rowdy, excited brothers, twin sisters Donna and Rodonna were dancing underneath a huge beach umbrella, the shelves behind me were filled with hats and backpacks, and I was about to fall over my counter from lack of sleep, when Louisa came over and told me to take off for the evening. "China, I think it's time for you to say good night," she said. "Put your clothes on and you come on back here and work tomorrow. I got this for the rest of the evening."

"But I can work a couple more hours, ma'am," I said.

"Not tonight. Honey, go home and go to bed. Hell, I'm about to drop myself."

"Yes ma'am," I said, disappointed. I went back to the dressing room and opened the door, just in time to see Star finishing up one of her personal dances with a shy round brother who owned a garbage dump on the other side of the tracks. The minute he saw me he pushed Star away from him and bolted like a teenage boy getting caught by his girl's father.

"What the?" Star yelled, putting her clothes back on. I snatched my bag and shimmed into my shorts and top in the hallway. When I was finished I went through the back door of the club. I was halfway down the block when Star came running after me. I could barely see her face with just a sliver of moon beaming through the clouds, but I'm certain anger was having a good time all over it.

"Hey, little high-school girl, you just cost me a lot of money," she said, jumping in front of me.

"Go away," I said. "I'm sure there's plenty more dudes you can cheat out of their money tonight."

"Cheat? Cheat nothing. Please, little girl, you wish you could work these guys the way I do. These men give me everything I want. Shoot, I got a nice car, a damn good apartment, jewelry, all kinds of credit cards. You wish you could be me."

"Not even in my nightmares. You just somebody that wanted to be something and ended up being nothing," I said.

"What? Who told you that, that stupid little Onyx? You don't know what you even talking about," she spat. "I've been places and done stuff you'll never even know about," she said.

"Oh yeah, I know about it, and so does Louisa. I don't know why she don't fire your trashy butt. I don't like you. You make me sick."

"'I don't like you. You make me sick,'" she mimicked. "You sound like a baby. And you think like one too, especially if you believe Louisa gonna fire me," she said, laughing an ugly laugh. "Louisa ain't gonna hardly do that. You really don't know nothing, do you, little schoolgirl? Just wait till you know what I know. You won't be acting like you better than the rest of us that work here at the club."

"I don't act like I'm better than anybody."

"Yes you do," she said with a smirk. "You act like you too good to dance and play up to the dudes. Hell, sometimes you even act like you too good to take the money them fools be offering."

"That's not true," I said.

"Sure it is. You act like it's some kinda crime to take money from idiots that don't even have enough sense to hang on to it. You really are dumb, as dumb as that little messed-up Onyx chick, running around here throwing her life away on a high. Little fool. I knew she was a loser when I met her. I knew she wasn't about to get her life back together. Ain't no way she was about to get cleaned up and get them kids."

"Yes she was; she told me. She just made a mistake. She slipped."

"Slipped nothing, girl, that fool ain't never stop using. You think Skinner was giving her drugs she didn't want? You think he tied her up with her swimsuit top and made her take them?"

"Naw," I honestly said. "I don't know why she did, but I know she took 'em herself."

"You don't know why? That don't surprise me. I figure you ain't never took nothing but a Tylenol. Well good for you, and good for you for knowing that Little Ms. Onyx was the one screwing her own self up. At least that's something you know. 'Cause you downright clueless about everything else, clueless—but one day you're gonna find out," she said, laughing.

"I gotta go. I gotta get home," I said.

"What for? It ain't like you got no kid or nothing to take care of," she yelled as I took off down the street.

"Forget you!" I yelled back. I wanted to go back and slap her face until it was as black as that stupid leather swimsuit she had on, but I left girlfriend to a harsher punishment. I left her standing there in the dark with just a sliver of moon to light up her angry pale face. It was one of the few spotlights she would ever get.

I didn't go home. I knew that Uncle would be waiting up to jump on my case about working so late, and I wasn't in the mood for it. I cut through the dark parking lot across the street from the club and walked in the opposite direction. In the darkness I tried to shake off Star's comments. She didn't know what she was talking about. I didn't think I was better than the other ladies at the club, and I hadn't been a schoolgirl since Amina died. Lately I wanted to be one again more than anything. I wanted to go back to before I got the call from Mrs. Mayfield about my daughter. It would be nice if I could be there again, if I could really be a fourteen-year-old girl who hated history class and enjoyed going to sci-fi flicks with my best friend. Star had no idea how much I wanted to go back to that, wanted to and couldn't. The truth is I needed to make the big bucks just like her. I owed it to my daughter, and Brother Agee who had put everything on the line for me. I sighed and headed for the safest route to Trip's house. It was the one that would take me well out of the way of the junkies and thugs that liked to prowl the streets and alleys after the sun went down.

The lights in Trip's house were all out when I got there. I was happy about that. I didn't want to have to explain to his moms what I was doing there in the middle of the night. I crept around the side of the house and pressed my head against the warm glass of his window. I couldn't hear a thing. It was completely quiet inside. I tapped lightly on the glass, then harder. I heard the bed creak and a low groan. So I rapped again, but no response. Finally, I checked the window. Sometimes Trip forgets to latch it before he turns in. I pushed up on the old frame. It screeched and I heard the bed creak again. A second later Trip appeared at the window.

"China, what the heck? I was just now trying to catch some z's," he said sleepily.

"Let me in," I said. He yanked the window up and I crawled through it.

"Girl, you must done lost your mind," he said, grabbing his king-sized *Outer Realm* T-shirt off of the chair next to the window, and pulling it down over his white boxers.

"No I haven't. I just didn't want to go home," I said, walking over to the bed and sitting down on it. He came and sat next to me.

"Why not?" he said, and yawned loudly.

"I just—" A couple of coughs came from the room down the hall and interrupted me.

"Wait, Shronda Faye sleeps like a cat. It hardly takes anything to get her eyes open, and she been acting all strange since you and her got into it a while back. I don't know what's up with her. I better close the door," he said, getting up from the bed and walking over to it. He closed it quietly and came tiptoeing back over to me.

"Why don't you want to go home?" he asked again.

"I just don't. I know Uncle is sitting there waiting to get on me about being so late."

"Probably," he said, running his hand through his long unbound hair. "I'm sure he is. It's his way of making certain that you haven't slipped on something and fallen through a hole into the center of the earth."

"Can you do that?"

"Theoretically yes, I suppose, but it would have to be one really deep hole."

"I know deep holes," I said. He yawned again.

"Yeah, you do. You certainly been falling your behind into them ever since I met you. I guess we both have."

"Naw, mostly just me. Can I stay here tonight?"

"Yeah, of course, if you give me the real four-one-one on why you're crawling up in my window tonight."

"I just told you. I don't want to deal with Uncle Simon tonight. Ever since Yolanda went away he's been all up in my Kool-Aid. He really misses her and them bad kids. Since they been gone he's been all over me. He wants to know what I'm doing all the time. Yesterday evening he even called the club when I didn't come home at my regular time."

"Good for him," Trip said, leaning back on one of his pillows. "That's what he supposed to do, look out for you. I hate you coming home so late too. In fact, I hate you walking home in the dark, period. I wish I was still walking you home each night."

"You can't. You have to get up for school early each morning," I said, lying down next to him. I pulled his corny *Star Trek: The Next Generation* comforter around me. "You really got to get rid of this kiddy stuff," I said.

"What I got to get rid of is having to go to school all the time. I hate year-round school. But please girl, this is *Star Trek*. If you ask me, it's the mother of all science fiction. The reason why people finally started giving sci-fi its due. My comforter ain't for kids. It's for true believers, folks with serious vision. And by the way, I didn't say you could stay yet," he said, tugging the cover back off of my legs. "Now with that said, break it down to me, my dark sister. Why you crowding me out tonight?"

"I'm not crowding you. There's plenty of room for both of us," I said, snatching at the comforter.

"If I say so. It is still my bed, girlfriend," he said. "Come on. Give up the issues."

I didn't say anything. I sighed and looked out the window. The leafy branches of the bushes next to his house looked like giant insect antennae waving about.

"You have giant bugs outside your window," I finally said. He looked at the branches too.

"I prefer to think of them as bug-shaped aliens from another planet. They came here to beam me up in my sleep, so they could examine a rare, excellent specimen of man, but my gal pal showed up at my window and screwed it all up."

"Shut up," I said, laughing. Another series of loud coughs erupted from Shronda Faye's room.

"We better whisper, my dark sister," Trip said. "Now what's going on?" I hesitated again for a little bit longer.

"If I did something really stupid would you stop being my friend?" I asked, turning in the direction of his face.

"Apparently not, because lately all you seem to do is stupid stuff," he said, and laughed.

"I'm serious," I said. "Would you quit being my friend?" He stopped laughing.

"Explain serious, and exactly what you're talking about."

"Just answer me. If I did something stupid would you still hang around with me?"

"Do what stupid? Girl, what are you going on about?" he said, turning to me.

"Something's happened."

"Something what?"

"Have you been by the cemetery lately? Have you seen Amina's grave?"

"Naw, I told you Mama been acting funny. I been hanging out here most of the time, trying to see what's going on with her."

"What is going on with her?"

"I don't know, she all moody, like it's a lot of stuff going on in her head."

"We got something else to be worried about. Something bad has happened at Amina's grave. Trip, somebody went and broke her headstone. Why would somebody do something like that?"

"Her stone? Somebody broke it?"

"Yeah, Brother Agee said the cemetery thinks it was some kids. They broke up a bunch of stones. Amina's was one of them."

"Aw man, I can't believe that. Who do we know would be that low-down? Most of the kids we know aren't into that kind of thing. Remember last year when that fool Akim tried to throw a Halloween party down there, and nobody showed up?"

"Yeah, I remember that."

"Yeah, me too. Everybody knew better, even them thugs like Reese and Duane, and them fools don't care about nothing. Man, I wish I could get my hands on the bastard that touched my little girl's grave."

"Me too. Anyway, now I got a problem," I said, pulling the cover back over my legs. "Amina doesn't have a stone anymore, so I have to start over, buy the whole thing from jump."

"What do you mean from jump? Wasn't there some kind of insurance on it? Can't you get something like that?"

"I guess not. Brother Agee says they don't cover a stone if

somebody deliberately breaks it. He says I just have to buy a new one."

"Okay, I see what you're saying. I understand that. What I'm still fuzzy on is the you doing something stupid part. China, what are you talking about?"

"I got into an argument tonight with Star," I said.

"That light-skinned mean chick at the club you're always talking about?"

"Yeah, her."

"Why?"

"She said things that pissed me off. I guess she was kinda right, though."

"Right about what?"

"She called me a little girl and said that the only way to make any money at the club was to get up on the stage."

"And that made you get into an argument with her? China, I don't know what you're getting at. What are you—oh no, no way, girl," he said quickly, sitting up. "China, you're not going to start doing that. You're not going to start taking your clothes off like them low-class heifers. No way in the world!" he shouted.

"Trip, you awake?" Shronda Faye's voice burst out. We both got really quiet, and we stayed that way until we thought she had gone back to sleep.

"China, forget it," Trip whispered when we heard her snoring.

"Trip, I told you somebody broke our daughter's stone. I have to replace it. Brother Agee added it on to our original agreement. I have to get it paid off in the same amount of time."

"That doesn't make sense," Trip said.

"I know it doesn't, but I don't have a choice. He says his boss is all upset because he made the agreement with me. I don't have a choice, Trip. I have to pay for a new stone or Amina won't have nothing. That's what he told me."

"Okay then, I'll pay the replacement costs. I'll get a job, and I got some comic books and cards around here that I know are worth at least a couple of hundred bucks. I'll sell everything, get the bill paid off that way."

"No, that's not what I want," I said, sitting up in the bed and shaking my head. "It's not what I want at all. Trip, I have to pay for the stone myself. It's my responsibility, not yours. I have to take care of it. I had her, you didn't. I have to be the one to make sure she's okay. I have to do it."

"China, we've had this conversation before. Amina was my kid too. What makes you think I don't need to do something for her?"

"I didn't say that, and I don't wanna get into it again. I'm doing this. I'm taking care of my little girl. She was mine."

"No, she was ours, and I've heard you say that so many times it's like a echo in my ear. It's like being stuck in a time loop where everything just keeps repeating."

"Okay, fine, then by now you should get it. I don't want your help with this. I need to do it."

"You wanted my help at first."

"You and your mama didn't have any money. That's what you told me, so I didn't expect any out of you, and I still don't. I need to do this on my own."

"By taking your clothes off for some dudes that would have a fit if they saw their daughters or sisters doing the same thing. You're gonna pay for it by exposing everything to some sorry dudes that don't know how to stay home and keep it real with their wives or girlfriends. China, what would make you think that's a good idea? Your mama raised you better than that, and your uncle would be crushed if he knew you were doing something so foolish and dangerous."

"It's not dangerous. It's just work, and the money is great," I said, raising my voice a little. "Star is right about that. It's where the real money is."

"Be serious, girl," he snapped. "China, quit trippin', okay. You see what happened to your friend Onyx Moon. You see how messed up she is."

"Onyx didn't get screwed up at Obsidian's, Trip. She came there that way. Louisa was being nice to her, simply trying to help her out with some decent work."

"Some decent work? China, your brain really has gone where no brain has gone before. You're trippin' hard and long if you think working in a place like that didn't have something to do with your friend hitting the streets again, trying to score from any fool she comes across. Trust me, my dark sister, it's all about where you work."

"Okay, fine, whatever, Trip. Stop being so ugly to me about it. I'm not going to keep arguing with you. I'm gonna do what I have to do. I know what I'm doing is all right. Louisa said it would be fine. Anyway, I don't need your permission. I was just telling you how it was going to go down."

"Well, I'm telling you how it's not gonna go down," he said sternly. "China, you're not going to start taking it all off at that stupid club or anywhere else. You're not going to start shaming yourself. If you do, I'm going to go tell your uncle, and I'll bet you he'll have you out of that place before you can even get up to the stage."

"What? Forget you, Trip. I don't need you to tell me what I can do with my life. You don't even know what you're talking about. You're not my husband or my boyfriend, and you sure as heck ain't my father. You don't get to tell me what to do, not today or ever."

"Okay, that's cool. I don't, but your uncle Simon does, and if you keep acting all ridiculous, I'm gonna run and tell him. Don't think I won't, China. You know I'll tell on you in a minute."

"Aw come on, Trip. Don't bring my uncle into this. Don't do that, Trip," I whined. "You'll just hurt him."

"No, you'll hurt him. If he finds out you're so-called 'dancing' for them dudes that come into Obsidian's, it will tear him up, and I don't care why you're doing it."

"I already told you why I'm doing it, and you better not tell him, Trip. You better not tell him or I swear I'll never say one single word to you again," I said, getting up from the bed.

"I don't believe that," he said.

"Believe it. I swear, Trip, if you tell him I won't speak to you again, ever."

"Then don't speak to me," he said, "'cause I rather you not speak to me again than watch you turn into some kind of slut."

"I'm not a slut, and you know that. Okay, fine, do what you have to do," I said, heading back to the window. The light in the hallway snapped on. The sound of footsteps could clearly be heard on the hardwood floor.

"Trip, what in the world is going on in there?" Shronda Faye yelled out. We dashed to the open window and I crawled out.

"Please don't say anything to Uncle Simon, Trip," I said as I hit the ground. "Just don't say anything, okay? Don't get me into trouble like that."

"China, I'll see you later," he said. He closed the window and went back to his bed. I scrunched down and took off through the alley.

CHAPTER 10

"My Albert told me a funny story this morning," Mrs. Waltrip said to me as she placed a plate of her peanut fudge surprise cookies on the counter next to an old schoolbook called *I Know a Story*. I picked up the book and thumbed through it as she talked. The copyright said *1953*. Inside were classic children stories, *The Three Little Pigs*, *Mr. Vinegar*, *Little Red Riding Hood*, *Goldilocks*, and *The Gingerbread Boy*.

"Amina and I love these," I said. "I can't believe this book was written before we were even born."

"Before a lot of folks were born; those stories have been around a very long time. Anyway, Albert was telling me this story that he read somewhere about this cat burglar."

"What about him?" I asked, picking up one of the cookies.

"Well, Albert says that there was this cat burglar. He was a big-time thief. He stole all kinds of things, but mostly he liked to steal jewelry," she said, walking over to the end of the counter. She pulled a stack of snake- and giraffe-shaped bookmarks out of her ruffled work apron and placed them on the side of the register.

"He stole jewelry and not cats?" I said.

She smiled. "Anyway, this burglar was good," she said. "He was so good that he hit all the great places to rob in the U.S. and then decided to go overseas. Through some other criminal folks, he heard about a lady in Switzerland, and went there."

"What kind of lady?"

"Believe it or not she was a famous chocolate maker. She was known all over Europe for her sweets."

"And had lots of jewels."

"You betcha," she said, taking her wire-framed bifocals off and wiping them on her apron. "She had lots of jewels, so when the burglar heard about them he went over to her house quicker than an uninvited relative to a backyard barbecue. He went over to her place and broke into her safe. Inside he found trays and trays of glistening jewels in elegant settings, and a golden bowl of loose diamonds. He took everything. He stuffed the bigger items into a small bag that he had. He also tucked some in his pants, underneath his arms, and poured the loose diamonds from the bowl right into his mouth."

"Wow," I said, and took a bite out of my cookie.

"Yeah, he was all loaded up when he headed back through the house. He opened the dining-room window to go back out, and just then a light clicked on. It was the beautiful lady of the house. In her hand she held a platter piled high with all kinds of mouthwatering chocolate candies and cakes.

"'You must be hungry from stealing all night,' she said to the burglar. 'Wouldn't you like to have some of my treats?'"

"She said that?"

"Yes, and the minute she did the burglar realized that he hadn't eaten all day because he was too busy planning his caper. He opened his mouth to tell the lady yes, and when he did all the loose diamonds spilled to the floor. They scattered everywhere, so the burglar bent down to retrieve them. When he did the jewels also slipped from underneath his arms, and fell out of the top of his pants. Frantically, he tried to gather his booty up, not knowing that the lady of the house had heard him sneaking in and had called the police before she offered him her treats. The law got there right as he was trying to reclaim the things he had stolen."

"They locked him up?" I said, laughing.

"For a very, very long time," she said, laughing too.

"Now that is stupid," I said.

"Yeah, the crook wasn't too bright."

"You bet. He shouldn't have let the lady get in the middle of his business. He should have hurried out with his stuff, and not let her jam him up." She stopped laughing.

"Is that what you get out of the story?" she asked, coming over and getting a cookie too. "I'm surprised, China. Is that really how you see it?"

"Well, yeah. The dude went there to do what he had to do, and instead of doing it he let somebody tell him different, distract him. It was dumb. He should have handled his own. He would have been all right if it wasn't for her."

"Is that what you think? You really think the low-down crook would have been okay if it wasn't for the owner of the house inter-rupting him?"

"For sure. He woulda made it if he hadn't of listened to her, and besides, we don't know if he was really low-down. I mean, we don't know anything about him. We just think he was a bad guy because he was stealing, but what if he had recently lost his job? What if he had a sick kid at home?"

"What if he did? Albert didn't say anything about that," she said. "He only said the man was a crook, a really stupid crook."

I shrugged my shoulders. "Maybe Albert didn't know the whole tale. Anyway, it was a funny story," I said. The bell over the shop door rang. Two old men came in, dressed in their summer straw hats and wobbling on dog-headed canes. "I need something for my grandson's birthday," one of the men said.

"What age is he?" Mrs. Waltrip asked, going over to him.

"I better jet. I got some errands to run," I said. Mrs. Waltrip waved good-bye to me as I dashed out of the door.

Six blocks later I found myself at the Original Sinbad's Fish Market. I was going to get some fish and crab claws so I could make gumbo for Uncle. I thought a hot bowl of one of his favorite meals would pull him out of the dumps. I was crossing the parking lot when a brand new multipassenger van pulled into the parking spot a few feet in front of me. A second later the driver's side flew open and out stepped Yolanda, or so I thought. She didn't look at all like herself. Her braids were completely gone. Her hair was relaxed and cropped short, like some of those professional chicks that worked in the buildings on Main. She had on a drab gray short-sleeved pantsuit, and her huge black handbag looked like the type of purse that your grandmother would take to a Saturday afternoon revival. She wasn't the fly Yolanda I was used to seeing at all. She looked like someone going to conduct a business meeting or prosecute a case down at the courthouse.

"Yolanda!" I yelled, hoping that a familiar voice would answer. She slammed the door and looked in my direction. It was her all right. I ran over to greet her.

"Yolanda, hey girl, what's up?" I asked with a big grin. She half smiled at me, the corners of her mouth not quite pulling into the full thing.

"Hey, China, what are you doing here?"

"Is that your ride?" I asked, pointing to the van.

"Yeah, Jamal's parents got it for me and the kids. It's got lots of room for my big crew. Everybody don't have to be all squeezed in together."

"Everybody? You got Eboni and the boys back?" I asked, walking over and running my hands over the smooth silver paint on the van.

"Yeah, Jamal's dad was good as his word. He called social services and some judge. The next thing you know that brother who took my kids away was bringing them back to my home."

"You mean their home, don't you? You left your place to live with them."

"I know that, China. I haven't forgotten. I'm just glad to have them back," she said, opening her handbag and reaching into it. She pulled out a folded piece of paper that I knew had to be a grocery list.

"I'm glad you got them back too," I said. She started walking toward the store and I fell into step beside her.

"How's your uncle?" she asked. "Is he still making them figurines out of clay?"

"You know he is. He'll be doing that until he passes away. It makes him feel good when he's creating things."

"So he's feeling pretty good? He's okay?" she asked. I caught her by her wrist.

"He's not okay. He misses hanging out with you, and I'm at work all the time, so he don't have nobody to talk to too much," I said.

"China, don't go there. You know I'm sorry about that. I miss Simon too. It was nice spending time with him. He always had some good advice, and he treated me like he really cared about my feelings."

"He did. He liked you a lot. He still does. You should come by and see him sometimes."

"You know I can't do that," she said, pulling away and walking toward the door again. "We already been through this. I care about your uncle, but I can't let nothing get in the way of me and my kids. I got 'em all back, China. We all living together under the same roof. That's all I care about. I got my kids back. I won't do nothing to get them taken away again. I'm only going to do right by them."

"And what about doing right about yourself? You know you probably ain't gonna meet nobody that cares about you the way my uncle does."

"I know that, but China, I can't be concerned about it," she said, stopping in front of the glass doors of the store. I got to do what's gonna make my kids happy, that's all. I get up every morning and go to work with Jamal's daddy now. I work in his office and help do the books. That's cool with me. You know I'm good in math. I finally get to use the brain God gave me."

"I guess you do," I said. "If that's all you want, to live in somebody else's house, and work at their job."

"Yeah well, I guess it is all I want to do," she said, opening one of the doors and going inside. "Anyway, right or wrong, I'm doing what I'm gonna do, China. You just watch out for yourself. I told you before, you're only a kid. You don't know everything. You don't even know how life is supposed to be. I'm sorry about Simon, I really am. But Jamal's dad kept his promise, now I'm gonna keep mine. Right now it's the only way for me to keep my kids, and I can't spend time with anybody who stands in the way of that."

"Uncle can't stand at all, or don't you remember that?" I said nastily.

"I remember, and I remember that you still work at Obsidian Queens, don't you?"

"I know where I work and I don't need Jamal's stuck-up parents to approve of it. I can do whatever I want to do."

"Yeah, I know. That's the problem."

"Okay fine. You know what, Yolanda. I'ma back off and quit sweating you about Uncle. Do what you want, enjoy having your bad-ass snotty-nosed kids back," I said, and brushed past her into the store.

"I already am. I'm enjoying them just fine," she hollered after me.

Back home I cut small cubes of wheat bread and tossed them into butter seasoned with garlic. I was making croutons for Uncle's side salad. When the cubes were good and soaked I spread them onto a metal cookie sheet, and placed them in a 425-degree oven. While they were toasting the phone rang and I hollered for Uncle to pick it up. A few minutes later he came rolling into the kitchen with the cordless receiver.

"It's Trip, honey," he said, handing me the phone.

"Don't let the croutons burn and your gumbo is in the refrigerator," I said.

"China, you didn't have to do that. You know I can always cook for myself. You ain't got to cook for me all the time."

"I know, but I wanted to do it," I said, and ran to my room.

I closed the door and spoke into the phone. "What's up, where you been?" I asked Trip.

"You know where I been girl, don't front," he said. "I been right here. You the one been trying to avoid me. I haven't heard from you in days."

"I'm not avoiding you. I just been busy," I said.

"Busy trying to see how you can embarrass everybody who cares about you?"

"Busy trying to handle my own affairs."

"Yeah, right. Anyway, China, I need you to come over here. There's something I really need to talk to you about."

"Something like what? Come on, Trip, I don't have time for this. You know I gotta go to work in a little while."

"I know, but China, I really got to talk to you. There's something I need to tell you. I've been asking around. Something funny is going on and I need to talk to you about it in person."

"Like what? Trip, don't try to hang me up today with nonsense. I already spoke to Louisa a few days ago. She told me it was cool with her if I started dancing. She said I could start any time I liked. All she had to do was put me on the schedule, so it's done. You're not gonna stop me from doing it now. You wanna tell Uncle, call him back and tell him. I'll deal with it when I get home."

"China, I'm not about to tell nothing. Just come by here, okay?

I got something I really need to tell you. Just stop by here before you go to the club. We need to talk."

"Trip, I'm not coming by there. I don't feel like arguing anymore. I already know what you have to say," I said, and I hung up the phone. No way was I going to listen to it again. I knew what he wanted to say to me. I had heard it over and over in my head for the past week, the part about me shaming myself and Uncle. What about the shame I was going to bring to my daughter? How would it look, me going back on an agreement I made in her name? Why couldn't he understand that she came first? I had made my decision for her and I was going to stick by it.

I opened my bottom dresser drawer and took out my new costume. It looked like something out of that African musical *Ipi Ntombi*, a tan bra and panty covered up by a detachable supershort beaded skirt that was adorned with some kind of animal-looking fringe. I glanced at myself in the mirror. I imagined what I would look like wearing the suit in some African village. Maybe I would be dancing with a group of other young girls, gaily celebrating the birth of a new baby, or maybe I would be wearing it on my wedding day. I would wear it for my handsome husband that I had just met. In it I would promise to be a good wife, promise to bear lots of kids. Later that evening, after all the guests had gone home, I would very shyly take the suit off for him, and only for him. I could see myself doing that. What I couldn't see was myself taking it off for the guys at Obsidian Queens, and yet that's exactly what I was going to do. I had asked Louisa if I could dance and she seemed very pleased with the idea.

"Sure, China, if dancing is what you really want to do, it will be great for you and the club. We can always use some new talent around here, and the guys do like 'em younger. Men are just like that. Back when I was in school my teachers used say that it was plain ole biology, men being attracted to girls young enough to be their daughters. It's always been that way. You go on and get up there on that stage. You make the guys happy, and get as much money as you need for your little girl," she said, lacing up the back of Sweet Petite's new corset swimsuit.

"Yes, Miss Louisa," I said. And that's exactly what I meant to do. I took my sundress off and put the suit on. As I was moving toward the mirror to get a closer look, Uncle Simon tapped on the door.

"China, you off the phone?" he asked.

"Yes sir," I said, pulling my dress back on. I adjusted it over my suit and opened the door. Uncle rolled in and stopped next to my bed. I sat down on it beside his chair.

"Did you get the croutons out?" I asked.

"Yes, and I made a salad," he said. "Are you getting ready for work?"

"Yeah, I gotta go in a little bit, but I'll be home earlier tonight."

"Good, I'm never comfortable at night until I know you're in the house."

"I'll be home early," I repeated, and got up.

"Well, what did Trip want? When he called he told me that he had to speak to you right away."

"He didn't want nothing," I said. "You know Trip. He's a drama king. He always has to make everything sound so important."

"Does he?" he asked. "Trip always seems pretty calm about things to me. He's pretty levelheaded about situations, hardly ever gets his buttons pushed. He's been that way ever since he was a little boy. I guess Shronda Faye been working his nerves lately."

"Ain't that the truth. I saw Yolanda today," I said steering him in another direction. His eyes perked up.

"You did! How does she like her new van?"

"How do you know she has a new van?" I asked, looking around the room for my backpack.

"I know," he said. "I don't have to see things to know what's going on."

"Oh, I better get going. I'm going to be late," I said. I spotted my backpack on the floor next to the window and retrieved it.

"Wait, before you leave I have something for you," he said, as I pulled it over my shoulder.

"What is it?" I asked.

He pulled two clay pieces out of his T-shirt pocket. I went over and took them from him. I recognized them instantly. They were two of the Amina figurines I threw away the morning after she died. I ran my fingers over the one of her sitting in his lap tugging at his beard.

"I thought I tossed these out of the window," I said.

"You did. I had Trip go out to the field with me and look for them."

"Why? You said you didn't want them. They're not the real thing."

"No, they're not, but I already have the real thing—you."

"Me? Uncle, I'm not Amina," I said.

"I know that, but she's in you, and as long as I have you, I have her. I needed to remember that again. With everything that's been going on lately, I needed to go back to understanding that. You do too. You need to remember that whatever you get into, she gets into too."

"You told me that already. What I really need to remember is these figurines ain't her," I said, tossing them on the bed. "They look like her, but they ain't her. So look, I'll be home early."

"Early or late, just come home yourself and not somebody else," he said as I walked out the bedroom door.

"I love you too, Uncle," I said. I went back to the kitchen and made sure that the oven was off. After that, I left for my shift.

As I went down the street I kept telling myself that I was confident about what I was doing. There was no way that I wasn't. Still, as I headed to the club I started to feel a little uncomfortable about

my decision. I thought again about what Principal Nesby asked me
a few months back. She wanted to know what I wanted to be when
I grew up. Back then I could think of lots of things I would like to
be, but none of them was an exotic dancer, none of them was being
the kind of girl that Mama and her girlfriends used to gossip about
when they relaxed kinky hair at the shop. I felt miserable thinking
about that, thinking that I would be someone that Mama would dis
with her friends. I didn't seem right, and yet Mama herself had done
things she didn't like for me. I remembered when she was working
at the Lovely Diva Salon with Mrs. Ritchie. One Saturday she spent
all day braiding this young sister's hair into some really intricate
braids that the girl had seen on a celebrity fashion Web site. It was
a great style, and the girl really did look like she could be on her way
to the Billboard Music Awards.

"Ooh, I love it!" she said, patting her hair with one hand, and
handing Mama three hundred bucks with the other. Mrs. Ritchie
reached out and grabbed the money before Mama could even get
her hands on it. She counted Mama out less than half of the bills.

"What's this?" Mama asked.

"That's your share. Carly is my client, and I would have done her
hair if I wasn't so busy today," Mrs. Ritchie said, placing the rest of
the bills in her bra.

"But I been working on her head since this morning, Mrs.
Ritchie. I don't think that's right," Mama said.

"Of course it is. This is my shop, and if you don't think I'm fair,
you can find another place to work. I'm already doing you a favor
by letting you keep your little girl here each day after school. Shoot,
you lucky I don't start charging you for daycare," Mrs. Ritchie said,
and walked off. Mama didn't go after her. She had recently gotten
out of beauty school and she needed to work in a place where she
could establish what she called a client base. Instead, she slipped her
business card into the girl's hand and told the girl to recommend her

services to all her friends. The girl promised that she would. When she was gone Mama stuck the rest of the cash into her smock pocket. She started sweeping the floor underneath her seat as if nothing had happened. I saw her hands, though. I saw how they trembled as she clutched the broom. She was pissed, but she held it all in. She was handling things the only way she knew how, taking care of herself, and mostly taking care of me. It would have cost her a lot more than three hundred bucks to put me in after-school care. She knew that. She knew how to suck it all in and make things okay. She did it all the time in bad situations.

What did I have to complain about? What Mama had gone through was much worse, getting thrown out of the house when she was just a teenager, having to figure out how to take care of a newborn and how to pay her bills all by herself. She had gone through years of hassle for both of us. How could I not go through just a little trauma for my child? Besides, I did have a nice body. Why shouldn't I let other people see it? Uncle Simon always said that if something wasn't working you should mold it into something else. Wasn't that all I was doing? Wasn't I simply reshaping the situation into the best possible outcome? The club got a new dancer, and I got money for my child.

A soccer ball rolled across the sidewalk in front of me. I tossed it back to a group of young Hispanic guys playing a soccer game under the shade trees of Grayson Field. They yelled thanks at me, and I went on to work.

By the time I got to work something new was plaguing me— physically, not mentally. I was itching. I don't know if it was the animal hair on the suit, or the material in the suit itself, but I was itching. I got to the dressing room and pulled my dress off. As I stood in front of the mirror the tiny red bumps were more than evident on my thighs and underneath my bra line.

"Shoot," I said. I rushed to the row of dressing tables, furiously opening the drawers. I was looking for some type of first-aid kit. The only thing I came across was a bottle of lotion and some baby powder that some of the girls use when they wear tight spandex suits. I poured some of the powder in my hands. I was spreading it on my thighs when the door to the dressing room creaked. I looked up and saw Star and Sweet Petite come in.

"Well, look at the little powdered sugar baby. What's the matter, high-school girl, you don't think you sweet enough for that crowd we got coming tonight? Don't worry, toffee cream. They'll take you anyway you come, as long as you come completely unwrapped," Star said, stepping out of her blue bicycle shorts. She left them on the floor and walked over to one of the dressing tables in her sports bra and nylon panties. While I sprinkled more powder into my hand, she opened a drawer and took out a plastic makeup case.

"Just ignore Miss Wanna-Make-Everybody-Unhappy," Sweet Petite said, going past me to the bathroom. She opened the door and took her button-down sweater off the hook on the back of the door. "I'm not dancing tonight, and it gets cold out there when you just sitting around in a swimsuit," she said, pulling the sweater on over her favorite gold-sequined two-piece suit. She came over to me. I stopped powdering my bra line. "Is that your new suit?" she asked.

"Yeah, Louisa gave it to me last week." I said.

"I guess it suits you," she said, looking it over. "You got long legs and nice thighs. You also got that pretty dark skin like some of them African girls have."

"Yeah, she looks like a real Kizzy Kinte," Star said, spreading pink blush on her cheeks with a huge brush.

"Be quiet," Sweet said. "You don't even know what you talking about. Kizzy was born in America. She wasn't no African girl."

"Well whatever. She ain't gonna be no girl either after tonight."

"Shut up, Star. You really don't need to say anything about this. Be smart, and just leave it alone," Sweet said.

"Sweet, you don't tell me what I can and can't say to somebody. I'm the star around here," she said, hopping up and getting into Sweet's face. "You know who I am. Don't go getting yourself into trouble."

"Don't go getting myself into what? Please, girl, you better get real, real fast. You may run other folks around here, but you can't run me. I bring in nearly as many clients as you do. And when it comes down to it, all we talking about is the cash. It don't matter who you dating, or how many of them nasty so-called dances you like to do, if you don't bring in the cash your behind will be out of here too. Now go on, and get outta my face before I forget I got 'sweet' in front of my name."

"Yeah, okay, okay, go 'head on and run your mouth, Sweet Petite. We gonna see how it all ends up. Schoolgirl, don't forget to shake it to the East, shake it to the the West, and shake to the one that tips you the best," she said to me.

I didn't respond. She stomped off to the bathroom. Sweet slammed the door shut.

"Heifer, I told you before, don't even worry about her. I knew when I first met her she was going to be as shallow and mean as she was attractive. I just had a feel for it. Forget her, she ain't nothing to even be concerned about. And remember, if you start dancing and you don't like it, you don't have to keep doing it. No matter what nobody say to you, you don't never ever lose control of yourself. If you ain't never got nobody else in the world, you got you."

"I got two somebodys," I said. "They just don't understand me right now, and I don't even have time for that."

"Time? Don't take this the wrong way, China, but you ain't got nothing but time. You're still young, baby. You got time to do whatever you need to do. You don't need to do everything at once," Sweet said.

"I'm not trying to do everything. I'm just trying to do one thing."

"I see that. I see what you trying to do. Anyway, you can chill and work your counter for now. Louisa put the schedule up a little while ago. You don't go on until late tonight."

"Really," I said, and sighed.

"Yeah, I guess she wanted to wait until the dudes with the big bucks showed up. It's better for you that way. If you're gonna put it out there you might as well get the best price for it."

"Price?"

"Yeah, or something like that. I guess I shouldn't have said it that way. I'll see you outside," she said. I put the powder back in the drawer and sat down in one of the chairs as she went out the door.

Price. She had talked about the men paying a price for me. It sounded sick when she said it. I read a book once about a young Japanese girl who gets sold to a geisha house. In the book the girl's virginity goes to the highest bidder when she comes of age. I remember how reading that part in the story made me feel. I didn't even know the girl, but I wanted to save her. I wanted to bring her home with me and Uncle Simon, where it would be safe, and all she had to worry about was being a kid again. I felt awful for her, but now I was going to be her. I was going to be someone that eager men would be willing to pay a price for. I needed the money, but nothing about that seemed right. I stuffed my dress into my bag and smeared on some copper lip gloss from Star's tray. When I was finished with that, I applied the same color eye shadow, and went to do my job.

Around ten P.M. my annoying itching slowly turned into fear. As I watched lady after lady get up and take her turn on the stage, I realized that I definitely was not ready to take mine. Every movement of their hips and thrust of their pelvises made me want to run out of the door. What was I thinking? How was I going to go through with my decision? I took a couple of backpacks from two college-age brothers who looked like they could have stumbled in from a late evening of studying at the community college. When I handed them their tickets one of them tried to mack on me.

"Say, you sho' is fine, girl. What's your name?" the young brother asked me. I tried smiling at him, but I couldn't. I shoved the ticket into his hand, and turned away. When I turned back all I saw was cherubs. Their chubby bodies were everywhere. They were sitting atop my counter, staring at me with their soft puddle eyes. And when I looked over at the stage they were there, too. I saw them flying all around, their halos glowing like celestial spotlights over the dancing girls. A little of my courage started to return. I had to dance. I said I would, and Amina's bill wasn't going to go away. I just needed to find a way to keep my word.

A Michael Jackson tune clicked on, "The Way You Make Me Feel." Swedish Lane came out wearing four-inch-heels and a red micromini dress. She danced up and down the stage, gyrating and twisting every which way she could, throwing her long platinum-blond hair. As expected, the brothers at the tables went crazy, whistling, hollering, clapping. Some were even waving bills at her, and she hadn't even taken off her dress. I wondered what was going on in the guys' minds, who they saw when they looked at Swedish Lane? Was she the sexy girl in high school who never gave them any play or the beautiful girl that worked bedside them at the burger station on their first fast-food job? Perhaps she was neither of those things. Maybe she was the hot model that they saw in their favorite chick magazine last month or the thong-clad girl on the poster in their garage. I wondered. I wondered who they would see in me when I took the stage.

"She really gets those dudes going, don't she?" Big Robert, the Angry Black Giant, asked, coming over to my counter, causing my cherubs to scatter. I shrugged my shoulders. He licked his plump lips at me as usual.

"You still don't like me, do you?" he asked. I ignored him. A short, bucktoothed brother that used to date one of Mama's old girl-friends walked up to the counter. I timidly handed him his baseball cap. He gave me a few dollars and left. I placed that money beneath the counter too.

"Naw, you don't like me at all, but you'll learn to," Big Robert continued. "A lot of the girls don't like me when they first start working here, but you'll soon figure out that it's better that you do," he said, leaning his huge body on the counter. He darted his eyes back to the stage. "You see how ignorant and crazy them dudes is acting over Swedish Lane? You see how they all trying to press up on her?" I looked over at the stage too, but still refused to say any-thing to him.

"Yeah, you see what I'm talking about," he said with a nasty grin. "You know I'm the only thing keeping them fools off of her. If it wasn't for me them dogs would be up there all over her. That's why she likes me, and it's why you gonna like me too."

"Big Robert, what are you doing hanging all over this girl when you should be over there next to the stage?" Louisa asked, coming up behind Big Robert.

"Nothing, Miss Louisa. I was just asking her how she was feeling tonight."

"She's feeling just fine, aren't you, sugar?" Louisa asked, pushing Big Robert away from the counter. He winked at me and went over to the stage area.

"I'm cool," I lied.

"Good, that's what I like to hear, honey. Because you know tonight is your time to shine. You're gonna look so wonderful up there in your new costume. I can't wait to see you do your thing. Now don't you even think of being nervous. Besides me, you're the prettiest thing in this club," she said, in a voice that seemed sur-prisingly vain. "You just go on out there and let the customers know that there's a *new star* shining on that stage."

"New and improved, I hope," Sweet Petite said, coming over too. She handed a folded piece of paper out to me.

Call Trip. He's called here three times, the message said in blue ink.

"Hilda in the office told me to give it to you," she said.

"Thanks," I said. I placed it beneath the counter next to the cash.

"You ain't gonna call him back? It looked like he really needed to talk to you."

"Naw, I know what he wants to talk about. It's cool. I'll speak to him when I get home."

"Of course you will, sugar," Louisa said. She pointed to the stage. "In another hour that's going to be you. I got some really nice music to go along with your costume. You're really going to be something to look at."

"I'm sure I will," I said. Then I looked down and I noticed that my hands and legs were trembling like I had just been left alone in a haunted house.

"Come on, Sweet Petite. Let me show you what I got special for China," Louisa said. She and Sweet Petite went to the back of the stage. I closed my eyes and tried to conjure up as many cherubs as I could. When I opened my eyes again, the cherubs were flying all around Swedish Lane and sitting atop every table next to the stage. I closed my eyes again and imagined the fiery pit they would fall into if I let my emotions get the best of me. I saw them falling right off the tables, falling into a cavern of smoky fire and stinky brimstone that had opened up in the floor. I couldn't let that happen to them. I sucked it up, like Mama did when her boss repeatedly cheated her out of money, like she did when her father threw her out into the streets. I was on in an hour. I didn't know how I would get through it, but I would. I had tried out to be a cheerleader once, in front of a bunch of stuck-up, bitchy girls. They dogged me out, said my jumps were whack, talked about my smaller boobs and my shorter haircut at the time. That was a horrible experience. Could getting up on the stage be much worse?

One hour passed like ten million. I handed men back their hats and bags, took their tips, told some I had a boyfriend, and gave others fake phone numbers. It was standard stuff, but what wasn't standard was how much I jumped when Sweet Petite tapped me on the shoulder. "Louisa said you're on in a few minutes, so you should go to the back of the stage," she said as I was writing new pick-up numbers on tickets.

"Okay," I said.

"I'll watch your counter until you get back," she told me, as I opened the gate and came out. I bumped into her. "You're trembling, baby? You okay?"

"I'm okay," I said. She caught me by the arm.

"Yeah, and that's why you look like you just came down with a bad stomach virus."

"I'm okay. I just need to take a deep breath."

"Maybe, you probably do need to catch your breath. Things is going so fast. But let me tell you this," she said, squeezing through the gate. "I'm sure you done heard this before. You don't have to go down this path. This life ain't for everybody. Don't let Louisa or Star talk you into something you don't want to do. You choose the way you want to go."

"Yes, ma'am, I know what you mean. I have heard something like that before. Last year my English teacher made us read a poem by a dude named Robert Frost, 'The Road Not Taken.' In the poem the poet had two roads he could take. He could take one that everybody had gone down or one that only a few people had taken. I liked it 'cause he took the one that only a few folks took."

"Really?"

"Yeah, plus it was a cool poem. I still remember all the words to it."

"All the words? Shoot, that's good. I don't remember nothing much from school. I guess that's another reason why I ended up here. Go on and do your thing, baby. I'll be right here if you want to talk to me when you through."

"Okay," I said. I walked shakily to the back of the stage, not having a clue what my thing was, and wishing that whatever it was, I was doing it at home. Swedish Lane had finished a second dance. With Big Robert's approval a crowd of guys had rushed the stage to give her money. She was laughing and wiggling it all about for them in her birthday suit, still giving them the best show she could for their bucks. I went to the back of the steps that led to the platform, carefully avoiding the cherubs that I had begun to conjure around me. Louisa was there in a striped pink-and-neon-green bikini that only she could pull off, and to my surprise Star was there also. She had on a pastel yellow suit that would have brought softness to her pretty pale skin, but as usual she had an ugly smirk on her face.

"Looks like the little schoolgirl is about to get schooled," she said.

"Be quiet, Star. I told you you could come back here, but not if you're gonna give this girl grief. Don't you dare make her nervous. You know she's doing this 'cause she has to."

"Yeah, her and all of us."

"Don't pay her no mind," Louisa said, taking me by the arm and leading me to the last step on the platform. "Don't you even worry about her, sugar. You just go up there and make you some money. Now this is your first time, so don't even worry about showing them too much. You just get up there and give them a little taste. They can see more next time. Come on down, Swedish honey," she hollered at Swedish Lane. Swedish Lane came walking past us.

"Good luck, China," she said.

"Thanks," I said. I closed my eyes and steadied my foot on the last step.

"Okay, I'll go up to the platform and get things started up," Louisa said. "You just be cool. Don't panic. Honey, all you got to do is one of them little rump-shaking dances you girls like to do today, and you'll be fine. And if you too scared, when you take your top off just hold it up in front of yourself. That's what I did my first time. Sugar, it won't hurt the men at all to be left with something to fantasize about."

"Yes ma'am. I'm okay. I'm really ready," I said—then I wasn't.

She left my side and I turned to stone. I was petrified, just like the day Principal Nesby came to tell me about Amina. *When you take your top off. My* top, not Star's or Louisa's or Swedish Lane's. The reality of that seemed to come to me more vividly as I stood on the final step, even more vividly than the cherubs that I could see gathered at my feet and flying over my head. Another memory about my mother came to me as well. I remembered how she said Grandpa treated her when he found out she was pregnant by the janitor at her school. She said he treated her like the garbage he took out on trash day, and that wasn't even the worst thing. It was the way he looked at her, like she was one of the crack hookers who tried to pick him up each morning when he stopped at the traffic light down the street. She hated him looking at her like that. It made her feel like she really was one of those girls. *"Don't ever do anything that makes people see you in a light you don't want to be seen in. People always say that it doesn't really matter what other folks think of you. Don't believe it. What other people think of you will eat you alive. My daddy's feelings completely gutted me."*

Completely gutted, that's what my mother said happened to her after she turned ugly in my grandfather's eyes. Was it also going to happen to me? How would I really feel when Uncle found out I was dancing? How would I feel when I saw the disappointment and disgust in his eyes? Uncle Simon loved me, as much as I loved my Amina. Would I still see that same love reflected in his face when he knew I was stripping it off for a bunch of dudes? What was I thinking? I couldn't go out there. I started to zone out more. My feet glued themselves to the floor. I saw the light click on over the wooden platform, but it seemed to me like a light beaming through a dusty window at the top of a deep cellar. Louisa began to speak. Her words sounded distorted to me, like I was standing at the other end of a long field, and they were being carried to me, on the wind, between the noisy rustle of shade trees. I could barely make them out: *welcome—talent—young—pretty. Be kind,* there was something about being kind. The music cued up, deep, intense African rhythms from the Motherland, the place where they say all life began. *"Get out there, girl,"* I think I heard Star say behind me. I didn't move an inch. "Get out . . . , girl," she must have said. My feet took root in the platform planks. I felt a hard shove, and I stumbled forward, almost tripped over my own feet. Claps. Loud claps. I was about to fall on my face and the men were clapping at me.

"Do—something, stupid—fool," Star hissed. Louisa appeared at my side.

"Go on, honey. Go on—men excited. Don't make me look bad," she said, shaking me hard. "Do—you—hear me? Honey, this is what you wanted."

Is it? I asked inside.

"Do something—girl," Louisa said. The men continued to clap. From the far end of the stage I couldn't see their faces, and I wondered if they *really* could see mine? Could they see how confused I was? "Move your hips—do—something," Louisa said. "Girl, what are—you—waiting for." The claps of the men grew louder, insistent.

"Move, fool," Star hissed.

"China, don't—be a baby," Louisa said. "Stop wasting my time." The men clapped harder.

"Move—your damn feet, girl!" Louisa suddenly yelled at me. The men began to yell too.

"Come on—baby, show—us something," I heard some voices say. "Come on, girl, shake your moneymaker."

"Go on, China, move your hips or something. Damn, if you make me look dumb you won't have a job tomorrow!" Louisa yelled. I started to snap out of my daze.

"Do you hear me, girl? If you cut a fool with me you'll be looking for another place to work. Sugar, do you want to work here or not?" she growled. The ugliness in her voice completely brought me back. I found my feet and started using them, but not to dance. I started to back up. The men started shouting again, and some of them began to boo. I kept moving backward, kept backing down the steps until I bumped into Star. She was still behind me, blocking my way, an angry wall of female flesh. "Where you going, schoolgirl!" she said.

"Get away from me and leave me alone," I said. I turned and pushed her with all my strength. She tumbled down the steps, and I rushed down them, with the men shouting and booing as loudly as they could. The sound system shut off. Louisa started talking in her purring sultry voice, trying to calm the men down. I went straight to my counter. Sweet Petite came out to greet me.

"You okay, baby?" she asked, as I squeezed by her through the gate.

"I gotta go," I said. I searched beneath the counter and quickly grabbed my tips. When I came out from behind the counter I found Star once again blocking my way. I pushed her a second time, and as I did she grabbed my top. It tore away with a loud rip. She swung it over her head a few times, then flung it toward the nearest table of men. It hit the floor, and a big buff brother got up and retrieved it. He started swinging it over his head too, as the whole club cheered on. I put my hands over my chest to cover my breasts and started for the dressing room, like I had done before.

"Wait up, schoolgirl! Where you off to? I thought you was

gonna take it all off. I heard you were gonna give the men a show they wouldn't forget!" Star yelled. She ran behind me and grabbed the back of my suit bottom as hard as she could. I pulled away, and to my horror the skirt and panty tore away too. They fell in a heap onto the floor. I was completely nude. This time the dudes went crazy, clapping and hooting, stomping the floor with their heavy feet. The brother who had my top grabbed me by my arm. He dragged me struggling from table to table while the other guys cheered him on.

"Say ya'll, ain't she worth that big-ass cover charge. Come on, girl. Don't be shy. Come on out and meet your fans. You what we been waiting all night to see," he said.

"Let me go!" I screamed.

"Aw, don't be that way, pretty girl," he said.

"Yeah, don't be that way, schoolgirl. Go on and dance for the men." Star laughed. "Go on and put on your show."

"Let me go!" I screamed at the guy again. He dragged me over to the table where his buddies were sitting and tried to throw me in one of their laps, but I wrenched myself free from his grip.

"Hey, come back here, young thing!" he hollered as I ran all the way back to the dressing room. When I got there I collapsed on one of the heart-shaped chairs, shaking and weeping. Seconds afterward Star and Louisa came through the door.

"China, what was that? I thought you told me you wanted to dance?" Louisa asked, without the normal honey or sugar in her voice. I didn't answer her. I got up and walked over to my bag.

"Well, answer me, girl," she said, as I fumbled around in it for my dress. I found it and slipped it on over my head.

"Yeah, answer her, China," Star said. "Don't be such a little girl about it. I wasn't trying to pull your drawers off. That was just an accident, but so what? Ain't nobody done nothing to you. I just helped you out. You say you wanted to make the big money, well, that's how you make it around here. You should be happy. All I did was give them guys what they wanted to see. Go on back out there and give them some more. Go get yourself some of them big fat tips."

"Just leave me alone," I said. I wiped my wet face and looked over at her. She was boiling inside. I guess she was angry at me for trying to take her place. I didn't care. I just wanted to go home.

"I changed my mind," I said to Louisa. "I don't want to take my clothes off for people I don't know. It's not nice."

"Oh, it's not nice. Is that what you just decided? 'Cause it seems to me that it was nice and *fine* not five minutes ago. You were ready to take it all off, weren't you, little schoolgirl? So don't be trippin' now, acting like you all better than everybody."

"I'm not better than anybody. I just want to go home," I said, bending down and zipping up my bag.

"You leaving?" Louisa asked. "You just gonna go, just like that, without even no decent explanation of why you went out there and made a fool out of me?"

"I wasn't trying to embarrass you, Miss Louisa. I just changed my mind. I'm sorry."

"You're sorry, you're gonna be a lot sorrier when you can't pay your bill off for your little girl. You're gonna be really upset when that happens. I can't believe you would do this to me. I just knew when you started here you were gonna be different. I had a feeling you were gonna be better than them other girls he told me to hire in here."

"What?" I said.

"Look, Louisa, quit trying to pull something out of this," Star said, getting in front of me with her hands on her hips. "Ain't no sense in trying to get this girl to do nothing or explain nothing to you. I knew when I seen her how this was going to end up. It was just a matter of time. I told my man that, but he don't listen to me. He always got to do things his way, especially when it comes to these young-ass girls. He's obsessed with them, and even worse, he thinks that just because they all desperate we can get them to do what we want them to do. I told him that about that Onyx girl. She was barely eighteen when she came here. I told him she wasn't nothing but a brittle twig. I knew she would snap at any time. I could see it wasn't gonna take much to run her back to the streets. He keeps sending us these damaged little girls. I keep trying to tell him better than that, but I guess them chemicals he works around all day is pickling his brain cells too," she said, rolling her eyes at me.

"What are you talking about?" I asked.

"Whatever," she said, stepping out of my way, all the while keeping an angry scowl on her face.

"It looks like you're right, Star. But it goes further than that," Louisa said. "We need to get all three of the guys to stop sending us girls. Damn, first I lose Kembra, and now neither one of the girls that your so-called boyfriend recommended has paid off. Go on, get out of here, China, and don't come back. I'll put whatever I owe you in the mail, but I don't have time to babysit no children. Get out, and stop wasting my time," she said icily.

I walked past her and Star, went back to the main club. Inside Swedish Lane had decided to give the men the show I was unwilling to give. She was dancing to my African music, her white skin making a strange contrast to the African tribal beats.

"You going, baby?" Sweet Petite asked as I went past the counter.

"Yeah," I said, still too out of it to even give her a proper good-bye.

"Good, just get out of here. This never was a place for you. I knew that when I first saw you. I can't believe Star did that to you. She know we don't ever treat each other the way these men sometimes treat us. That's a rule we got around here. It wasn't right. Anyway, I guess it's all over now. You go find another way to handle your business. You don't want to spend the next few months or even weeks working with a low-life heifer like Star."

"Yes, ma'am," I said. I went down the long hallway of the club. Big Robert was hanging out at the door.

"You can come back any time you want. Just come by and talk to me. I'll get your job back, if you real nice to me," he said, and smacked his fat lips.

"Get away from me," I said, and pushed open the door. I squeezed by him and went out. I walked down the steps and crossed the manicured grass. With my emotions tied in a knot, I welcomed the long dark alleys I was about to cut through to get to my house. In the darkness I could hide from other people, and maybe even from myself. I was a little ways up the sidewalk when someone came jogging across the street toward me. It startled me for a second, but as the figure came nearer I breathed easy. It was Trip. He ran over to the sidewalk.

"China, I've been trying to reach you forever. Why didn't you return my calls?" he asked.

"I didn't get them," I lied.

"Didn't get them? China, I must have left ten calls at your work and home."

"Trip, I said I didn't get them," I said. I wrapped my arms around my chest, and kept walking. He cut in front of me and stopped me.

"I gotta tell you something, China. Something's not right."

"I'm tired, Trip. I don't want to talk about anything. I just want to go home," I said.

"Me too. I've been across the street all night, just waiting on you. That big giant brother wouldn't let me in the door."

"Good, you didn't want to be in there," I said, holding back my tears.

"China, something weird is going on," he said. "That's what I was trying to tell you. I don't know what it is, but something ain't quite right."

"Trip, what are you talking about? It's late."

"China, I went by Amina's grave yesterday."

"Okay."

"Her stone was there."

"I know, Brother Agee ordered an emergency replacement. I told you that, Trip."

"Are you sure, China? Are you certain about that?"

"Of course, I told you that was the reason why I needed extra cash."

"I know you told me, China, but I swear that's the same stone."

"What are you talking about, Trip? I told you, Brother Agee replaced it."

"No no, I don't think he did, because it looks the same."

"It's supposed to look the same, Trip."

"Naw, that's not what I mean. I mean it doesn't look like anybody's been there for a while, and I didn't see any pieces of broken stone anywhere."

"They probably just cleaned them up," I said, trying to get around him. He cut in front of me again.

"Maybe, but I just don't see how they replaced that stone so quickly. It took a lot longer for them to put it there in the first place."

"Did it?"

"Yeah, and there's something else. Remember when I told you that I put a story idea on her stone?"

"You said you taped it, I remember."

"Yeah, but at first I tried to do something real dumb and put it on with one of them big pushpins Mama keeps in the tack board by the refrigerator. I thought it would be cool to do it that way, so I could use the same hole again if I wanted to give her another idea. I wasn't trying to hurt the stone or nothing. I really thought I could do it, you know, like last year when I helped my cousin put down his wooden flooring. We had to hammer the squares right over the wood and into the concrete. I thought if I could hammer into concrete I could probably hammer into stone. Anyway, like I said, it was really stupid. I wasn't even thinking when I did it, and I didn't want to tell you because I thought you would get mad."

"I wouldn't be. I told you I liked that you gave her the story. Let's talk about this later, Trip. Uncle Simon is waiting on me," I said, wiping my face again with my hands.

"Okay, I'm sorry, my bad. I know something's wrong, but I still have to tell you this," he said noticing my wet face.

"What is it?"

"China, when I tried to hammer that stupid pushpin in all I ended up doing was making some scratches on the stone. The pin wasn't going in at all, so I went down the street to buy some tape."

"Is that all? Okay, Trip, okay. That's no big deal," I said.

"Naw, you don't get it. China, those scratches are still on that stone where I made them. They're right on the top, near the left side. Somebody took the plastic bag with the story off, and maybe wiped off all the dirt, but the scratches are still there, right where I made them. China, that can't be a new stone. I know it's not."

"It's got to be, Trip. Brother Agee told me that it was broken, and it needed to be replaced."

"I know what he told you, but I know what I saw. China, ain't nobody put no new stone there."

"Are you sure, Trip?"

"Have I ever lied to you, girl? Don't I always tell you the truth?"

"Oh God," I said. I walked back to a nearby telephone post and leaned against it. I knew he was telling the truth. I could feel it. My mind shifted back to Star and Louisa's conversation. Snippets of it started to run like an instant replay in my mind. I saw Star glaring at me with her angry face. I saw her lips move and say the phrase "*I guess them chemicals he works around all day is pickling his brain cells too.*" Chemicals, what chemicals? And pickling whose brain cells? A confusing and sickening answer slowly came to me. I knew whose business she was talking about.

"China, I'm sorry," Trip said, coming over and standing next to me. "I know this is all freaky, but there was nothing wrong with Amina's monument. I know there wasn't."

"I believe you, Trip," I said, breaking into fresh tears.

"China, don't cry," he said, wiping my face. "I don't know what's going on, but we'll go home and talk to your uncle Simon. We'll figure it out. Don't cry. Whatever's wrong is going to be all right."

"Trip, I need to ask you a question. Do you think it's possible for something really awful to be going on all around you, and everybody know about it but you?"

"What are you talking about?"

"Just answer me."

"I guess so. I saw an *Outer Realm* once where the earth was about to be destroyed by meteors, and everybody was moving to the moon. The families were going by ship, and there wasn't a lot of room, so each family could only take one kid. In the show this family had two girls, just a year apart. One was frail and smart, the other one was a dunce, but really strong."

"Which one did they choose?"

"They chose the dunce girl. They figured she would survive the long journey. For weeks they made plans and prepared for the trip, but they never told the frail girl that they were leaving. She didn't know she was being left until the day she saw the ship was ready to take off. Wasn't that awful?"

"It was really cruel," I said. Then I broke into sobs.

"China, what's wrong? What else is going on?" he asked.

"Trip, I think somebody did something really mean to me."

"Who? Are you talking about one of them brothers at the club?"

"Yeah, something like that. I think it's his club, Trip. I think it belongs to him."

"To who?"

"Brother Agee. I think it's his club."

"What are you talking about, China? You mean he's one of the owners?"

"I think so. I think he is. I don't feel good, Trip," I said. Then I ran to the curb and threw up.

CHAPTER 11

For nearly a week Trip's come over to my house and helped out Uncle while I've stayed locked up in my room crying and obsessing over the story Trip told me the night I got fired from the club. I've wondered how the girl could have been so stupid. She had to have known. There was no way that her family could have planned to leave the earth without her being aware of it. She had to have seen the packed bags in the closet, and the extra dried food items that were finding their way into the shopping basket. She just didn't want to see, like I didn't want to see what was going on at the club.

I'm still dazed by it, but it turns out that Brother Agee is indeed part owner of the club. After the club was built one of the owners decided that a gentlemen's club wasn't his thing and dropped out. He sold his share of the club to his cousin, Donald Agee, who had recently inherited some cash and wanted to buy into a business. So Donald Agee, or Brother Agee as I met him, became the third owner of the place. And that wasn't his only investment—it turns out that Brother Agee isn't just a worker, he *owns* part of the funeral home that I buried Amina from. How much he owns I couldn't find out, but when Uncle asked around, Perry down at Perry's 24 and 7 Beer Joint said that he thought it was at least 40 percent.

"I don't know why you asking. But yeah, that dude Donald Agee, he definitely owns a big chunk of that Obsidian Queens club *and* that

funeral home. He was in here talking about it one night. He was saying that renovating the home from a pet-funeral parlor to a place for
real live folks cost a lot of cash, cash that Ms. Aldrich didn't have.
From what I gathered Ms. Aldrich was seriously in the hole when
Agee told her he would help her out with some cash, just as long as
she let him in on the business and let him work some of the customers every once in a while. I thought that was kind of weird. But
hey, I stay out of other brothers' business and hope they stay out of
mine," Perry told Uncle, while he was getting into his gold Caddy
in front of the store.

What did that mean—"work some customers"? Brother Agee
apparently had plenty of money. Why would he even want to work
at the home and push burial packages to people—to me? That's
what he did. He sat down with me all caring and kind while he sold
me a package that he knew I could never afford. He told me that he
didn't really want to make a deal with someone so young, but he
trusted that I would do whatever it took to get the bill paid. I certainly did that. I walked all over the neighborhood until I found the
one place that would pay enough money to settle the bill, the one
place that he happened to be part owner of. "I have papers that say
I'm legal, old enough to do what I want," I told Louisa. The funny
thing is she never asked me to see them. Not in all the time I
worked at the club did girlfriend ask. She never wanted to see if my
papers said it was okay for me to work at a place where you were
supposed to be at least twenty-one to get in the door, a place where
they served alcohol.

Why didn't she care? Trip said it was all about the Benjamins, and
in a way that was true. It was about money, but not the money that
they could make from me passing back hats at the counter. It was about
the money they could make from me stripping off my clothes. How
could I have been so dumb? Why didn't I see that I was being set up?

And yet, was I really set up? Brother Agee didn't send me to the club. I sent myself. I took myself there and agreed to work behind the counter, and when I needed more money I agreed to dance. I never asked who owned the club, and I wasn't bothered by the fact that the owners never showed up. Brother Agee had lied to me about Amina's stone being broken, but was it really his fault that I never went to visit my daughter's grave? He knew it, you bet he did. I'm sure when he asked, the caretaker there told him that I never, ever showed up. So he played me, and he would have kept on playing me as long as he could get away with it. Still, when I thought about what had happened, I couldn't quite get my head around it. I raked in the dough at the club and took it as fast as I could down to the funeral home. When I got there I sat across the desk from Brother Agee, while he told me how proud he was of me, took back his own cash, and put it back into his funeral parlor. It was a win-win situation for him, but I still couldn't understand why he had done it. My head swam from the ugliness of it, and how I had let it hurt my child. I wanted to do something wonderful for her, and because of him I had tricked myself into doing something terrible. Everything was tainted now. I felt like the beautiful flowers etched into her bronze coffin were withered and decayed. I had decayed them—and that was what I was going to have to live with. I had no choice. I knew that the night I tried to dance at the club, but yesterday I got a final phone call from Brother Agee. After that, there was no use in trying to deny anything to myself. I saw him for what he was, but mostly I saw myself.

"Good morning, China. I heard you weren't feeling too well, so I thought I'd call you instead of asking you to stop by," he said, all concerned like, when I picked up the phone.

"What do you want!" I flared.

"Oh dear, I know why you're upset," he continued. "I guess you've found something out. I heard your uncle has been asking questions about me all over town. I—"

"Are you Star's boyfriend? Do you own Obsidian Queens?" I asked, cutting him off.

"I am, and I do. I never said I wasn't one of the owners of Obsidian's. I have a right to make a living. It's a legitimate business, and I'm a legitimate businessman."

"You're a creep. How could you do something like that to me?"

"Something like that to you? Did I really do something wrong to you, or did you do something to yourself? Wasn't it your idea to go take a job at my club?" he asked, in a matter-of-fact way.

"I didn't know it was your club. You never told me you were one of the owners."

"I didn't have to. That's part of being grown, or as you say, 'legal.' You get to make your own decisions. My decision was not to mention the club. Your decision was to go get a job there. It was your idea alone, just like the big funeral you knew you couldn't afford to pay for. I stood right here in this room and watched you fly in your uncle's face about it. You told him you could do what you wanted—so you did. No, I didn't do one single thing to you."

"You lied to me about my little girl's stone. You told me it was broken!" I yelled.

"Oh yeah, I did do that. Only it was simply an honest mistake. It turns out the cemetery was wrong. There were some stones broken, but your little girl's wasn't one of them. It was just a little mix-up. I'm sorry about that. It was all just a mistake. Now I can let you know this very minute that you're all paid up. You don't need to come see me again."

"I don't want to see you," I said. "I hate you. You're a dirty dog, and I'm going to tell everybody in this neighborhood what you did to me."

"Oh, are you going tell them how you went to Louisa and asked for the job on your own, and then asked her to be a dancer, when you felt like you weren't making enough money? Are you going to tell them that?"

"Yeah, I'm going to tell them that," I said.

"You do that, and you'll truly let everyone know that what happened really was your fault."

"I know it was mostly my fault, but you're still a creep," I said.

"That's your opinion. Your receipt's in the mail, China. You can't prove that I've done anything wrong, little sister. Go on, tell whomever you like. There was nothing unique done to you. I treated you the same way I treat all my customers."

"I know, that's why I'm going to tell them all to stay away!" I yelled, and slammed down the phone.

Then there was nothing to do but wait for the receipt in the mail, the receipt that would confirm how foolish and immature I had been. I rolled over in my bed and wished I could go to sleep and never wake up again. A knock sounded on my door.

"China, you up yet, baby?" Uncle's voice said. I didn't answer. The door creaked and I heard the sound of his chair rolling in.

"China Cup Cameron, I want you to get up and get out of that bed right now. It's time for breakfast," Uncle said sternly.

"Uncle, I'm not hungry," I mumbled.

"Well, I am, and I don't like to eat by myself. I've been doing that for months, and I hate it. I like to see your pretty face across from me."

"I don't want anything to eat. Uncle Simon, just leave me alone." He snatched the covers off me, and I lay there curled up in my Snoopy gown.

"China, I've left you alone. I left you alone when you decided to cut me and everybody else out of Amina's arrangements, and I left you alone when you decided to take your behind down and work at that club. I left you alone, even though it was harder than anything I've ever done in my life. You know why I did that?"

"No," I said.

"I'm not sure either. I really did think you would come to your senses in a little while. I had no idea that it would turn into this. Baby, I really was just trying to keep us from hating each other. I remember how things were with your mama and my daddy. When she wouldn't do what my daddy wanted, the screaming would go on for hours. My daddy would call her every low-life name he could think of, and at the end of every argument she would end up yelling out that she hated him, and I knew she did. Even after she got her life together she hated him. I didn't want that for us. When we first moved in together I was terrified. I didn't know how to raise you. I made a ton of mistakes, but whatever problem I created, you dealt with it and moved on, just like you did when your mama died. I guess that's why I left you alone. I figured eventually you would move on from Amina's passing too. I didn't expect things to turn the way they did. I couldn't see how bad it was going to get."

I turned over and looked at him. His scruffy, graying beard was gone again. He didn't look young though, he looked like I felt inside, ragged and beaten down.

"I turned it bad, with help from that no-good Brother Agee," I said. "He helped me ruin everything."

"He did do that," he said. "He's a lowlife for sure, and I'm going to contact somebody and see what can be done about it."

"Good, I hope he gets what he deserves, but I did this, Uncle Simon," I said, starting to tear up. "It was mostly me. I was the one who decided to go work at the club to buy things that my child would never even see."

"Why?"

"I don't know. I guess I didn't want to let go of Amina. I didn't want to admit that she was gone. I had to let Mama go. I hated that. I used to have nightmares about it all the time, and it was awful at school. Most of the kids didn't have a daddy, but everybody had a mama—everybody but me."

"I know, baby. I'm so sorry about that," Uncle said.

"I know. Anyway, I couldn't deal with losing Amina, too," I sobbed. "I didn't want her to go away."

"Me either, baby. And I know how much all of this hurts. Now get dressed and go say good-bye to your child. Can you do that?" he asked.

"I don't know if I can."

"I can't do it for you, China. I want to, but I can't."

"I know," I said. "You can't handle my stuff. Can you handle yours?"

"China, if you mean Yolanda, that canoe done already fell over the falls."

"No, she said she couldn't come around anymore because I was working at the club. I don't work there anymore. You should go and tell her."

"No, Yolanda did what she needed to. She has her children to worry about and I have you. I'll leave her to the life she chose for herself."

"What if it's not really what she wants?"

"Then she'll have to come to me and tell me that," he said. I sat up, and he leaned in and kissed me on the forehead. His lips felt warm and comforting. "I'm gonna go and fix you some oatmeal and toast. Come and eat it, if you feel like it," he said.

I nodded. He rolled out of the room.

I didn't go eat my breakfast. I couldn't stand the thought of food in my stomach. I got dressed and I left the house. I didn't go to the cemetery right away. I did what I did the day of Amina's funeral. I walked all over the neighborhood. I stopped at the Princess and the Pea Bookshop and listened to Mrs. Waltrip tell me one of Albert's stories. I sneaked into school, said hi to my homegirl Alejandra while we watched the girls' track team jumping hurdles in the bright morning sun. I peeped in the window of the resale shop and watched the large, friendly sister dress a unisex mannequin in a flowered dress with a bell skirt. I went by Bobby's Rib Shack and talked with his new wife, Marisa, as she placed vases of plastic flowers on the picnic tables. I even poked my head into my old church and listened to the senior choir practice a new version of the hymn *Holy, Holy, Holy.* In short, I did everything I could to avoid going— and then I finally went. I made my way through the dense brush that led to the side of the gate where Amina's grave was, and peered at her headstone from a distance. I couldn't quite make out the engravings on her red granite stone or the cherub carved in the center, but I knew it was her grave. I could feel it, like I felt her soul drifting away from mine the moment she died. I knew she was dead, the reality of it flowed into every chamber of my heart. I wasn't ready to say good-bye to her, though. You could never say good-bye to a child that you had carried for nine months.

"You're not going in, are you?" Trip's voice suddenly asked beside me.

"No, I can't," I said.

"I figured you wouldn't. I told your uncle that when I came by this morning, but he said that you needed to try and do it anyway."

"Did you come out here to try and get me to do it?"

"Naw, nobody can make you do anything. I just wanted to tell you something."

"What is it?"

"It's about Kembra. She came over while I was coming out of class yesterday."

"What did she want?"

"She said she heard about what happened at the club, and she was sorry. She told me she knew what Louisa had in mind for you, and she should have let you know. Anyway, she said she was glad you decided not to dance, and some other things."

"What other things?"

"Stuff she wanted you to know. She told me that Brother Agee was her stepfather's cousin, and it was her stepfather that sold him his share of the club. She said that her mother and stepfather got into a big fight about the club, when her mother found out she was working there."

"Why was she working there?"

"She said her stepfather told her she could make a lot of money and probably get a new car."

"She bought the car herself, with money from Obsidian's?"

"Yeah, she made a lot of cash until her mother pulled the plug. Her mother threw a fit and threatened to get a divorce, so her stepfather sold the club and Kembra quit working there."

"That's good. Louisa and Star would have made her dance."

"Yeah, you're right."

"What about Onyx? Did Kembra say anything about her?"

"Not much. She just said that Onyx started working at the club after her brother died. She said that Onyx was a really good friend to her until she got back on the drugs."

"Onyx didn't have a brother? She told me she did, and so did Sweet Petite."

"She had one, but he passed a little while back from AIDS. I guess that's how she met Brother Agee."

"Probably, who knows? Everybody over there lied so much. I don't know what the truth is."

"I don't either. Anyway, Kembra said Onyx's brother was a great guy. He worked with gang kids down at the Lyons Center."

"He did?"

"Yeah."

"Great, we should go down to that center and see if anybody's heard from Onyx. Maybe she went over there for help. She certainly never came back to the club."

"Naw, even on dope she knew it wasn't a good place to be.

Anyway," he said, taking a piece of folded paper out of his shorts pocket and placing it in a Ziploc bag, "I came here to put a new story idea on my daughter's grave. I read it to Mama yesterday. She liked it a lot."

"Shronda Faye liked your story idea?"

"Yeah, she told me it was intriguing and interesting. She told me to send a copy to the *Outer Realm* folks."

"Really, your mama said that?" I asked.

"Yeah, she even gave me a stamp to mail it," he said, with a big grin spreading all over his handsome face.

"Man, that's a surprise."

"Yeah, it is. We talked a little last week. I came home from school and found her sitting in my room reading all my stuff. When I asked her what was up, she told me that she may have been wrong about my writing. She said that I should give the TV stuff a try, and if it didn't work out for me I could always go into the military like her."

"She said that?"

"Yeah, she said that I should keep sending my stories off. She won't hassle me about it. She just wants me to do the best I can with my life."

"Wow, good for her, and you. What's the new story about?" I asked. He hesitated a minute, then reached over and squeezed my hand.

"You'll find out when you can go over and read it for yourself, my dark sister," he said. After that, he trotted off to find the gate opening. I watched him go through it, then I watched him take a spool of tape out of his pocket and tape the story idea to Amina's stone.